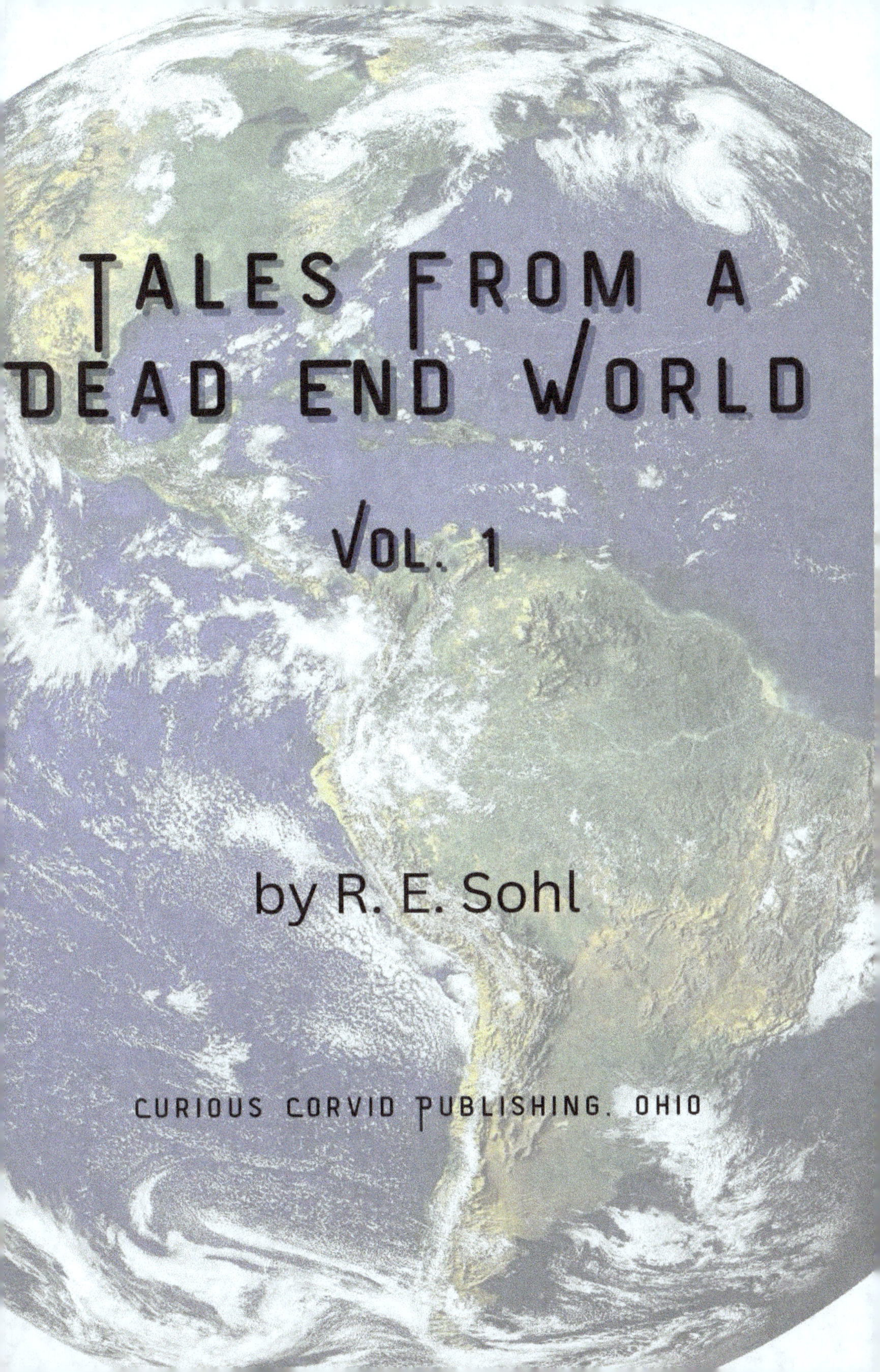

TALES FROM A DEAD END WORLD
Vol. 1
by R. E. Sohl
CURIOUS CORVID PUBLISHING, OHIO

INTRODUCTION:
THROUGH A GLASS, DARKLY

Greetings and salutations! The volume you now hold in your sweaty little palms is a collection of short stories (and even a few vain attempts at poetry) written by yours truly. It is based upon several sources recently given to me by the associates of my old friend, Matt Spike, P.I., under his direction. These sources run the gamut from Matt's own case files to a volume of the *Magna Historia Mundi,* written by Matt's wife, Dr. Naomi Waters-Spike, the esteemed professor of history.

Several of these stories predate the events of my previous novel in this series, *The Shadow of Death.* Three stories happen about a year prior to that one: *Tears of Akshani* (set in 10,000 BC!), *The Vivisectionist,* and *The House on West Bay Ave.* Two more occur *during* the events of that story, namely *There's Always a Bigger Fish* and *The Golden Inquisition,* which were held back because they would have revealed spoiler details about the main story but nevertheless deserve to be told in their own right.

Two of the stories presented here directly tie into the locations, characters, and key concepts from the second novel in the series, *Beyond the Veil of Death.* These are the aforementioned *House on West Bay Ave* and *The Golden Inquisition,* while *Odin's Back Scratcher* takes place shortly before the opening of *Beyond the Veil of Death* in 1997. Due to all of that, this volume is designated as being *Book 1.5* in the series.

Some of the stories will expand your understanding of the world and events of *The Shadow of Death*, while others will grant you a gentler landing into *Beyond the Veil of Death* and help illuminate certain aspects of that novel.

As always, all the names have been changed to protect both the guilty *and* the innocent. Certain artistic liberties were taken. Thus, what follows can be regarded as one possible interpretation of these events, rather than a definitive and reliable record of what occurred. As needed, specifics were changed to protect the secrets of the Guilds – should anyone fail to be sufficiently dissuaded by the inherent absurdity of some of these tales and decide to take them too literally.

Don't go down that particular rabbit hole, my friends, for that way lies only madness and grief.

Anyhoo, enjoy!

-Robert Enrico Sohl

A SPECIAL NOTE ABOUT THE CAPITALIZATION OF THE WORD "GOD" IN THIS BOOK

It is a normal grammatical convention these days to only capitalize the word "God" when referring to the deity worshipped by the Abrahamic religions of Judaism, Christianity and Islam. All other deities are "gods" with a lowercase letter g.

In this book, as well as any of my other works we will be deliberately *ignoring* this rule.

The reasoning behind this is that following this rule reflects and reinforces a cultural bias in Western society which automatically assigns a place of primacy to the God of the Abrahamic religions, implying that any other Gods are therefore lesser, false, or purely mythological.

This seems terribly disrespectful, not to mention inaccurate as many of these other Gods which are seen by Christians, Jews and Muslims as being mythological have modern day worshippers to whom such beings are quite important.

The author does not wish to contribute to this cultural bias, while sadly being keenly aware that choosing to do so is akin to shouting into a hurricane!

It is the author's opinion that all faiths should be treated equally, as they are precious to the individuals who practice them. This also applies to respecting the decision *not* to adhere to any such belief systems. It's perfectly fine to have a preference for one God or a group of them, or to completely disregard this entire God business as so much hokum, but it's not my place to abuse language to unconsciously suggest which of these choices is the only "correct" one.

TABLE OF CONTENTS

EXCERPT FROM THE *MAGNA HISTORIA MUNDI* BY DR. NAOMI WATERS-SPIKE:

THE TEARS OF AKSHANI

Author's Note: Many of the most ancient records pertaining to the history of the Great Houses of Assassins were either lost in the War of the Assassins or were destroyed along with the Shadowmen's Citadel in 1995. I couldn't believe my fortune in discovering this fragmentary account in the archives of the Lodge of the Black Wolves, one of the more obscure chapters of the Reformed Greater Guild of Assassins. The head archivist, or "Memory Walker" (which is his rather charming official title) was kind enough to provide this translation from the original M'bogish without much arm twisting on the part of Director McDowell.

The Memory Walker of the Lodge of the Black Wolves shared one other bit of information with me. His only other visitor who has ever taken such an interest in this manuscript was a young wizard who visited him many years ago, who went by the unusual name of Dexter Sinister. This is the only remaining piece of what appears to be a personal journal kept by Ashkani Dhwarna, the Grand Matriarch from whom the surviving Assassins all claim descent.

It is presented here in its entirety in English for the first time.

Many would be surprised to learn my people have ever shed a tear, given that they think of us as nothing more than heartless killers. We are killers, it is true. The best killers in the world, a fact in which we all take great pride. But heartless? No. Many sights make my heart hurt these days, ever since the world broke.

For example, today, when I led my people through the rubble of the once great city of Khalsa. It was a city I had visited many times in the past but which now lay choked in ash and ruin. I had to battle to hold back the tears. It was a battle which I lost.

It wasn't the sight of the formerly grandiose pyramids, now burnt and crumbled, that upset me so. No, it was the awful vision of children dressed in rags who darted in and out of the collapsed structures like rats, scavenging for any scraps of food they could find. Orphans of the war, reduced to living like animals. I had been a mother once, and it pained me to see children living like this. Such things were common now. With the near total collapse of civilization, the few who remained would do anything to survive.

I wiped the salty drops away before my clan could see them, trying to focus instead upon the task at hand. I was leading my people, the Bringers of Death, through what was left of the city in order to meet with Thoth and hopefully bring about an end to this madness. We silently wound through the craters that had once been streets in a long single file line. My loyal assistant Fahja, as ever by my side.

Many of my people must think I have lost my mind. To ally our clan with a sorcerer? One of the very ones who have brought about this devastation. So far, we have survived by staying out of the conflict, dedicating ourselves only to protecting our own assets from raiders.

Yet there comes a time when one looks upon all the suffering in the world, and cries, *"enough!"* Indeed, it is my judgment that unless this war comes to an end, and soon, there will be no more life left anywhere in the whole world. If allying with a sorcerer is the way to stop it, then that is what I shall do.

I had no reason to trust Thoth beyond my own instincts, but he was not your typical mystic. A most powerful magic user indeed, he famously abandoned his Order in protest when the war began, an act which won my respect. He disappeared not long afterwards. Many believed he was dead, and I was among them, as it had been so long since there had been any news of him.

Until the night when he came to me in a dream and explained his scheme.

He told me that he knew I would be open to his plan because he had seen into my heart when he was in my dreams. Once he explained what he had in mind, I was more than agreeable to it. It was a desperate plan, but in those times horror was cheap and hope was rare and I was willing to give almost anything a try. I felt in my bones that extinction was the only thing which lay on the current path. Everything depended on this plan.

I consulted my [1]Wayfinder Stone to check our position.

I was pleased to see we were still on the correct path. With hand signals, I communicated this to Fahja. As he signaled back to me his understanding, I noticed his face tense up as he caught sight of something in the distance. I followed his gaze and saw it too: shadowy forms scuttling through the tumbled down stones and other scattered wreckage ahead of us.

These were no mere children. These shapes were much bulkier, and the outlines of weapons flashed in their hands. Instinctively, I pulled my [2]stinger from beneath my cloak and signaled to the others for battle-readiness.

They attacked in force from the gloom, it looked to be seventy or more of them. I was astounded by their boldness. Our clothing was not subtle, could they not see we were the

---

[1] *A "Wayfarer Stone" was a magical device, an enchanted stone, with a map etched into the surface that moved as its user moved. They were once common during the Long Ago Beforetimes, but few modern examples survive.*

[2] *A "stinger" was the ancient equivalent of a handgun. They fired poisoned darts and, enchanted like most sophisticated devices of the era, they never ran out of ammunition. The darts were magically replaced in the barrel immediately upon firing. As well, they could only be fired by their rightful owners by speaking a personalized "kill word", though very experienced magic users had been able "hack" them. The deadliest and rarest varieties, such as those used by Akshani and her clan, were also enchanted so that they never missed their target. Thus the intention to kill and the act of doing so became one and the same for them.*

Bringers of Death? How desperate must these people be to dare attack us?

My heart heavy, our stingers hissed out their deadly issue at the oncoming horde, dirty-faced and dressed in their filthy, torn scraps of fabric. Our swords sang as they whipped through the air, cutting down those who ventured too close before the toxins from the darts could take effect. I took no joy in this fight. There was no honor to be found in taking down hungry people who had nothing left to lose but their lives. The slaughter was carried out with grim efficiency, and when it was over, I sighed at the ground before me, slick with blood and littered with twitching, frothing, poisoned bodies.

I couldn't dwell on it. I kept my weapons drawn as I gave the signal to continue moving forward. If we didn't reach the entrance to Thoth's hideaway before sundown, we could expect more attacks like this and I was eager to avoid more pointless killing.

Fortunately, we encountered no further resistance and reached the remains of a temple. Inside in a deep vault was a door we needed to get through, but it was blocked by a large chunk of stone that had been deliberately placed there. Child's play for a mystic, to us mere mortals it presented more of a challenge and with levers made of slender trees from outside and ropes from our field packs, we were able to shift the block.

The door was magically locked, but my Wayfinder Stone contained the correct sequence of symbols to press on the frame of the door, along with the proper spell-words to intone while doing so. It made me uncomfortable to wield such magic but there was no help for it. The titanic door swung open with an ominous scraping noise and revealed the swirling multicolor lights of the Maelstrom. Few of these doors remained in the world these days, we all paused for a moment in awe of it, both old soldiers and the striplings alike. Presently we all partook of the [3]*tjuba root* to minimize the effect of such travel on one's stomach, then linked hands and plunged into the swirling vortex.

We emerged in a vast underground cavern lit all around by a series of small, magically generated suns. Before my eyes had even adjusted, Thoth appeared, and I was not afraid because I knew him. He told me he believed he knew the secrets of my heart from entering my dreams. I would be

---

[3] *This reference to "tjuba root" is most intriguing. The problems with traveling via Maelstroms through the Place Between Places will be well known to those likely to read this volume. It appears the ancients had a natural way of combating this nausea, and further research will need to be done to determine what the tjuba root was and whether this plant still exists today. Rediscovering this plant could be of great help in deployment of the United Guild Forces in some future crisis. Doors such as this one is what enabled the rapid rise of the original global civilization. These days, such portals only survive at the bottom of the ocean, and of course only the members of the Ancient Brotherhood of Mariners know their locations and how to activate and navigate through them. Although expeditions are currently underway to locate land-based examples which are rumored to still exist*

lying if I did not admit that I also believed I had captured a glimmer of his own inner nature during such an intimate exchange. I had been struck by the sense of peace and wisdom which radiated from his being at that time. It was an overwhelming sense of firmly grounded *rightness* which I had never experienced. Indeed, I longed to feel it again. It was more like meeting a God than a man. As I now regarded him, I had to remind myself that he was all too mortal.

Before me stood the man from the dreams. A tall, dark-skinned man with a clean-shaven face, which was unusual for such an aged mystic. His head was similarly shaved clean and reflected gently the many balls of sunlight. He wore the deep purple robes associated with the members of his former Order. His eyes burned with determination and kindness.

I should not have been surprised he anticipated the exact moment when we arrived. It was said there are few secrets not known to him. Indeed, my own dealings with him had proven it true.

He cleared his throat, his eyes flicking to my retinue before returning to me. "Thank you all for coming so promptly," he announced in a sonorous voice. "Akshani, it is both an honor and a privilege to at long last meet you in person."

He raised his hand, giving me the standard greeting, which I returned. As I did so, I found it remarkable how at peace I felt in his presence. We had never met outside my dreams, but this meeting had the quality of being reunited with an old friend.

He went on. "It pleases my heart that you are here, but you will forgive me if I find it difficult to smile. We are almost ready to begin the ritual, and as you know, it is a most solemn occasion. You may observe it, Akshani, if it interests you to do so?"

I told him it did, and it was a decision I would come to regret. At that moment, however, I wished only to see such a renowned worker of wonders in his element despite knowing the ritual in question involved sacrifice. Death, and lots of it. But such things, I reasoned at the time, couldn't bother me. I was the Matriarch of the Bringers of Death, and I had seen enough blood to last a thousand lifetimes. Bloodshed was our currency.

I went alone. While the rest of my clan took the opportunity to rest and eat, Thoth led me to the enormous chamber where the ceremony was to be conducted. I couldn't tell if it was natural or hewn from the rock by some unimagined power. Made of the same stone as the chamber we arrived in, the entirety of it had been carved from floor to ceiling into figures of all sizes and descriptions, along with many symbols that were meaningless to me. We stood on an outcrop overlooking the level below which was thronged by a crowd of Thoth's followers large enough to obscure all parts of the voluminous floor. From my dreams I knew these to be the many magic users who had no interest in the war, or had come to hate it, as I did. I hadn't seen so many people gathered at one time since the last of the great metropolises had fallen only a precious few year earlier.

Thoth chanted a few words, and the text of the spell appeared writ large in the air above us. In a cracked voice he then turned to his people and thanked them for the sacrifice they were about to make. He swore to them it would not be in vain, that he would make sure what they freely gave that day would bring about lasting peace. I also felt moved and found myself fighting back tears, despite having promised myself I would not show such weakness for a second time that day. To display such emotion was not our way, although this was a tradition that I often wrestled with maintaining. I could grasp the logic in presenting ourselves to outsiders as emotionless killers, but why maintain the illusion even amongst ourselves? I often mused to myself that being honest with oneself took a certain kind of courage, that it was a strength, rather than a weakness.

Such idle thoughts were soon swept aside by the spectacle unfolding below me. I gasped when, at a signal from Thoth, as one everyone below raised their ceremonial daggers and slit their own throats. Old, young, even a few children, it didn't matter. In moments the floor below was a chaos of slick glistening red, the only sound their choking gasps as they died. I knew well the sound of a throat being cut, but never a thousand at once! It still haunts me to this day.

Thoth spoke the words of his spell, and with each word chanted, it disappeared from the text hovering before us. Then I took a step back as first one, then more, then many and all of the souls of the people below rose from the bodies and formed into bright balls of energy!

As Thoth continued his spell, they flew towards him, hovering in a space between his outstretched hands like a galaxy of fireflies. As his tone intensified, they merged, until where there had been a thousand small points of light, there was but one large brilliant one, the heat of so many lives warmed my face even at this distance. As he spoke the final words, the ball cooled, approached him, and fell into his hands, the flesh of which still popped and sizzled.

I meant to shout but stayed my voice as I looked into his eyes and saw no pain there. No, that's not right. There was pain, but it was the look of a man's heart being torn out, tempered by the steel of cold determination. What he had just done ran counter to everything he had ever believed in, yet at the same time it didn't. For in this instance, he believed the ends justified the awful means. The deaths of his closest friends, allies and even his own family. There could be no other choice made when the alternative was the loss of all life on Earth. Still, it meant that he was now alone. Utterly alone. Moved by all of this, I placed a reassuring hand upon his arm. I made the gesture without even thinking.

His head tilted in my direction, and I caught his eye, which glinted in gratitude. "It is done."

"Will it work?" I asked, my voice tiny and hoarse. It surprised me.

"It must," he said with finality. "Now, go. Leave me. Rejoin your people and get some rest. Tomorrow, Gods willing, we will end this war forever."

I bowed—not sure why, as I'm not one for bowing—and hurried from the chamber. That night I would have the first of my countless nightmares about the writhing, dying masses who gave their lives to create Thoth's Orb.

At Thoth's urging, we spent much of the next day training and sharpening our skills. Though his Orb was expected to make what we had to do next easier, it was a folly to believe it would be easy.

The great mage was not idle. He spent the bulk of his hours in astral projection. Gathering information, he explained to me, regarding the precise locations of our targets and their defenses. At long last, Thoth arose from his meditations. He gave me a gleaming magical pearl that would connect our minds together, so he could quickly and quietly direct our actions.

Thoth bade us follow him back to the massive doorway through which we had arrived. He set a new course for us as he waved his hands over the symbols hewn into the doorframe and chanted the words of activation. Once more, the rainbow lights of the Maelstrom called to us.

Before we departed, he turned to me. "There is one more matter." He unsheathed his bejeweled dagger and ran the tip across his thumb. He allowed a drop of his blood to fall upon the Orb clutched in the crook of his arm. In response the Orb lit up and in my mind I swear I could feel a thousand souls cry out to greet him.

The ghost of a smile played at the corner of his lips. "Now we are ready," he said, and with that, he took my hand and pulled me to the threshold of the door and beyond . . .

When we arrived at the other end of the door, we were inside the Eternal Palace. I recognized it immediately from the many [4]Story Stones I had seen set within these walls.

---

[4] Story Stones" were the ancient equivalent of movies or television. But instead of projecting the story onto some external surface, it projected directly into one's mind. They are still sometimes created and used in the instruction of young magic users. As well, a large cache was recently unearthed in the ruins of the Eternal Palace, which I am excited to have been told I will be given access to once they have been sorted and cataloged. It does not make up for the unimaginable wealth of knowledge which was lost when the Order of the Golden Path was annihilated, but with this discovery it is our hope not all of their secrets have been lost for all time.

Thoth communicated to me using the enchanted pearl which I now wore in my ear. He wore one as well, and through this link, he showed me the way to the private rooms where the Celestial Emperor and his queen lay slumbering. We had appeared only a few floors below it. Guards patrolled these corridors, but with the Orb in our possession, they would be helpless and unable to cast their spells. These guards were, like many of their kind, too arrogant to make use of enchanted weapons or other devices, which were not affected by the Orb. Enchanted items were below them, meant for the common folk unschooled in the arts of the highest magics. Dependence upon them dulled one's ability with the mystical arts, or so the thinking went. It worked to our advantage.

We needed to dispatch any sentries we happened upon as silently as possible, lest they raise the alarm. Thoth's Orb would prevent them from using their magic to defend themselves, but we could still be overwhelmed by sheer numbers or set upon by magical beasts. The latter Thoth assured me I should not fear, however, for he had seen no such beasts when he scouted the place earlier. At least, none which could fit inside a hallway.

With chilled blood I remembered it said that more than one Leviathan stalked the waters surrounding this island. Command of such monsters would do them no good in this battle. Nevertheless, the thought of them shook me. Years earlier, I had seen those monsters snap the largest sailing ship I'd ever seen like it was a bundle of twigs and I hoped to never look upon one of them again.

I returned my focus to the task at hand. Thoth's plan required that once we had killed the Celestial Emperor and his paramour, we would turn our attention to the Grand Vizier. Next would be General Hsua, also known as the butcher of Magdov, who also resided within these walls.

We encountered guards outside the doors to the Emperor's apartments. We set upon them unknowing, blades gleaming in the moonlight and stingers firing off their lethal payloads. We cut their vocal cords first as much to silence their cries of alarm as out of habit, as we'd all been trained to do when fighting spell casters. A silent spell caster is a dead spell caster. The Orb made irrelevant such concerns, but our conditioning was such that it was done without thought.

We burst into the room. The Emperor jumped to his feet but remained silent, too haughty to beg for his life. His queen clutched the bedsheets to cover her nakedness. How I laughed as the Emperor tried to cast a spell, only to find it impossible. This great villain had been the cause of all this trouble. His reckless ambitions had launched the conflict. I took great pleasure in seeing one so accustomed to wielding great power realize how utterly helpless he was.

I flipped through the air, landing upon the feather soft bed and took off both of their heads with one swing of my blade. The satisfaction I felt as this tyrant's head rolled off the bed and landed with a thud on the floor below is difficult to put into words even now. I bathed in his blood enjoying it like a sudden summer storm as it erupted like a geyser from his neck.

My only regret was this architect of such wanton destruction and his whore wife should have such a quick and simple death. I would much rather he be dragged behind a horse nude through the streets of all the cities of the world which fell to ruin at his command. Alas, he had made sure no cities were left, so this would have to do for now. *We have a larger mission to worry about,* Thoth reminded me though our mind link. I could not allow myself to get lost in the blood lust. With a reluctant sigh, I agreed.

Killing the Grand Vizier was no test of our skills. He lay asleep like a babe, in the grip of some pleasant dream while the world around him burned. It had been rumored that the Vizier was the one who had first planted such poisonous dreams in the pliant mind of his Emperor, that he was the true power behind the throne. He constantly beat the drums of war yet was too frightened to ever lead an army into battle. I felt great satisfaction in ridding the world of such a coward.

The so-called great General Hsua did not live up to his reputation as a mighty warrior without his magics to aid him. We cut him down with barely a struggle. The simplicity of this task was disappointingly anticlimactic. I was hoping to have my own mettle tested by one so renowned, but alas it was not to be. Still, I smiled knowing that the general whose countless atrocities had earned him the hated nickname of "Butcher" could never again sanction such crimes.

Wherever we left corpses, we left behind Story Stones to educate those who found them what must come next, and the consequences if they didn't.

Our mission completed, the time came when we were to take our leave of the Eternal Palace. Outside, Thoth [5]deactivated his Orb with a word.

Thoth set a new course for us at the door, first unlocking the magical protections which prevented the two factions from using these doors to attack each other. It was a testament to Thoth's skill as a mage that he could perform such a tremendous feat. Soon we were on our way once more.

---

[5] *The ability to deactivate an Orb is, unfortunately, one of the countless secrets of this elder age which has been lost to time. Today there is no known way to deactivate an Orb once it is turned on. Too bad. It would certainly make my life a bit more convenient sometimes!*

This time, we emerged in the [6]citadel of Thoth's own people. Or at least, those who had been his people, before he turned his back on them forever. Of course, he would say that they turned his back on him first with their own mad ambitions, and he would not be wrong.

We arrived ready for possible dangers. Thoth had warned us that unlike the other faction, his people used magical creatures, specifically [7]Man-Wolves as guards.

I had no fear of the Man-Wolves, as I had faced them before. They were fast, strong and only stingers that fired darts of silver or other purified metals seemed to have any effect on them, but if you could cut off their belts, they quickly transformed back into helpless, naked men. All the people of my clan knew of this weakness.

Moments within our arrival inside the citadel, the Man-Wolves had our scent and were upon us. We dispatched them as quickly as we could, but not before they tore out the throats of two of my finest warriors before the belts could be severed. I'm ashamed to admit I struggled to defeat the one

---

[6] *My research has indicated the location of this citadel now lies buried beneath the waves of the Black Sea. This was the original headquarters of the organization which today we now know as the Temple of the Old Gods, though they did not call themselves that then.*

[7] *Man-Wolves" were created through enchanted artifacts, namely, the wearing of an enchanted "wolf belt" dedicated to the Great Wolf Spirit. Such monsters (and much worse) were commonly used throughout the Great Magic War as living weapons.*

that leapt onto me, its hot stinking breath filling my nostrils as it slavered over my face, jaws chomping at the air mere inches from the tip of my nose. Worse, this one had no belt to cut off! I had heard rumors of such monsters: Man-Wolves created by surviving an attack from another Man-Wolf. They were physically weaker but could only be killed by weapons made from pure metals. Fortunately, Thoth came to my rescue, burying his ceremonial dagger of pure iron into the back of the beast repeatedly until it fell off me. Thankfully, my armor had protected me from its massive claws.

The scuffle alerted nearby guards, but these were all too human and with the Orb as our ally they presented no great challenge. Still, wary that all this noise would wake up the entire castle, we hurried on our way.

We broke into the room of the Great Shaman first. She did dare to try and beg to preserve her miserable existence once she realized she was unable to use her magic. Perhaps she thought the presence of Thoth would save her, but he had no mercy left, no patience for her since their war of liberation had turned into one of conquest under her leadership. In her own way, she was worse than the Celestial Emperor and his lot. They made no secret of their thirst for conquest and empire. But the Great Shaman had sought to create an empire for herself under the false promise of liberating those whose freedoms had been stolen by the Emperor's warlords.

I can stomach a monster that makes no effort to hide what it is. But I cannot abide by a hypocrite who comes to you with the open hand of a friend only to bury a dagger in your back with the other hand.

I had lost my firstborn child to her armies. My beloved chosen heir. This had happened before we retired from the conflict. In fact, the depth of this loss had been why we sat out the remainder of the war, although I would never have admitted this to my own people. The loss had made me want to do nothing more than hold onto and protect what I still had left to me. I couldn't shake the feeling that my selfishness had helped hasten the doom of the world. Perhaps if we'd played a more active role we could've ended this war sooner? Such questions will always torment me.

We silenced her lies forever, sickened by her unseemly cowardice. I felt immense satisfaction knowing that the witch who was ultimately responsible for the death of my baby was now in one of the Twelve Hells where she belonged.

We moved through the next few wings, eliminating her most loyal advisors and generals. As before, we left the stones behind wherever we went. We encountered resistance on exiting the castle, but at this point they were a mere annoyance.

This time, the door returned us to Thoth's caves. Despite his distaste for such bloodshed, he seemed more relaxed, more at ease, when we returned. I decided it was grim satisfaction. Even with the pearl out of my ear, his emotions were an open book to me.

He sat on a square outcropping of rock I hadn't noticed before and turned to me. "That went rather smoothly, all things considered. Better than I hoped, in fact."

I agreed darkly, my thoughts returning to the two warriors we'd lost to the Man-Wolves. Yet it could have been far worse. "Now what?"

He sighed. "Now, we wait. Give them time to understand what has just happened and consider our ultimatum. In a day we will see if they will join us at the meeting place."

That next day was filled with interminable waiting. Yet I noted that the distant sounds of war – constant sounds of distant explosions, which we'd all been able to hear even this deep into the Earth – had finally ceased.

Thoth, as usual, spent the day in meditation, which is to say he wasn't present at all in spirit. He was off somewhere in his astral body, gauging the reactions of the warring sides to the previous night's events.

The only time I did see him that day, he appeared to be in good spirits. "They will be there tomorrow. They're scared, yet oddly hopeful. We pruned the most radical elements from their trees. Those who are left now are as tired of this war as we are. I foresee a favorable outcome, but it will be a long and difficult road. There are many details to be worked out and much work to be done before the rebuilding can begin."

It was as Thoth had prophesied. When the new leaders magically teleported to the small island where I, Thoth and my people stood awaiting them, the great mystic immediately activated his Orb, trapping them there for the moment.

"Gentlemen, I see you got my message," Thoth stated, all business.

"Indeed!" The new Emperor, Vishan Dragonrider, barked, and repeated verbatim what the Story Stone had said. "End this war now, or we shall end you as easily as we ended your leaders. You have no defense against us. We will keep coming for you until all of you are dead if you do not cooperate. You have abused your power, used it to break the world, now you must use these great gifts to fix it. Meet with us in one day to discuss how."

He cleared his throat, adding, "Yes, blunt enough, I'd say!" His voice conveyed a mixture of fear, awe and respect.

The new Great Shaman bowed to Thoth. "I should have known it would be you who was behind this! They all said you were dead, but I never believed it. What exactly do you propose?"

Thoth gathered his robes about him. "An immediate end to all hostilities. The globe will be divided into separate, equal spheres of influence. Emperor, your people will control the Eastlands. Great Shaman, your people shall control the Westlands."

The two leaders looked pleased by this pronouncement. They each believed it left them in a more secure position than they were currently in.

Thoth's voice dropped lower in warning. "A war of this magnitude must never occur again. Never again will magic be used for conquest. To this end, only the members of your respective organizations will be allowed to use the higher magics. Your most sacred duty, going forward, will be to prevent the common people from discovering these secrets lest a new faction arise that will abuse this power as we have. Outside of our three factions, there will be no use of magic, or enchanted items, by anyone. The common people will use their wits and their muscles and craft tools to do what once we did."

The Great Shaman scowled at Akshani and her retinue. "Three factions? Do you mean to equate these common assassins with our people?"

Thoth drew himself to his full height, which was considerable. "There is nothing 'common' about Akshani or her people," he replied icily. "They shall be the keepers of this new order and the guarantors of its peace. They will bring death to you, your descendants, all those who know the secrets of the Titans, if they must. I have given them this power, and even now, in your impotence to work even the most rudimentary of spells, you feel it."

The Emperor slapped Thoth on the back. "Very well, no need for threats, friend! We are as opposed to the continuation of this conflict as you are. We have already been speaking to one another. We were both horrified as our old leaders became increasingly obsessed with using magic for domination. From now on, I declare that my Order shall be known as the Order of the Golden Path, and we shall seek the perfection of the human spirit through magical means over the pursuit of earthly riches."

Thoth looked less than enthused at his touch, but he didn't reject it. "I'm pleased to hear that. I suggest that you three meet here regularly, to chart out the future shape of this new world. Also, you should come up with a way to resolve your conflicts peacefully, perhaps through ritualized combats rather than actual wars?" He smiled at them indulgently, as a parent to a child.

"This is all well and good," the Great Shaman objected, "but no magic outside of our organizations? What a smaller, meaner, more primitive world it will be! Already, the common people who have fled the conflict zones are reverting to tribalism."

Thoth shifted ever so slightly so the Emperor's hand fell from his shoulder. "Yes, for a time, for perhaps even a very long time indeed, your estates will be the only true bastions of civilization. Yet I have foreseen a time when the common people will work out how to do most of the things we are used to doing through magic with the aid of machines."

The Great Shaman laughed at this idea. The Emperor did too. It did seem a ludicrous thought that mere machines could ever do what only magic did. Thoth appeared pleased to hear them both laughing over the same thing. It had been a very long time since anyone had heard much laughter in this world.

We all agreed to meet there again in a week's time. Thoth deactivated his marvelous Orb long enough to allow them to leave, and for us to teleport back to his caverns.

When we returned with the news of our success, my people broke into a raucous celebration that would last well into the next day. My people are not above showing jubilation at the sight of victory. It's the more vulnerable kinds of emotions that they eschew.

That night, he asked to see me in his room, and when I entered, he looked up from his desk. "Akshani, thank you for all you've done. Thank you for believing in a crazy old man and his wild dreams."

"It's been my honor," I told him, and I meant it. But why did this feel like a goodbye? Surely, we had so much work left to do together. I decided to head him off. "You can't leave now!" I said, more desperately than I intended. "We still need you! I still need you!" I nearly slammed my fist on his desk.

He shook his head and chuckled. "Nonsense! Things are finally on the correct track. All is now as I have foreseen. The peace will hold for millennia to come. There will be more wars, countless wars, but they will be wars fought with machines and never again Magic War, at least not on the scale of this one. I have already shown you how to turn the Orb off and on, but I suggest that once I am gone, you always leave it activated, so it can never be taken from you."

My eyes flicked to the Orb on his desk, his ceremonial dagger next to it, then back to him, a terrible sense of foreboding seizing me. "But where will you go?"

"I wish to be reunited with my friends, my family again," he said quietly.

He means to join the Orb, I thought with horror. There was only one way inside the Orb and we both knew it.

I lost all control. The tears flowed down my face freely, and for the first time in my life, I was not ashamed of them. I did not turn away or wipe them away. They were the least I could offer as a tribute to this great man, who had brought peace to this shattered world. I realized with an unburdening sense of freedom such a naked display of emotion was nothing to be hidden away and denied. And I had known it all along. It had taken Thoth to make me see. It must be why he chose me.

I would teach this truth to my clan. I would change the ways of my people, to make us into something better than what we were. Thoth knew that I would fulfill my plan to transform my people into the kind of noble guardians he desired to safeguard the future. It was just one of the many things he'd foreseen.

My hand trembling, I reached out with strength to take his. He took it with a warm smile. His skin felt delicate, like the petals of a flower. I stammered. I could not find the words.

"Tears for me, Akshani? I am honored, for I know what that means for you, but don't mourn. This is a happy occasion for me. Now, farewell. I know that you will succeed." With that, he released my hand and in the same movement swiftly seized up his dagger and plunged his dagger deep into his chest, while chanting his arcane words. As he slumped in his high-backed chair, I spied his spirit as it flew out and entered the deactivated Orb that sat upon the desk before him. It glowed for a moment as he became one with it.

Though my vision remained blurred tears, I wasted no time. I pulled the dagger from his chest, and as he had commanded, reactivated the Orb with a drop of his blood from the tip of it.

I cradled his head to my chest. "I will never forget you. I will see to it that the world never forgets you."

I am a warrior, not a scribe, but I entrust this chronicle to no one else. I write it to keep that promise, so that the world may never forget the man who sacrificed everything, including ultimately himself, so that the world may know hope once again.

Author's Note: So ends Akshani's narrative. She did make good on her promise that the world would never forget Thoth. The ancient Egyptians regarded him as a God. The ancient Greeks believed that he was the equivalent of their God Hermes. Even well into medieval times and the early Renaissance, he was remembered as Hermes Trismegistus, the wisest of all mages, though their rationales for that belief were completely wrong.

Thoth was an unusually powerful sorcerer with vast knowledge unknown even to his contemporaries. They say that for a living person to touch an Orb is an unpleasant experience and 'spooky,' but Thoth himself seemed to believe it was an afterlife realm unto itself. So, it may be the souls within it do not merely power the device, but are aware within it and are at peace.

Thoth lives and is with his family. Absent contravening evidence, I choose to believe it.

THE VIVISECTIONIST

From The Case Files of
Matt Spike, PI

Part One: The New Digs

The chill of winter clung to the air like a bad memory, biting into Matt Spike even inside the idling moving van. He considered turning on the engine and letting the heat blow on him, but it would be a good while before the engine warmed up enough. He hoped it wouldn't be too much longer before his parents showed up with the keys to this place.

He sighed when he thought about how he could have had half the van unloaded in the time he'd been sitting around here waiting for them. He'd spoken to his dad on the phone the prior night and asked why he couldn't just tell the building superintendent he was the landlord's son and get him to let him in. His father had shot that idea down, insisting on personally letting him in for reasons he wouldn't go into.

Matt studied the unremarkable brownstone that was to be his home. It wasn't much, and it certainly wasn't in the best of neighborhoods, but he couldn't complain. It was *free.* Lord knows he couldn't afford an apartment of his own in this city without having to put up with multiple roommates, let alone one with office space. This place, modest though it was, would have to serve as both until his business took off and he could afford better accommodations. It had taken some verbal arm twisting to get his father to let him have it, that and his mother nagging his dad into acquiescence. She could always be relied upon in a pinch.

Now here he was, about to strike out on his own, with his very own detective agency. He couldn't help but feel a surge of excitement at the idea. His childhood dreams were finally coming true. He was a real life private eye now, living in the big, bad city. He'd already been working as an investigator at someone else's agency for several years now, part-timing it while going to college, and getting enough experience to apply for his PI license.

Now the time had come to spread his wings and take flight on his own, and he just hoped it didn't all come crashing down before his dad grew tired of indulging his eccentricities.

The lights of his parents' Oldsmobile swiped through the left-hand mirror as they pulled into the open space behind him. *It's about fucking time.*

He jumped from the cab as his father exited his car and rounded on him. "What took you guys so long? I've been here for over an hour."

"You know what traffic is like trying to get into this city," his father Frank, said through gritted teeth. His tone told Matt he should be grateful he had come at all.

Matt's mother, Sheila was still struggling to pull herself out of the car, her ostentatious fur coat making a challenge of it. Impractical in the extreme, but she insisted on wearing it, practically begging for someone from PETA to come along and toss a bucket of red-dye-for-blood on it.

Still, he looked at her jealously. *At least someone here is warm.* He buried his freezing hands into the thin pockets of his tan trench coat, wishing it was at least lined.

His mother, finally extricated, ran toward him and smothered him with hugs and kisses.

"Oh my Matt! I've missed you so much!" They hadn't seen each other since Matt had come back home to Jersey for Christmas. It was early March, so that was almost three months ago now, an epoch in mom-time.

"I've missed you too, Mom," he said, not realizing how true it actually was until he said it and found himself choking up a bit. For a moment he was a child again, buried in the warm, comfortable embrace of his mother's bosom. Then, almost as soon as it had come, the feeling was gone again.

His father's voice ground like a dying car transmission. "C'mon. Let's get this over with. I oughta get my head examined, letting you talk me into this! Staying in this fine piece of prime real estate rent free! I should make you the new Super, so you can at least earn your damned keep for once!"

Matt rolled his eyes. This was probably the third or fourth time he'd heard some variation of this same exact sentiment out of him. "You really trust me with a hammer? Or a plumber's wrench? Besides, I can't be a Super and a PI at the same time!"

His father spat. "The phone will be ringing off the hook with new cases, I'm sure.

"Thanks for the support, dad," Matt said drily.

His father scoffed and continued to rant as he led the way up the concrete steps and into the building. "My son the Private Eye! *This* is what I paid for four years at Columbia for? With your brains, you could have gotten a nice business degree so you could take over the family business someday. I never should have let you read all those silly detective books as a kid! Bargain-basement Sherlock Holmes, you reckon? It's time to grow up and stop playing pretend!"

Matt's mother shot her husband a dirty look. "Oh, give it a rest already! It's too late to whine about all of that now. I think it shows initiative that he wants to start his own business. He's his own man, not just a carbon copy of you! We're here to support him today!"

His dad cast her a look. "I'm supporting him all right! Living rent free in New York City!" He shook his head. "Think of all the money I'm losing out on! This whole thing is nuts. There's no money in being a gum shoe."

Matt breathed out through his nose, hot dragon steam in the cool air. "That's not true. As an independent contractor, I can charge whatever I want. Some of these guys really make bank! My old boss was living pretty large."

"Bah! Selling your time, how many hours in the day you got? The *real* money is in real estate!" His father chuffed.

Matt almost laughed out loud. At this moment, his father reminded him too much of Lex Luthor in *Superman: The Movie*. He even sort of looked a little like Gene Hackman.

"Even so, there's more to life than making money, Dad."

"Oh yeah? Really? Like what?"

"Ahem!" Sheila cleared her throat theatrically. "Do you notice anything different around here, Matt?"

Matt looked around. They had arrived in front of several rows of mailboxes. Nearby was a bronze plaque with a directory of the businesses that had offices here emblazoned upon it in rows of removable plates. This building was zoned for both commercial and residential. A few businesses had offices on the first couple of floors and the rest were apartments. Most of the offices in this building were vacant and had been for years. Despite his father's grandiose claims, this was anything *but* prime real estate. He really wasn't losing much of anything by letting Matt set up shop here, and at least the space would be used for something other than housing rats.

Matt noticed something new on the plaque and smiled. "Matt Spike Investigations. Nice." It all felt a little more real now, seeing it written there in black and white, or rather black and bronze.

"Yeah, yeah. Really cool. Let's all get a move on already, okay?" His father repeatedly jabbed at the elevator call button with one pudgy finger. Eventually the ancient elevator arrived, and its doors croaked open

They all entered, and Frank's eyes took the measure of the space. "Ya think you'll be able to fit yer bigger stuff in here?" Matt was mildly surprised; the man's tone was practical, not biting.

He wondered how long it would last. "The couch might be a tight fit, but I think it'll work. You mean there's no freight elevator?"

"In this place? Dream on!" His dad laughed humorlessly.

Matt found himself wishing his father had let him have an office on the first floor, but that had been out of the question. Those offices were "prime real estate" in the old man's eyes, even if no one else's.

The elevator reached Matt's floor, and they waited for the doors to open, long enough for Matt to wonder if he was going to die here. But they did open.

"Someone's coming to service this thing on Thursday," Frank muttered as they exited.

As they stepped out into the hallway, a rat the size of a small car went skittering by. Sheila screamed and grabbed onto her son's arm as if to climb him.

"And an exterminator is scheduled to come in next week, I think," Frank added.

His mother had had it. "This place is a dump! I don't want to hear another word out of you about Matt staying here for free. *We* should be paying *him* to live here! How can you live with yourself?"

"I live with myself just fine when I see the balance in my bank account, thank you very much, and it keeps you in fur coats. Where do you think all that money comes from?"

She pulled her coat around her, and huffed, "I just didn't realize some of these properties were so . . . shoddy."

He led them down the hallway, and he wasn't done. "People just don't want to work anymore. Is it my fault good help is so hard to find these days? I *was* hoping that maybe my boy, my only son and heir, would be able to help me out with keeping on top of these things, but noooo! All he wants to do is run around the city playing Dick Tracy!"

She grabbed her husband's arm. "Hush now! You're going to ruin the surprise with all your negativity."

Matt smiled. "Surprise? So *that's* why you insisted on giving me the keys in person!"

"Is that what you've deduced, oh great detective? Took ya long enough!"

He had. It wasn't a stretch, not once his dad refused to offer a believable reason why Matt couldn't get the keys from the Super. But he didn't want to spoil the moment for his mother, whom Matt had no doubt was the culprit behind setting up whatever it was.

And there it was. On the frosted glass window that was set into the door was painted the words, "Matt Spike Investigations – *Truth is Our Business!*"

He ran his fingertips across the words. "Truth is our business, huh? That has a nice ring to it! Did you think of that, Mom?"

She gushed like a rig in Texas. "You'd better believe it! This cheapskate sure as heck wouldn't do anything this nice for you. Good thing you have a mom who loves you!"

"I love it. Thanks, Mom!" Matt kissed her on the forehead. "Truth is our business! It's perfect! I need to put that on my business cards!"

Matt's dad shook his head in disapproval, but it had a different quality than before, and when he spoke, the tone was softer. "Ya know, Matty. I might be more enthusiastic about this new venture of yours if it didn't include changing the family name. It's like you're ashamed of your roots, ashamed of *us*."

That hit Matt like a gut punch. "It's nothing like that, Dad," he said, but now that it was out there, he wasn't so sure of it himself. After all, he'd fought through miles of red tape to legally change his last name, and he'd told himself it was because it was too long and difficult for people to pronounce correctly...bad for business. But the truth was he'd always hated his Polish last name that, to him, marked him out as something "other" when all he wanted to do was blend in. He hated being the target of every truly tasteless joke in the book about dumb Polacks. And yes, when he was growing up there literally was a popular series of books called "Truly Tasteless Jokes" and each of them had an entire section devoted to jokes about Polish people. He'd pretended to laugh along, to show what a good sport he was, going along with it to have friends. But inside there was always the anger. The *shame*.

So, was his father really so wrong? Wasn't he at least a little ashamed of his heritage? Years later, after much of the pain left over from his childhood had faded away to a dull throb and he was more open to embracing his ethnicity, he would wonder if changing his last name had been a mistake. However, that was a long way off in his future. At this moment in time, throwing off the yoke of his family name felt like having a great burden lifted from him. It felt like exactly what he needed for a fresh start.

His father deserved an explanation, and he'd give the best he was prepared to give. "Look, dad, back in school, everyone used to just call me 'Spike' because it was the only part of our last name they could pronounce. 'Matt Spike' became a part of me and all I did was make it official. Don't take it personally." He put his hand on the man's shoulder in a way he hoped was reassuring. "It also happens to be a good marketing move, it's nice and punchy! I think it sounds cool."

"It's not cool," his father shot back. "Sounds like the name of a damn porn star."

Sheila glared at him. "A 'porn' name, huh? And how would you know that?" she demanded archly.

"I'm a man of the world, I've been around," he blustered without looking at her. "In my younger years, of course."

"Of course," she echoed skeptically.

"'Spike' sounds tough," Matt put in, desperate to get back on topic. Like Mike Hammer, it's a really good name for a PI."

"No, it's *not*. It doesn't sound tough at all! It's stupid! You didn't think it all the way through, son. A spike is something that gets hammered, driven down, it's passive. In life, you don't want to be a spike, you wanna be the thing that's doing all the hammering, not the thing getting nailed! It makes you sound weak!"

Matt sighed. "I think you're reading too much into this, Dad. And....a spike can be something that pierces through all the lies and deceptions, and nails down the truth."

Matt's father stared at him long enough for Matt to think he'd won, but no such luck. "Hmmph!" His father said but had nothing more.

"Are we going to stand around all morning arguing in the hallway, or are we ever going to go inside?" Sheila asked impatiently.

"Oh. Yeah." Matt's father dug in his coat pockets and held up a set of two keys on a ring. "The little key is for your mailbox downstairs. The big key is for the deadbolt." He unlocked the door and it squeaked open.

They walked into a large, spacious room. A door in the far-left corner led into a room behind, and through the door was a room with a single window which faced out onto the street. Off to the side was a tiny bathroom.

As they moved through the rooms, disappointment darkened Matt's mother's face. "Where's the *kitchen*? How do you expect him to eat?"

"This is an office, not an apartment," Frank offered, and waved toward one of the walls. "There's plenty of room to put in a fridge. And an oven, if he has to."

Matt didn't want yet another fight. "Yeah, it's okay, Mom. I still have my mini fridge from college, a microwave and a toaster oven. I've been living with a set up like that for years." He chuckled. "I never trusted my roommates not to steal my food otherwise."

She wasn't going to be so easily put off. "You're not in college anymore. You should have a real kitchen! And what about a sink? How are you going to clean your dishes?"

"I'll just use the sink in the bathroom, Ma, it's fine. Relax."

"Washing dishes in the bathroom!" she scoffed. "The very idea!"

"Calm down," his father broke in. "The kid says he's fine with it. Who are we to argue? Now let's get that van unloaded, and maybe we can beat the five o'clock rush out of the city."

It was all Matt could do to resist belting out a 'hallelujah.' He was eager to get settled and get started on his new life.

They spent the next hour hauling things into the office. His father complained the loudest when they had to bring his couch up. "Why is this damned thing so heavy? You got a dead body hidden inside, to kick off your business?"

"It's a fold-out, Dad. All steel and mattress," Matt said tiredly. It was what Matt had been sleeping on for the past few years. His father was right about one thing, though, in a way: it tended to stick and was such a pain in the ass to make it bed-like, nine times out of ten he didn't bother and just slept on it as a couch. He didn't really mind; he was used to living like that.

Once the van was cleared out and returned to where it was rented from, they all went out to dinner. It was his father's treat, and he didn't let Matt forget it, especially when he ordered the steak.

"Well, I hope your business is a success, son. Once you start turning a profit maybe you can finally afford to pay me some rent?"

"Sure, we'll see how it goes once I start getting on my feet." It sounded reasonable enough. Matt wished his father would stop plucking that string on his tiny violin. Beyond that he'd never hear the end of it from his father if he couldn't prove himself as anything other than his father's lackey, he'd never really feel like he was his own man who wasn't still beholden to his parents, if he couldn't make good.

But his mother had other ideas. "Oh no! We don't need to start charging him! We should just let him stay indefinitely for free. It's the least we can do for him, he's our only child! We've got plenty of money, and you can never get all the offices in that building filled anyway. Now that I've seen it, I can certainly understand why!"

"Plenty of money?" Matt's father scoffed. "Baby, there's no such thing!"

Despite his complaints though, Matt's mother eventually won out on the argument.

She always did.

Part Two: Getting a little Randy

Once he was back in his new place, Matt set about halfheartedly unpacking. The first thing he unpacked was his gun, a matte black nine-millimeter pistol he usually carried when he was on a case, though thank God he'd never had occasion to use it. Truth be told he wasn't sure he had it in him to shoot someone else and wasn't in any rush to find out either. And the sound of the thing kind of terrified him; they were so much louder than in the movies.

His boss at the detective agency he used to work for had insisted he get one though. It wasn't easy. New York City had some of the toughest gun laws in the country, but his old boss knew how to grease the wheels to speed up the process.

Matt tried unpacking a few more things, but after spending so much time with his parents he was dying for a smoke. He didn't dare light one up while his mother was around, as it would be sure to trigger a lecture. Despite how cold it was, he decided to smoke out on the front steps of his new home. He wanted to watch the sunset over the city and felt like he could see it better outside than through the single grimy window he had.

Matt slipped into his fedora and his trench coat on his way out the door and down the hall. Dressing the part of a PI always made him feel a little stronger and less vulnerable, like a knight strapping on his armor. As the chill air hit him, though, he was reminded how badly he needed to get a trench coat that was a little thicker. This one wasn't much better than wearing a sheet, but it was all he could afford at the time. At least it had plenty of pockets. One could never have enough pockets! He dug inside one of these marvels of textile engineering to extract his crumpled pack of cigarettes and silvery Zippo lighter.

As he sat there, watching the diminishing sun daub the clouds with brilliant hues of orange, red, pink, and yellow, a calmness washed over his soul. It was more than just the nicotine. Watching the sunset was almost a religious experience for him, about as close as he ever got to one. His anxieties about striking out on his own were temporarily extinguished by the majesty of the spectacle in the sky. He watched the people on the street rushing around and pitied them for missing this slice of beauty.

He thought about what his next move *should* be, which was to finish unpacking all his shit and get the office looking somewhat presentable should he be fortunate enough to get a client tomorrow, which was his first official day open. Yes, that's what he *should* do. But he already knew it probably wasn't what he *would* do.

What he *would* do when this cigarette was done burning would be to give Sara a call.

Sara Berry was the closest thing he had to a girlfriend at the moment, although it was more accurate to say he was her frequent "booty call." He'd met her a few months earlier, when he'd attended a convention for private investigators that was held at the stately old Manhattan hotel where Sara served as the "Hotel Detective," which meant that she was in charge of security.

She was almost ten years his senior. A former NYPD officer, she was smart, sassy and also sultry. She was exactly the sort of woman he'd always hoped to be with someday. She was also very independent, as she'd already been through one disastrous marriage and had vowed to never go down that road again.

He was feeling more and more frustrated with their current "arrangement." Not so long ago, a relationship with no strings attached to it like that would've suited him just fine, but he'd done enough sowing his wild oats in college and was entering the phase of his life that was about getting serious about settling down. God help him, he was even starting to think he might want kids. He thought that he might be falling in love with Sara but whenever he brought up the subject she became irritated. Her response was always to tell him she cared about him, just not in that particular way. But when they were deep in the throes of passion, when she was crying out his name like a plea to the heavens, it was hard to believe her.

In fact, today. He recalled how she had been into helping him move until he mentioned it'd involve meeting his parents. "Meeting your folks?" she said. "I don't think so, Spike! Wouldn't want to give them the wrong impression about the two of us."

At least she didn't lie, but she laughed, like it was some kind of joke.

He wasn't sure why it bothered him so much. She *felt* like his girlfriend. They did pretty much all the things people did in that sort of relationship. Hell, most of the time *she* was the one calling *him*, and not just for a booty call either. She called when she was lonely, she called when she was bored, she called whenever she needed a shoulder to cry on.

And he always answered the call too. Good, old, reliable, Matt.

What a sucker he was! As far as he knew, she wasn't messing around with anyone else, at least regularly. So why not call it what it was? And why did putting that kind of a label on the relationship matter so much to him anyway? Was it all just an ego trip? Would the fact she was so unattainable in that way make her even more irresistible?

Did he want to be the man who finally tamed her and made her break her vow?

All he knew was that whatever it was they had going on between them, it didn't feel entirely healthy. He often felt used and underappreciated. Yet he couldn't stay away. He was powerless. He knew he'd call her tonight, and if she agreed to it, he'd come over and one thing would lead to another as it always did. It was like a fucking addiction, like any other drug.

Jesus! What was wrong with him? Why couldn't he just find a nice, normal girl to settle down with who didn't have all the hang ups Sara had about having a deeper kind of relationship? His mind drifted back to some of the women he'd known in the past. He was full of regrets for the opportunities he'd missed out on. One particular woman from his past was still always crossing his mind: Naomi Waters. They'd known each other as far back as Middle School, when Matt had first moved to the sleepy Jersey shore town of Barnegat, but they hadn't really become good friends until High School.

Matt's friends had convinced him to take the school's "Improvisational Acting" class. "It's an easy "A", they assured him. "You just goof around like we do when we make movies, but you get graded for it – leniently!" They hadn't been wrong, either. Matt and his buddies made their own silly comedy movies with a camcorder for fun, and the class was like doing that, except without a camera.

Naomi was also in the class, and that's where they first became close. He'd had a thing for her since the first time he saw her. No, a *pull.* She was the first girl he'd ever struck up a conversation with for no other reason other than that he was smitten with her. Everything about her seemed right, like recognizing a kindred spirit.

Matt took one long, last drag off of his cigarette before flicking the filter into the gutter.

He hadn't asked her out. His courage and confidence never extended that far, and now, she was far away and spoken for. Maybe he hadn't felt worthy? Either way, someone else had swooped in, someone who wasn't shy about going after what they wanted. Shortly after graduation she was married and pregnant. He didn't go to the wedding.

He'd even seen her son once, when he ran into her at a WaWa convenience store on a holiday break from college. The kid was a cute little guy. Had Naomi's eyes, and it made him sad. He couldn't help feeling it should be his kid, if he'd just believed in himself a little more.

He and Naomi chatted for a bit. She was taking some night classes at Ocean County College, to get a jump on a distance learning program at a more prestigious school. She gave him her number.

Matt never called. The old feelings came flooding back, if they had ever left, and he knew his intentions in calling her wouldn't be pure. He didn't want to be *that guy!* She seemed happy, secure. What right did he have to try and take that from her, or take her son away from his father? And what if he failed, as he almost certainly would? It would mean the ruin of a valued friendship, forever tainted, pleasant memories shit upon.

He shook his head and stood up. *Ah, Naomi! The one that got away. How she haunts me to this day!*

So lost in his rueful thoughts of the past, he didn't even see the kid on the steps until he'd already bumped straight into him. The kid was tall for his age – almost as tall as Matt – and Matt stood out in a room. Definitely somewhere around fourteen or fifteen years old: his face hadn't yet grown into his nose, his forehead and cheekbones were that kind of red always associated with the first flush of hormones, and his upper had a generous helping of peach fuzz Matt was convinced had not yet known the touch of a razor. Thick glasses perched atop that nose, and he wore a stained tee shirt and baggy jeans. The kid was a little plump and, Matt decided with the help of a chance breeze, smelled like he had just rolled out of bed.

"Sorry, kid. Didn't see ya there," Matt said, and waited for the kid to get out of his way..

The kid didn't get out of the way, and instead stared up at Matt with his round face. "No problem! Hey, aren't you that private eye guy? Matt Nail or something?" His breath reeked of Cheetos.

"Spike," Matt said. "Matt Spike, is the name. Actually."

"Oh yeah, that's right! Spike, not Nail! Duh! I saw you move in. My name's Randy Grumman. I live on the floor right above you. Are you a real detective?"

Matt did a double take. "Don't I look like a detective?"

Randy studied him for a second before responding. "Yeah, you've got a trench coat and fedora but that's such a cliché. I didn't think that private eyes dressed like that in real life. "

"Well, *this* private eye does dress that way for real. Plus, it's cool."

"It's not *that* cool," Randy replied undeterred.

What's with this kid? If ever there was a poster kid for daily toilet dunking, it was this kid, and Matt was about to say so when the kid spoke up again.

"But I *do* think detectives are cool. Sometimes I stay up all night reading and I love to read mysteries. I especially love Sherlock Holmes stories. Hey! If you ever need a sidekick, you know, like Dr. Watson or something, just let me know."

Sure, kid. That would be a good look for me, a grown man hanging around with a teenager with personal hygiene issues!

Matt nevertheless was flattered by the attention. The kid was obviously lonely and needed a friend. It wasn't too long ago he'd been in the same boat, though Matt liked to think that even as a teen he took better care of himself than this kid did.

Hell, truth to tell, Matt felt like he was *still* in that boat. Since moving to the city, he hadn't made many new friends, at least not the kind you could really depend on, as evidenced by the lack of help he'd gotten in moving in. The only person he could really confide in was Sara, and he was mostly on his way to being convinced she only tolerated his yammering because she hadn't yet tired of fucking him. Yes, he sure could use a real friend too, but he didn't think he'd find it in this pudgy, underaged misfit.

Matt took a step to the left. "Sorry kid, I don't do sidekicks."

The kid followed, still standing in the way. "Well, then maybe I can be more like one of the Baker Street Irregulars or something? Run errands and keep my ear to the street for you?"

Matt glared at him. "Maybe," he said through gritted teeth. Internally he was thinking there's no way he wanted to encourage this kid to hang around his detective agency. The whole encounter was coming off to be a little creepy anyway. Was he stalking Matt?

I really should just tell him to buzz off and never bother me again, Matt thought, but didn't have the heart to do it. The kid's enthusiasm that a PI was working out of his building was so earnest it was almost infectious. He probably would have felt the same way at that age, considering how obsessed with detective stories he'd been.

Matt took a deep breath. "It's been nice meeting you Randy, but I really need to get moving. I've got lots of important detective stuff to do, ya know?" Of course, the only important "detective stuff" awaiting him were two rooms of boxes badly in need of being unpacked, and he'd already resolved to shirk that responsibility tonight if Sara was amenable to his coming over to her place. He shifted around Randy, again.

This time the kid didn't move to stop him. "Oh, I totally understand! Keep me in mind if you need a little help!"

Matt rolled his eyes at that last comment and entered the building. Once he was inside his not-kitchen, Matt rang Sara's phone. Once she picked up, he tried talking her into coming over to his place, thinking that maybe once they were done messing around, she might stick around and help with the unpacking.

Not surprisingly, she laughed at the idea. "The only people who love that part of town are the slumlords, Spike! It can get dangerous down there at night, sorry. Besides, you don't even have a proper bed! You should come here; my place is *much* nicer."

Matt sighed at the superficially obvious excuse, and the explicit lure of a proper bed...She could handle whatever nocturnal dangers this part of the city could conjure up. She was one tough cookie. It was part of what he found so attractive about her. But he had to admit that her place, a well-appointed suite in the swanky uptown hotel where she worked, was a far more pleasant environment in which to conduct their activities than his worn leather couch. So he headed over there in his beat up old Hyundai Excel with the usual mixture of genuine excitement and helplessness about the inevitability of it all.

Part Three: Lean Times

The next week crawled by at an agonizingly dull pace.

Matt found he had no trouble finding time to unpack, in fact he seemed to have nothing *but* time on his hands. He hadn't received a single phone call from a prospective client. The only calls he got were from his mother checking in on him, various long distance phone service providers trying to entice him to switch to them, and the occasional booty call from Sara. He passed the time vegging out in front of his TV watching his favorite noir detective movies, playing video games or reading while waiting for the damned phone to herald the arrival of some much-needed business.

Sometimes, he'd sit and listen to big band and swing music. Immersing himself in these relics from a bygone age which he only knew of through movies and books was usually oddly comforting to him. Something about the era of the 1930's and 40's had always called to him, it all felt *right* somehow. Yet even this outlet provided only cold comfort. He couldn't enjoy any of it when he felt like he should be out there doing *something*. He felt too guilty just sitting around by the phone. But what else could he do?

He began to fall into depression. Perhaps his father had been right after all? Was he just pursuing a pipe dream? He couldn't stomach the idea of crawling back to him and telling him he was right and asking for a spot in the family business. If anything, he'd lived much of his life in defiance of becoming like his father, at least ever since he'd become old enough to take the measure of the man as an equal and found him wanting.

No! Matt thought. *I am a real detective! I've already worked as an investigator for the past few years, I won't give up now!*

Of course, the difference between then and now was that he'd worked at somebody else's detective agency. An agency that had been around for years and had a solid reputation. But now that he was out on his own, it was frighteningly obvious to him how much having a good reputation was to getting any business. He also wondered if he wasn't spending enough on advertising. He thought about running some more ads, but when he looked at the ever-dwindling numbers in his bank account and the diminishing food stocked in his mini fridge, he felt that he couldn't risk it. How much longer would he continue to coast on the savings he'd managed to stockpile? Something had to change, and soon.

In the end, he'd had to swallow his pride and call up his old boss and mentor from the detective agency he'd recently left. A man by the name of Alan Collins.

"Hey Alan, how's it going?" Matt said casually.

Alan chuckled. "You know how it is, same shit different day. So how have you been since you decided to become my competition?"

Matt winced. "Not so great, actually. I can't seem to attract any clients."

"I'm sorry to hear that," Alan said, sighing heavily. "You're a straight arrow with a real talent for the game. You play like a cynic but you have a love of people and I always admired that. That's rare, especially in this gig." He cleared his throat. "I tried to tell you this was a bad idea. You're good, kid, but green." A pause. "You know there's a place back here for you if you decide to pack it in."

Matt wanted to shout "Yes!" but didn't. "I don't think I'm ready to call it quits just yet. It's hardly been about a week so far. I was wondering though . . . if there were any cases that you turn down, if you might want to send them my way?"

Alan sighed again, this time longer and deeper as with wind rushing from a cave, and he didn't mince words. "You know that I only turn down the really kooky cases. Or the ones that I think might be a little too dangerous. Or morally compromising. Are you sure you want to take on that kind of shit?"

Matt cringed, knowing he sounded desperate, but the problem was, he was. "Yeah, that's no problem. Right now,

I'd take on anything. Better dying on the street than of boredom. Maybe."

"That's dark," Alan remarked after a pause. "But all right. Sure. I don't suppose I mind helping out an old friend. But watch yourself, don't get so desperate you'll do anything you might regret. Or might not live to regret."

"Thanks, Alan. I appreciate it, I knew I could count on you."

"I just hope I'm not making a mistake. You should see some of the nuts that want to hire a PI sometimes! Well, I guess you *will* see what kinda nuts I'm talking about soon enough. Just be careful, Matt. And remember, my offer still stands."

"I will, thanks again Alan." He was grateful that Alan was willing to take him back. He'd certainly rather go back to working for him than go to work for his father.

"Eh, be careful what you wish for. You might not be so quick to thank me later! See you around."

Matt swallowed, his mouth dry. "Bye, Alan."

Days dragged by, and Matt was beginning to wonder if Alan would come through for him after all, and how long he could make the ramen soup last, when a call came in. He had just made a chipped cup of mix-in coffee.

"This is Matt Spike? The detective?" The voice was tremulous and small, like a little girl's.

Not a prank call, please don't be a prank call. "Yes, the one and only! How may I help you?"

"Well, I think my cat has been kidnapped, and I'd like to hire you to help me get her back."

Dammit. "Forget it, kid! I don't look for missing cats! I'm not Ace Ventura, Pet Detective ya know! This is a serious business I'm trying to run here! Don't waste my time by calling back, or I'll find out who *you* are and tell your folks what you've been up to!" He slammed down the receiver.

Matt slumped, held his face in hands between his knees, not knowing if he should scream or cry. Was he ever going to get a case?

The phone rang again, and he stared at it like it was a viper ready to bite him. He wished he'd taken note of the number on the caller ID before he'd hung up. With resignation, he picked up the receiver.

"Hello, thanks for calling Matt Spike Investigations. Truth is our business! This is Matt speaking, how may I help you?" he said as he always did, each time more resolutely, now with all the excitement of a train announcer.

"You should be ashamed of yourself, a grown man yelling at a little girl and hanging up on her like some sort of a bully!" a woman's voice shouted at him. "Don't you have any idea who just called you?"

Matt looked to the heavens for help. *This is hell. I am in hell.* "No, I don't know who she is, nor do I care. But I can tell you're busting to enlighten me, so go ahead." He took a sip of his coffee, which had gone cold.

"That was Lily Vanderhoff, and she was completely serious about hiring you!"

Matt sprayed his coffee all over his desk at that name.

"Clyde Vanderhoff's kid? The one who thinks she's an actress?" He asked while wiping the caffeinated dribble from his chin with one sleeve.

"She *is* a *very* talented actress, actually," the woman on the line sniffed.

"So, then this is Mrs. Vanderhoff, I presume?"

"Then you presume incorrectly. Mrs. Vanderhoff is far too busy and important to deal with something this trifling. I'm Lily's nanny, Ms. Knots."

"Of course, you are," Matt said drily as his mind raced. He wasn't interested in reading the drabble of the social columns, but even *he* knew about Clyde Vanderhoff and his daughter. It was such a notorious story at the time that it reached Matt even under the rocks he used to crawl under.

Clyde Vanderhoff was born with a silver spoon in his mouth, courtesy of one of the city's oldest and richest families. He'd first made a name for himself in the Eighties when he doubled his inheritance through a series of risky

Wall Street investments. Recently he was in the news because his ten-year-old daughter Lily wanted to be a star on Broadway. However, even the Vanderhoff fortune couldn't buy her a leading role. No casting directors would give her anything other than bit parts. So, Clyde put on his own show for Lily to star in. No mere puppet show, he'd purchased the rights to adapt the *Madeline* series of children's books – apparently his daughter's favorite – as an off-Broadway musical. The reviews were mixed to terrible, yet daddy moneybags continued to sink his fortune into the endeavor.

Fuck it! Maybe I'm not so above playing a little Ace Ventura after all? Matt thought. Time to show a little humility. "Okay, I'm sorry I hung up on the girl, Ms. Knotts. Surely you can understand that I thought it was a prank. I don't typically have kids calling me, and you have to admit that the idea of having your cat kidnapped is pretty out there."

"I suppose. That's what the last detective we tried to hire told her," she said dubiously. "I believe his exact words were 'this case is too kooky for me, but I can refer you to someone who might be interested.'"

Matt almost laughed. *Alan wasn't kidding about 'kooky.' But he threw me a major bone by turning down a case that could have such a lucrative payoff, and I owe him, if it does.*

The woman's voice warmed, just a little. "As for having her call you herself, I did think it was a poor idea personally.

But Mr. Vanderhoff insists on instilling a certain degree of self-sufficiency in his daughter."

"I see," Matt said indulgently. "Are you free today? I'd be happy to arrange a time with you to go over the details of this case here at my office." He shifted papers looking for a pen and found one.

"Today? I'm afraid that's out of the question. Lily has two shows to perform. There simply isn't any time. Perhaps tomorrow morning? It will have to be quite early, however. Around 8:00 a.m.?"

He didn't usually start until 9:00 a.m., but who was he to argue. "Sure, that's fine. Do you have the address?"

"We do."

"Well, good," Matt remarked, mildly surprised. "I look forward to getting to the bottom of this for you." He rubbed his chin and said, rhetorically, "Who on earth would want to kidnap a cat?"

Ms. Knots answered. "This cat is a Savannah, one of the rarest and most expensive breeds on the planet."

"You don't say!" Matt said several moments after remembering to breathe.

Matt had never heard of this kind of cat. He didn't know much about cats at all. He'd never owned one. His mother had always insisted on maintaining an immaculately clean home, and this excluded any pets that shed hair and dander.

An endless series of fish he could never quite manage to keep alive for very long were the only type of pet Matt had been allowed to have when he was growing up. What was the old saying? "Every boy should have a dog". Well, Matt was the boy who never had a dog. Or a cat for that matter. It was something he dreamed about rectifying someday.

"Was there a ransom note?" Matt inquired.

"You can't very well have a kidnapping without a ransom note, now can you?" Ms. Knotts replied in an exasperated tone.

"Or a catnapping," Matt quipped, eliciting a groan from Ms.Knotts over his punsmanship, but his next question was more serious. "Did you show the note to the police? What did they make out of it?"

"Unfortunately, they didn't take it seriously, despite the Vanderhoffs being generous regular patrons of the policeman's ball. It's been quite frustrating. That is why we are pursuing alternate lines of inquiry such as yourself. Lily is very attached to this poor, sweet animal, whose safety might be in danger, yet nobody wants to treat this matter with the gravitas it deserves."

"Well, don't worry too much about it. Here at Matt Spike Investigations, gravitas is our business." Matt put in while hoping that he wasn't laying it on too thick. *I already have the job. No need to keep on kissing her rich ass so hard.*

"Oh?" Ms. Knotts replied humorlessly. "I thought *truth* was your business?"

"Yeah, that too!" Matt said to salvage the situation.

"Well," said Ms. Knotts after a long breath, "we can go over the finer details of the situation when we see you tomorrow morning, Mr. Spike. 8 a.m. sharp. You will not be late. Remember that it is rude to keep a lady waiting, especially one as influential as Lily Vanderhoff."

"I'm looking forward to it!" Matt said, not looking forward to it. Seeing this snobbish woman in person was tenth on his top five list of things he'd rather do tomorrow. That said, the prospect of getting out of the office and actually working on a case – even one as silly as this one – excited him, but not nearly as much as the prospect of finally getting some money flowing in did. Still, he groaned inwardly at putting money first. *My God, I'm turning into my father!*

But he did remember one thing before hanging up. "Ms. Knotts . . . please be sure to bring a copy of the ransom note with you."

"But of course," she said condescendingly. "Goodbye, Mr. Spike. I will see you at 8 a.m. tomorrow."

"See you then, goodbye."

The receiver clicked with finality and Matt smiled. Perhaps his luck was changing?

Matt told Sara all about this new case as he lay in her bed that night, tracing his fingers along the smooth, supple lines of her marvelously long legs.

She turned toward him; her head propped on her hand. "Geez! Alan must really like you to hand a case like this over to you! You should charge them at least double your normal rate. These rich bastards can afford to pay it, and you need the money."

"Price gouge them?" Matt said, still running his fingers up and down those legs. "I don't think so. That's the sort of shit that my dad would do."

She shrugged her bare, statuesque shoulders, "That's the sort of shit that people have to do to make it out here. The sooner you learn to accept that, the happier you'll be."

His fingers stopped, and he looked her in the eyes, debating standing on principle versus his chances of getting laid in the future. The ease of the choice surprised even him. "Well then I guess I'm just doomed to be a miserable bastard for the rest of my days," he told her.

Part Four: The Sordid Details of the Abduction of Mr. Fluffy

Matt woke up early enough to ensure he would greet his illustrious potential clients on time. It wasn't easy. He'd been up rather late at Sara's place the night before and, quite frankly, she'd worn him out. Also, he had an unfortunate tendency to sleep through alarm clocks. However, through sheer force of will he'd forced himself to wake up on time, and after half a pack of cigarettes and two cups of coffee that could peel the paint off of a battleship, he was more than ready to face the day.

He straightened up his office as best he could. It wasn't all that much of a challenge as it was still rather spartan in its contents, mirroring his bank account.

At precisely 8 a.m., a pair of silhouettes appeared through the frosted glass of Matt's front door. One tall, the other short. The tall one's hand made a sharp, staccato rapping sound on the window.

"Come in!" Matt called, hoping he didn't sound too gruff.

In walked a tall, model thin woman wearing a dark, tight-fitting dress. Her hair was a bob of tight, brunette curls. A designer handbag was slung over one shoulder, and her expensive-looking heels clicked like carpenter's nails on the rough hardwood floor of the office. She looked about as thrilled as most people did when they had to visit this crumbling structure, only more so. Matt guessed that she was only a few years older than he was, and beautiful, but in a cold and remote way, like a softball-sized gemstone under glass. For some reason, that air of inaccessibility made her all the more attractive to Matt.

Matt's eyes scanned down to Ms. Knotts' companion, who was without doubt Lily Vanderhoff. He'd seen her in the papers and on television. Small in frame, she looked to be ten or eleven years old but was actually thirteen, if he remembered correctly from what he had read about her. A slightly built ginger little thing, she looked like a better fit to play Little Orphan Annie than Madeline.

Not dressed like a child either, or with a child's bearing. She wore a mink stole wrapped around her shoulders and an outfit to rival Ms. Knotts' in style. It absurdly struck Matt that this child looked much more adult in the fur than his own mother.

"Please have a seat," Matt said, and gestured to a pair of well-worn chairs he'd rescued from the Salvation Army.

Ms. Knotts did so, though with a clear look of distaste that she should have to suffer such an indignity. Lily, on the other hand, sat with no apparent judgment, and fixed him with her intelligent eyes.

Whether intended or not, it was an unexpected gesture of respect from the young scion, and with an inner wince, Matt recalled how he'd yelled at the girl just the day before and decided an apology was in order. "Ms. Vanderhoff, I'd like you to know that I'm sorry about how I spoke to you yesterday over the phone."

"Please, call me Lily," she said in a crisp voice, and with an exaggerated wave of dismissal Matt guessed she acquired from seeing the adults in her life do a thousand times. "And think nothing of it, it's water under the bridge. Just bring back my Mr. Fluffy safe and sound, and all will be forgiven. There will be a substantial bonus in it for you as well."

Matt blinked at the mention of "a substantial bonus." *Could this get any better?* "Mr. Fluffy, huh? So that's the name of the, um . . . victim?" He tried to sound serious, but it was difficult under the circumstances.

"Yes, it's a rather misleading name though. While it is true that she is somewhat fluffy, she's a female cat and not a male. You see, there was some confusion about the sex when I first obtained her, and I stubbornly refused to rename her once the discrepancy was brought to my attention. Ah, I was so young and precocious then . . ." Lily said wistfully.

Matt had to stifle a laugh at the idea of this little girl nostalgically pining away for her younger more innocent days, but he sensed something more. Gone or suppressed was the nervous and uncertain person Lily had been on the phone yesterday – replaced with this one who had a kind of over the top, forced air of sophistication and confidence. Here was someone who was desperate to be taken seriously, to prove herself worthy of the respect adults often take for granted.

In an odd way, he felt a certain kinship with her. Were they so different? She was a child of privilege using her family's fortune to chase after her dreams. Although Matt's family couldn't boast anywhere near the kind of wealth that the Vanderhoffs possessed, his dad had done pretty well for himself in the real estate game. Matt's life had been pretty comfortable up until he went off to college, and most of his discomfort in life since then was self-inflicted. Wasn't Matt basically doing the same thing Lily was? Taking advantage of his family's assets to advance his own ambitions? And like Lily, didn't he also often hide his true self behind a facade – in his case, his perhaps cartoonish idea of how a "hard boiled" private eye was supposed to act?

Matt snapped himself out of his reverie. "So how long have you been acquainted with Mr. Fluffy?" The words felt strange coming out of his mouth.

She blinked as if to hold back tears. "Three wonderful years. We're quite inseparable! I bring her with me everywhere. That's why she was at the theater with me when she went missing."

Three whole years! Yeah, I'll bet you were so different back then! Matt thought with bemusement.

"I see," Matt said, making a show of taking notes. "So, she was abducted from the theater?"

"Yes. I usually keep her on a leash, but when I or Ms. Knotts are unable to attend to her, she's kept in a cage in my dressing room. A very spacious, nicely appointed cage, I might add. Really more of a mobile kitty apartment than a cage. That's where she was when she went missing last Tuesday. We were doing an evening show and when I returned to my dressing room, she was gone." Her voice cracked.

Ms. Knotts reached into her designer purse and produced a folded square of paper. "This is a copy of the note that was found inside the cage."

Matt had to stand up in order to retrieve it over the length of his rickety surplus store desk, and when his fingers brushed the woman's hand, it was every bit as cold and frosty as her general demeanor. He studied the note. Typewritten, and the kidnapper (catnapper?) had made multiple errors and had bothered to fix them with correction fluid. It read: "I have Mr. Fluffy. She is safe for the moment, but what happens next depends entirely upon what you decide to do. I will contact you again soon with my price for her safe return and where we can meet. Keep the police out of this or Mr. Fluffy will suffer the consequences."

Matt snapped the note with his index finger and addressed Lily. "Mind if I keep this?"

"Certainly, it's merely a copy," Ms. Knotts answered for her with a wave of her hand identical to the one he'd seen Lily do earlier. "The authorities have the original."

So that gesture comes from Ms. Knotts, Matt thought idly, and wondered how many other things she'd picked up from the older woman? He eyed the woman surreptitiously as he sat down and realized she was also putting on something a show herself. Perhaps trying a bit too hard to prove that she fit into a world of high rollers that she hadn't been born into? Was she the one who was really behind this? Maybe she resented having to raise someone else's child? Did she feel that she was underpaid for her services? Could you ever really pay someone enough money to mother a child that wasn't their own, if the affection they received from the child wasn't compensation enough?

It was tough to read the woman or gauge the closeness of her relationship with Lily. She was utterly glacial, impenetrable.

"So, despite the warning in the note, you still decided to contact the police," Matt said drily.

Lily blew out a breath. "Yes, my father insisted on doing so. He hoped the police would set up an ambush for the kidnapper when it was time to do the exchange, like in the movies. I suppose they still could when the time comes. It's been over a week now and I haven't heard anything further from the kidnapper, I'm starting to fear that I never will. That's one of the reasons why we decided to hire a private investigator. That, and the fact they were treating the whole thing like a joke! Do you know that if a person is kidnapped, they immediately turn the case over to the FBI? But because an animal was the victim, they wanted to hand it over to Animal Control! My father had to raise quite a fuss to get them to treat it like the theft of a luxury item." She banged her fist on the arm of her chair.

Matt felt for her but tried to keep it professional. "Do you happen to have a copy of the police report?"

"No, but we can certainly obtain one and fax it to you, assuming you have a fax number." Ms. Knotts said airily.

"I do," Matt said after counting to three. "Good. Any idea how the official investigation is going so far?"

Lily barked a laugh. "What official investigation? As far as I can tell, all that the police did was interview a few people that same night, take the ransom note with them, and tell us to call them if we heard from the kidnapper again."

"They only spoke to a few people?" Matt asked, flabbergasted. "Obviously it was either someone with regular access to the backstage area, or they're working with someone who had that kind of access. With a production as big as yours I imagine that would be a pretty big list of suspects." He couldn't believe their incompetence; they really weren't treating this seriously. Was it so surprising though? Clyde Vanderhoff had ruffled many feathers and made many enemies in his time. So many that even his great wealth couldn't buy him a fair shot at getting justice.

"They limited the list of suspects to people who had access to a key to my room, despite my telling them that I had left it unlocked that night."

"They interrogated me as if I was a common criminal!" Ms. Knotts exclaimed, drawing a surprised glance from Matt. It was the most emotion that he'd seen the woman display aside from projecting an air of general haughtiness. He noted she gripped the armrests of her chair so hard her knuckles were white. Obviously, it had been a harrowing experience for her. However, he couldn't blame the cops for questioning her, she was certainly at the top of his list of suspects too. He made a mental note to be particularly delicate when it was time for him to question her himself.

"Who else did they speak to? Who has a key?"

She pulled her spine straight and settled herself before answering. "Aside from myself and Lily's parents, only the members of the janitorial staff have a spare key."

Matt nodded once and turned his attention to Lily. "But *you're* sure that the door wasn't locked?"

"I usually leave it open. The cast and crew, all of us, are like a little family. Door locks are rarely used. Which is another reason why this stings so badly. Besides, they all know that their jobs depend on my father's continuing support of the production. It would be stupid to jeopardize all of that by stealing from me."

"Not if the payoff far outweighs what they'll get working for you," Matt said half to himself. He could understand the cops wanting to narrow down their pool of suspects, but if she really didn't bother to keep her dressing room locked, then practically everyone in the whole damned production were suspects.

He rubbed his temples, as his head throbbed at the prospect of how many people he'd have to talk to in order to get to the bottom of this. "Do you have a picture of the victim?" Matt was curious to find out what such an expensive cat might look like.

"Yes, of course." Lily produced a rectangular leather wallet from her purse, from which she extricated a photo that she handed to Matt. It showed Lily smiling next to a grayish brown cat with black stripes, and extraordinarily large ears made to seem even longer by curved tufts of hair on the ends. They almost looked like a pair of horns at first glance. A cat like that would definitely turn lots of heads, but he wasn't sure he'd ever be willing to pay thousands of dollars for one. Then again, he didn't have piles of money just sitting around idly either.

He wondered if a cat like that would still fetch a good price on the black market. Maybe the kidnapper wasn't stupid enough to risk getting caught trying to collect a ransom in order to profit off this theft? Matt had no idea how to go about searching for illegally obtained exotic pets, but it was something he would have to figure out soon.

He held it up. "Do you mind if I hold onto this? I can return it to you when the investigation is over."

"Keep it," she said, seeming brighter. "We have the negatives; I can always make more." She looked at him hopefully. "So, you're going to take the case? You're going to help us?"

"Yes. It would be my pleasure." Matt was surprised to find that he meant it. It would be genuinely good to be doing something other than haunting this office waiting for the phone to ring, even if this case did sound like it might be something of a pain in the ass with a low probability of a happy outcome. He was also surprised to find that he liked Lily Vanderhoff, despite the media writing her off as a spoiled little rich kid with no real talent. All Matt saw was a little girl who was scared she might not ever see her pet again. A little girl who maybe wasn't being treated fairly because her father had a reputation for being kind of an asshole.

He could relate to that.

"Thank you! Please bring Mr. Fluffy back! She's my only real friend in the world!" Lily exclaimed, a single tear falling from each eye and threatening to be followed by many more. Matt thought he caught a look of jealousy cross Ms. Knotts porcelain features, but it was gone as soon as it appeared, and he couldn't be certain he hadn't just imagined it.

Again, Matt's heart was touched by the sincerity of Lily's plea. All her pretensions of trying to impress him with how adult she could be had vanished, to be replaced by true vulnerability. She was indeed just a lonely kid who longed to be reunited with the only living thing that loved her unconditionally, that didn't judge her because of who her parents were or how vain her ambitions might be.

The rest of that visit to his office was spent going over the boring details of what hiring him entailed and signing paperwork. Ms. Knotts looked almost insulted by what Matt's hourly rate was, even though it was comparable to what most

PIs charged at the time. Then again, she always looked as if everything around her had slighted her in some way. Matt realized he could have gotten away with inflating his price as Sara suggested, but he didn't really regret not doing so. He wasn't in the business of taking advantage of people. That wasn't to say he was comfortable discussing all these details. When he worked for Alan, he was just assigned his cases, and these kinds of things were already hammered out by an office secretary. Matt hoped someday he'd be able to hire someone like that to deal with all this dull business stuff so he could focus entirely on solving his cases.

They all agreed Matt should begin his investigation as soon as possible, so it was arranged he would come by the theater when it opened later that day. The entire cast and crew would be encouraged to cooperate fully, and he would have access to the entire building.

When they left his office, Matt rubbed his hands together in anticipation. He had a lot of work ahead of him.

Part Five: A Gilded Cage

Matt arrived sometime past noon at the theater. Despite not being on Broadway, it was still as large and impressive of a set up as any he had seen there. Not terribly surprising since this production aspired to capture the feel of such a show. As he'd been instructed, he told the people at the box office who he was and was ushered through a side door. The building manager, an old fellow named McDermitt, gave him a quick tour of the place.

Matt inquired about the security at the theater, specifically if there were any surveillance cameras covering the exits. He was disappointed by McDermitt's answer, which was to bark out a bitter laugh at the very idea. Apparently, the only part of the theater that was covered by cameras was the box office area. Matt doubted the thief would have taken the cat out back through the front doors. Of course, this raised the question of how the thief got the animal out to begin with. How did they entice Mr. Fluffy out of her cage and into whatever they had carried the animal away in? If they had a cat carrier it must have been concealed in some way, as it would have been noticed otherwise.

Matt asked to see all the exits to the building. He noted most of them couldn't be opened without triggering an alarm, including the one closest to Lily's dressing room. McDermitt assured him that he was the only one who could disable the alarms. The only exit that wasn't alarmed led to a back alley that was completely walled off, and for that matter was almost constantly populated by various employees on smoke breaks. With the possibility of other options thus eliminated, the idea of walking out the front doors didn't seem so unlikely anymore, so Matt asked to see the security footage from last Tuesday. That turned out to be a possible dead end because the cameras barely caught anything outside of the confines of the actual box office. They had been set up to make sure that the employees working the window weren't pocketing some of the cash for themselves. The footage they'd captured that day was completely useless to him.

Matt began interviewing anyone that he could corner for a few minutes. It wasn't easy at first, as the place bustled with people trying to do their jobs and was an intractable problem until he took a smoke break in that back alley. He discovered that, sooner or later, almost everyone ended up there, they felt more relaxed and willing to talk while having a smoke.

Be careful what you wish for. Between the cast and the crew, there were well over a hundred people working on this show or involved in maintaining the building, and Matt began to feel overcome by the enormity of his task. Most would have been working the night of the theft and eliminating those few cast members who would have been on stage during the time window during which the theft must have occurred didn't help much. At times like this he wished he had a partner to divide up the work with, but he doubted it would be any time soon before he could afford to hire any additional investigators.

All that said, Matt enjoyed being in a theater again. It brought him back to his high school days, which for the most part were happy. He'd enjoyed his "Improvisational Acting" classes, although he was a mediocre actor at best, and a poor singer at a school that mainly put on musicals. Being in a theater again made him think longingly of Naomi, whom he'd first started to grow close to while they were both in Improv class together. He wondered what she was doing right now? Did she sometimes wonder the same thing about him?

Matt also checked out the scene of the crime, Lily's dressing room. Dominating one corner was an enormous cage with golden colored bars. Considering who had bought the cage, he pondered if they were gold-plated. He eliminated that they might be solid gold because in that case they would've taken the cage and left the cat.

According to his client, the cops had already dusted for prints and found nothing, and it wouldn't do him any good anyway because he didn't have access to any of the federal databases of fingerprints. There was no lock on the cage door, it was just a simple latch. The thief wouldn't have needed to possess any lock picking skills to open it up. Mr. Fluffy's food bowl sat inside the cage, half eaten, along with the fanciest looking litter box he'd ever seen. Matt figured Lily didn't have the heart to touch any of it until the cat came home. He hoped it wouldn't become a memorial.

Matt hung around long enough to watch a performance of the show, mostly from backstage, while exploring to get a feel for where most of the cast and crew would be while working and score the occasional interview. True, he couldn't devote his full attention to it, but to his surprise, he found it wasn't half bad. He also felt that while Lily wasn't going to set the dramatic world on fire, she had some talent and didn't deserve some of the savage reviews she'd gotten in the press.

Unfortunately, the attendance at the show wasn't all that great. It was far from being a packed house. Half the people attending were probably there to see if the show was truly the train wreck the media portrayed it as. With some guilt Matt had to admit to himself he'd assumed it was and had the same morbidity curiosity. With such low attendance, he wondered how much longer Mr.Vanderhoff would continue to throw his money away on this venture.

Speaking of the big man, there was no sign of him nor his wife, and not that it mattered. He was strictly prohibited by

Ms. Knotts from speaking to them, let alone interviewing them.

"They're not suspects. They didn't steal their own cat, so there's no point in bothering them. It's ridiculous enough that the police wasted their time doing so," she informed him in her typically airy way.

Matt knew damned well that sometimes people did seemingly crazy things like that, but he couldn't think of a single plausible motive to do so. Even if the Vanderhoffs had a big insurance policy on their pet, he couldn't imagine they needed the money, so he didn't argue. He wasn't looking forward to meeting Clyde Vanderhoff anyway. He had a reputation as a difficult, abrasive man. He would probably act doubly so to someone who he'd see as a paid subordinate. After the show, Matt congratulated Lily on her performance, something that he'd never thought he'd be able to do with such earnestness. He told her he'd return the next day to talk to more people and began the trek home. He tried not to think about how much work was still ahead of him and how unlikely it was that he'd be able to crack this case. He had no promising leads so far, or even a theory about how it was pulled off. Then again, he'd only talked to slightly under a quarter of everyone who worked at the theater. He hoped the next day's activities would yield a break.

Starved, he grabbed some fast food and polished it off on the drive back from Manhattan to Brooklyn. When he got back home, he decided to have a smoke out on the steps to clear his head. He could smoke inside, but he'd been cooped up all day and the weather had been warming up lately.

As he walked towards the front door, he spotted that weird kid Randy sitting out there on the steps, and briefly reconsidered, but where would he go? He sighed. The kid seemed to always be hanging around on these steps. He'd already ended up watching his beloved sunsets through the window of his office many times because of him. In the end, he decided he'd be damned if he was going to continue to allow some kid to stop him from doing what he felt like doing.

When he stepped out the door, he noticed that the boy was reading a book, using a small flashlight. It seemed like a pretty odd thing to be doing out here on the street at this time of night.

Randy turned his head to see who it was, and greeted Matt nonchalantly, like they were old friends. "Oh, hi, Matt," he said.

"Hello," Matt said noncommittally, and turned away more than he had to to light his cigarette.

Nothing more came from Randy, so Matt turned back to observe him, and actually felt sorry for the kid trying to read a book with the dubious assistance of a dim flashlight. Inwardly cringing at possibly starting a conversation he didn't really want, he said, "You know, you're gonna ruin your eyesight reading in the dark like that don't you?" More cringe: it wasn't lost on him how much he sounded like somebody's dad.

"I already have," Randy said enigmatically and tapped the side of his glasses. He looked up from his book. "My brothers are making too much noise right now, so I came out here. Sometimes I try to drown out all the noise they make with my headphones and my Walkman, but I'm afraid if I do that too much, I'll end up hurting my hearing. I'd much rather be blind than deaf. I love music too much to be able to deal with being deaf. At least if I was blind I could still read using braille. I'd rather "see" the pictures in my head than what reality has to offer up anyway. It's usually better."

Matt found that all poignant and was glad to know it. "I didn't know you had any brothers." He blew out a puff of smoke.

"Yeah, two of them. But they'll be out of the apartment soon, now that they're both adults. They're talking about getting a place of their own together. Then it'll just be me and my Aunt, and I'll finally have a little peace and quiet for a change."

Matt imagined what it must be like with so many people crammed into a space that likely wasn't bigger than his tiny office. No wonder the kid was always out on this stoop! He probably had very little privacy.

Another puff of smoke. "What're you reading there, kid?"

"Twilight of the Gods," Randy said, flipping up the book slightly. "It's Norse mythology, specifically about Ragnarok, that's what they called their–"

"Apocalypse," Matt finished. "Yeah, I know. I've read it."

Randy's eyes got big. "I didn't realize you were interested in mythology."

"Sure. I read that one because the Thor comic books got me curious about the Norse stuff."

"Yeah, it's really *stimulating*, isn't it?"

"It's not bad," Matt said, warming to this. "I like all that fantasy stuff though. Yeah, I like *Lord of the Rings*, and especially anything to do with King Arthur. I even used to play AD&D with my friends."

Randy looked wistful. "I have all the AD&D rule books. My brothers will hardly play it with me anymore though now that they're older."

Matt groaned inwardly, hoping the kid was just being honest and not trying to guilt trip him into playing the game with him. He was often bored in his office, but not *that* bored. He decided to subtly change the subject.

"What I really like is Star Wars. That's probably what got me into fantasy in the first place. If you think about it, it's just fantasy set in space more than it is serious Sci Fi. I see all kinds of echoes in it if that Arthurian stuff I'm so into. I mean, Luke gets his father's "magic" sword, just like Arthur did, right? And it marks the beginning of his life changing, of him having to grow up – what Joseph Campbell calls "The Hero's Journey." Obi-Wan Kenobi is the Merlin character, "a crazy old wizard" and mentor. They even have an incestuous relationship between a brother and a sister, just like Arthur and Morgaine."

Randy nodded eagerly. "I've noticed all those parallels too! So you've read Joseph Campbell too? You really are into mythology, aren't you?"

Matt leaned back against the handrail. "I just like a good mystery. Mythology is mysterious. Magic is mysterious. Fantasy stories have both elements in abundance. I have to confess though, I never actually read Campbell, although I've always meant to. Back home where I used to live at the Jersey Shore, our local community college has its own cable TV channel. They used to play old video tapes of Campbell's actual classes. I used to watch them all the time because I knew that he influenced George Lucas."

"Yeah, I know. Lucas used to be one of his students." Randy said.

"Yup." Matt acknowledged. "Those Joseph Campbell classes were always really interesting. They gave me a whole new appreciation for mythology. I'd sit through them, even though the picture quality on those old videos was totally shitty! Like, I mean so shitty they'd make your eyes wanna bleed, ok? I'd usually listen to them while I was doing something else because they looked so bad. But the content of those old lectures . . . that was pure gold."

He had to reluctantly admit to himself that it felt good to have someone around to geek out with for once. Sara was many things, but nerdy was not one of them. And forget about his parents. And did he have any real friends? He was alarmed to realize how lonely he was.

"I'm jealous," Randy went on, oblivious. "It's almost like you got to take one of Campbell's classes for free. There's nothing that cool on any of the local cable channels in this damned town."

"Yeah, it was cool, but honestly I can barely remember the details of most of those lectures nowadays, just that I thought it was some good stuff at the time. He's supposedly working on the prequels now, you know? George Lucas, I mean. I wonder how closely that's gonna follow the story of Arthur's dad, Uther Pendragon. I can't wait for them to come out."

"I dunno," Randy said sagely. "My gut tells me that you probably shouldn't mess with a classic, and I always try to listen to my gut."

Matt couldn't help but glance down at the kid's expansive waistline and resisted the obvious joke. Instead, he said, "That's probably some good advice. The other investigators at the detective agency where I used to work always used to say how important it was to trust your instincts when working a case."

"The Jedi say so too."

Matt grinned with his lopsided smile. "Yeah, they do, don't they?"

"So, are you working on any interesting cases lately?"

Matt shrugged and put out his cigarette with the toe of his shoe. *Hell, why not?* Going over what he knew with someone else might help him to see something he'd missed. And besides, the kid seemed unusually bright for his age, maybe he'd offer some fresh new insight. Randy listened in rapt silence as Matt laid it all out.

Matt didn't stop there, and went on by discussing his insecurities, which surprised him. "It's hard not to feel like it's completely hopeless with so many damned suspects. Sometimes I wonder if I'm wasting my time at the theater. What if the ransom note is just a total red herring to throw everyone off? Like maybe the thief is gonna sell it on the black market instead of trying to collect a ransom? Maybe they've already sold Mr. Fluffy? If so, I don't know how I'd ever get her back. I don't have the first clue about how to start looking for her on the black market for exotic pets. I don't even know how to find that black market."

Randy looked away in thought for a moment, then back, and said, "What does your gut tell you about the ransom note being a red herring?"

Matt didn't answer out loud. He already knew he wasn't listening to his gut when it came to that possibility, and that's what was really bothering him about how he was handling this case. He was probably trying to ignore his instincts because he was so afraid of having to delve into the shadowy and possibly dangerous world of black markets. But if the shoe fit . . . he had to consider the possibility.

"I think you should look for someone who seems the least obvious," Randy continued. "Perhaps even someone who might have a motive other than money."

"Someone with a motive other than money?" Matt scoffed, but he had to admit this was a new angle that hadn't occurred to him. "You mean like a crazy cat lady?"

"Yeah," Randy continued, undeterred. "Or any serious animal lover. It could be that they want to keep a cat that rare and cool looking for themselves."

Matt tilted his head, considering. "If that's true, it would have to be someone who's a real loner, somebody who doesn't socialize much with their coworkers. Otherwise, they'd spot the cat if they ever came over to their place." He looked down at Randy as if seeing him for the first time. "Thanks, kid. You've sure given me a lot to think about."

"Anytime! I'm always happy to help out!" Randy beamed, but then seemed to lose all interest in the matter. He turned back around, clicked his flashlight back into life and picked up reading his book right where he had stopped.

Matt was bemused at being so effectively dismissed by a teenager, but he didn't mind, and left Randy to it. He had to admit he'd underestimated the boy, and he had just demonstrated he was useful to have around. *Still not ready to take on a sidekick*, Matt thought with a chuckle.

Matt didn't call Sara that night, being too busy poring over the copious notes he'd taken interviewing the employees at the theater. His talk with Randy had energized him to find something he'd overlooked. Maddeningly, nothing did, and he fell asleep at his desk, too tired to even go to bed.

Part Six: Breaking the Ice

The next day after his talk with Randy, Matt decided he needed to take a closer look into Ms. Knots as a suspect. After all, she'd set off plenty of his alarm bells the first time he'd met her. What was it Randy had said? To look for someone who didn't have monetary gain as a motive. He'd wondered about the nature of her relationship with Lily. Did she love the girl or resent having to raise her? The woman had seemed so frigid that it was impossible to imagine her loving anyone.

Perhaps stealing the cat was her twisted way of getting back at Lily or her parents? A way for her to derive cruel satisfaction from hurting them without losing her job? Was she really that sadistic? She would be a firsthand witness to Lily's grief, watching her deal with the loss of her pet day after day. Did it give her some sick thrill to know that she was the cause of it all?

A vengeful nanny with no other outlet for her rage sure sounded more likely than the idea that a crazy cat aficionado had made off with Mr. Fluffy. Besides, he wasn't looking forward to another boring day of trying to interview the staff. He was beginning to feel overwhelmed by the enormity of that particular task. It felt like he was wasting his time on it.

He knew that he was making lots of assumptions, but his conversation with Randy had also reminded him of the importance of trusting his gut, and his gut had told him that something wasn't quite right with that woman. He couldn't shake the feeling that she was hiding something. He recalled that the only time she'd come close to displaying any emotion other than icy condescension was when she recalled how the police had interrogated her. Was she really so insulted to be treated "like a common criminal" or simply terrified that they'd eventually pull the truth out of her? Well, too bad! She'd have to deal with him questioning her and soon.

But first, he decided that he'd like to try and get a little background information on her if possible. It may help him to better formulate what kind of questions he needs to ask. But how to do this? He wondered if they had some useful information on her at the Vanderhoffs business office? She was an employee, after all, wasn't she?

He already had the address and phone number for their corporate headquarters. Ironically, it had been given to him by Ms.Knots herself so that he could get paid for his work. After having his customary morning cup of joe and a smoke, he dialed the number printed atop of one of the forms Knots had given him. He'd already called over there once to get the list of employees at the theater and copies of their applications. He'd been assisted on that occasion by a friendly and helpful young woman (well, she at least *sounded* young over the phone) named Genevieve. When someone answered the line, he asked to be transferred to the HR department. As he listened to the phone ring, he crossed his fingers, praying that she'd be the one to answer the call again today.

He smiled when he heard her voice on the other end. "Vanderhoff Enterprises! Human Resources Department. This is Genevieve speaking, how may I help you?"

"Hey, Genevieve! It's Matt Spike, I was hoping you could help me out again?"

"Certainly Mr. Spike! What can I do for you today?" She asked with undeniable enthusiasm. Matt suspected that helping him out, even in some small way, made her feel kind of important. It was probably the most exciting thing that happened to her during her dull otherwise workday. People tended to romanticize private eyes. Hell, he was exhibit-A when it came to doing that.

"I just needed some information on another employee."

"I'm pretty sure I faxed over the records for everyone who works at the theater. Did I miss somebody?" she said uncertainly.

"Oh, don't worry, you did great the other day. You were thorough. No, the person I need information on this time isn't an employee of the theater. I was hoping you could send over information on Ms. Knots."

"Ms. Knots?" She paused. "What kind of information do you need about her?"

"The same stuff I wanted on the others. A copy of their job application and resume, plus info on her pay rate."

She let out a long breath. "The financial information should be no problem. But I don't know if we have an application on file here for her. You see, she's actually Mrs. Vanderhoff's cousin. I don't think she ever had to bother with filling out an application."

Now it was Matt's turn to play the silent game. He was left speechless by this latest revelation. He had no idea that Ms. Knots was related to her young charge.

Ah, the power of nepotism rears its ugly head! he smugly mused to himself, then immediately realized what a hypocrite this made him. Here he was, sitting in an office his father was paying for and judging Ms. Knots for taking advantage of her family connections.

"Mr. Spike? Are you still there?"

"Uh, yeah sorry. I guess I was just a little blindsided by that information. Can you look around for her application anyway? If there is one on file, it could be really helpful to me."

"Of course! I'm always happy to help in any way that I can.

"Great! I really do appreciate it," judging her to be sincere, and took a chance. "What do *you* think of Ms. Knots, Genevieve? What's your personal take on the lady?"

He thought he'd lost the game because she didn't speak for a moment, but she did and lowered her voice conspiratorially. "I don't know her very well at all. She's only been in here a few times, for routine things. But I always felt like she was a little cold. You know, aloof and kind of arrogant."

"Yeah, I know what you mean. I felt the same way around her. She's a real ice queen, isn't she?"

"Oh yes, totally! I swear the temperature in the room goes down a few degrees as soon as she walks through the doors!" She giggled. "I do hear that she's very devoted to Ms. Lily though. Everyone says she takes good care of her, so there's that."

"Well, I suppose that's the important thing, isn't it? What else do you know about her?"

"Not much really. I wasn't here when she was hired. I just know to jump when she says jump, if I want to keep my job. She speaks for the boss's daughter, so that puts her high up in the unofficial chain of command."

Matt felt a pang of guilt. "I'm not going to get you in any trouble by asking you for the file on her, am I? If so—"

"Nonsense! We were told to cooperate fully with *any* request for information you might make. That includes the resident ice queen as far as I'm concerned."

"Thanks, I really do appreciate that."

"Say, do you really think she had anything to do with the kid's missing cat?"

He hummed. "I don't know, but I sure intend to find out! Can you think of any reason why she might want to do such a thing? Have there been any disagreements between her and the Vanderhoffs or Lily that you know about?"

"No, not really. What makes you think she could be involved?"

"Nothing specific. Just following up on a hunch."

"Well good luck. I'll get whatever information I can over to you as soon as possible." She confirmed Matt's fax number one more time.

Matt hung up the phone and tried to digest the new information. He didn't get very far before the annoying sounds of his fax machine's modem interrupted his train of thought. Genevieve had wasted no time in sending over information on Ms. Knots' pay. Matt whistled as he read the numbers off the page. She was certainly well paid for her work. It didn't eliminate a financial motive, as her designer wardrobe showed that she obviously had expensive tastes, but it did make such a motive seem more remote. Then again, there was really no limit to some people's greed was there?

Anyhow, he didn't sense greed coming from her. That wasn't what raised his suspicions. No, if she was involved, whatever this was about it wasn't about money. It was far more personal than that. She was hiding something; he was sure of it. And he was also sure that she hated Lily's parents. There was just something about the way she came off when she mentioned them. She wasn't shy about throwing their name around to get what she wanted, but beyond that he felt like she had little use for them. And now to discover that Mrs. Vanderhoff was her own flesh and blood? What family feud might be fueling her attitude? He could only guess.

He examined the fax one more time. It also had Ms. Knots' address on it. He was just starting to get familiar with this part of town, but if he was correct wasn't that address only a few blocks away from his own office, in an even rougher neighborhood than the one he was in? Why on earth would someone with the kind of salary that Ms. Knots was pulling down choose to live in a dump like that?

His phone rang, making him jump. He snatched it up roughly as if annoyed with it for so rudely startling him out of his speculations.

"Mr. Spike? It's Genevieve again. Guess what? Good news! I found her application! Apparently, she had to fill one out as a legal formality before we could take her on. I'll send it over in a moment. I hope it helps."

"That's great, Genevieve! Nice work! You're a real doll! We'll make a detective outta you yet!"

"Aww, thanks! That's sweet of you to say," she said, her voice billowing. "Let me know if there's anything else I can do to help."

"I will. Goodbye."

"Goodbye."

Matt rubbed his hands together with excitement as he waited for the fax to come though, practically ripping it off the printer when it finally arrived, the modem noisily trumpeting its arrival like a chorus of drunken angels.

He scanned the pages and was stunned by what he read.

According to the application, Ms. Knots (whose first name was Cathy) was a high school dropout. Matt was flabbergasted because she put on such a good show of being so poised, proper and sophisticated. He had expected to see an expensive college or finishing school on her resume. He had to remind himself she'd gotten her job because of her relation to Mrs. Vanderhoff, not because of her qualifications. Indeed, he didn't see any real qualifications at all. Was this her secret, that her air of uptown class was all an act? Or was there something else running deeper below the surface? He noted that his estimate of her age had been close. She was almost five years older than he, which meant she was pushing thirty.

Armed with this new information, Matt decided it was time to return to the theater and confront her with his findings. Doubtlessly she would be resistant to being questioned considering how much the police interrogation had ruffled her feathers, but she would have to go along with it. Like all the Vanderhoff employees, she was duty bound to cooperate with his investigation.

He could barely contain his excitement on the drive over to Manhattan. He felt he was tantalizingly close to cracking this case wide open. Maybe he could even bring poor old Mr. Fluffy home safely. He hoped so, and for more reasons than simply collecting the bonus Cathy Knots had hinted at if he did. He genuinely liked Lily Vanderhoff and his heart went out to her. He wanted to see her reunited with her beloved pet. He wished his dad could understand that, sometimes, as a PI you had a real opportunity to help others and to do some good in the world. It wasn't all about the money. Reuniting some rich kid with her cat might not seem like much but reuniting a young child with her beloved friend was.

Of course, the reward money certainly wouldn't hurt. He knew that was the only language his dad spoke. What was it he loved to say? "Money talks and bullshit walks!" If he could show him how lucrative investigative work could be, then maybe his dad would respect him. He was shocked to discover how much that idea pleased him. He spent so much time telling himself that he didn't need that man's approval, that having the respect of someone he barely respected himself was meaningless. But the truth of the matter, the truth that he tried so hard to hide from himself, was that he really *did* need his dad's stamp of approval, badly. Deep down, he was still a little boy himself, waiting for the pat on the back from daddy that he never got. Sure, he could play his dad's game, dance to his tune and join the family business, but that was the easy way out and would make him feel cheap and disingenuous. It simply wasn't who he was, it didn't hold any interest for him.

No, if he was going to get Dad's sincere blessing, he wanted it to be for being himself. He wanted his dad to see the value in what he did. He needed to be appreciated for who he was rather than what his dad wanted him to be. He wanted his dad to eat his words, to admit that all the hours he had spent reading detective stories and watching old film noir movies hadn't just been a useless escape from reality, but rather preparation for a well-paying career. A career which meant a hell of a lot more than just taking advantage of people desperate enough to tolerate living in crumbling old rat traps.

Yeah, he'd show the old man! And he'd show Sara too! Show her that he was more than just a good fuck, that he was a real man, a man who was going places. The kind of man who could be a good provider and give her all the kinds of things that a classy woman like her deserved to have. He'd show 'em all! He was so close to doing so he could almost taste it. Cathy Knots was a lady with lots of secrets and he'd crack through that icy exterior and dig out those secrets no matter what it took.

But did those secrets include the biggest one of all? The whereabouts of Mr. Fluffy? He had a theory for why she hated the Vanderhoffs so much. A theory that might explain her motives in taking the cat. Now it was just a matter of putting it to the test.

Matt pulled up to the theater and parked. "Showtime," he said grimly as he popped his fedora onto his head.

Matt found Cathy Knots in Lily's dressing room. They were between shows and Lily's math tutor was going over a lesson with her. Ms. Knots sat in a chair nearby, reading a newspaper with her typical blasé coolness. She wore a daringly short skirt today, and his eyes couldn't help but be drawn to her shapely, nylon covered legs. On the ends of those legs were a pair of the brightest, tallest and spikiest heels Matt had ever seen. He didn't have to know much about women's shoes to know they cost a month's good salary.

She barely looked up as he entered the room. It was quite a contrast to how Lily greeted him. The young girl fixed him with her cherubic smile and bounded from her chair towards him. For a moment he thought she was going to throw her arms around him in a hug.

"Matt! I'm so glad to see you! Have you got any good news for me yet?"

His heart broke from her green eyes glistening with expectation. "I'm afraid not, Lily. I'm still working on it. But I promise I'll get to the bottom of it all soon!"

"I'm sure you will!" She told him.

He was heartened to see Lily's face perk up, and hoped he wasn't making empty promises. "I'm sorry to interrupt your lesson. I was wondering if I could speak with Ms. Knots in private for a few minutes?"

The math tutor, a tiny, balding middle-aged man answered for her. "Don't be sorry. We were done here anyway." He stood up to make his way out of the room.

"Yeah, it's no trouble. You can talk to her in here if you want. I have a few scenes I need to rehearse on stage right now anyway." Lily replied. She looked over at Ms. Knots, eyebrows raised. "If that's okay with you?"

Ms. Knots raised one of her own eyebrows and folded the paper in her lap. "It makes no difference to me," she sniffed.

Lily bounced out of the room. Matt shut the door behind her and walked the few steps to Ms. Knots, keeping a respectful distance. He kept his eyes on hers, willing himself not to focus on the pleasing curves of her legs.

She spoke in her precise, over-enunciated way. "I was beginning to wonder if you'd ever show up. I was surprised you weren't here this morning. I'm sure you still have many people left to interview. Unless, despite what you've just told Lily, your absence means you've already settled on a suspect?"

"Now who's trying to play detective, Cathy?" he said, deliberately using her first name to judge her reaction.

Her lip twitched. "I wasn't aware we had become on a first name basis, *Mr. Spike*. Am I to take it I have somehow piqued your interest?"

"Nothing so dire. Just a few routine questions and being thorough. You strike me as the kind of person who appreciates thoroughness."

"I do. You have already been provided with a copy of the police report. I fail to see what you could ask me that they haven't already covered. They were quite thorough themselves in their questioning of me, I assure you! You already know my whereabouts on the night when the

unfortunate event occurred. What more is there to know?"
Her leg swung a little as she said it.

Matt took a deep breath. *Focus.*

Focused, he could tell he was going to have to dive right in and go for broke if he was ever going to break through her icy shell, but it was risky. If he chipped away too hard, he could end up shattering his chances of solving this case into a thousand pieces.

"The police report doesn't tell me why you hate your cousin so much, Cathy. But I can guess. It must not be easy, is it? Having to be so dependent on your rich relations? But you never finished school, so I'm guessing you didn't have many other good prospects. Not if you want to keep yourself in fancy heels like those. It must not be easy, being a charity case. Kind of humiliating, isn't it? I'll bet you'd do anything to stick it to them. Even something as petty and cruel as arranging to have their little girl's pet go missing."

Cathy's eyes flashed, giving him a curt smile accessorized with a golf clap.

"That's impressive. You've done your homework," she said in a think Brooklyn accent so heavy it was difficult to understand. He had to muster all his control not to flinch at the contrast. The real Cathy Knots had finally stood up. It had been easier than he expected to coax her out. Maybe she was sick of hiding?

"But you've got it all wrong, Sherlock. Sure, I hate my cousin Vivian. That bitch likes to pretend she's *so* much better than the rest of us, because she fell backwards on her heels onto a rich guy. But she comes from the same place as the rest of us! She's nothing special, just a cheap showgirl who caught Vanderhoff's eye and suckered him into putting a big fat ring on her finger. She likes to hold her money over our heads and never misses a chance to remind me I owe everything to her. But Lily, she's a different story. I love that girl like she's my own daughter. Hell, I'm the only one who does! That's *why* I put up with it all! For Lily! I would never do anything to hurt her. These clothes? I hate those too. It's an act, yes, a façade. But for *her*. I have to pretend to be so prim and proper or these people won't take me seriously."

Matt didn't know what to say. Her transformation from an overly formal governess into a good old working-class girl complete with cuss words was so sudden and complete that it left his head spinning. He struggled to process what she'd just confessed to him. He wondered why she'd dropped the pretense so suddenly for him when she'd maintained it with the police.

"Why should I believe you? You've already admitted that you hate the Vanderhoffs and shown me that you're not what you seem. How do I know this isn't all just another act?"

She leaned in, crossed her arms over her lap. "Okay, look here's the deal. I admit I was a bit of a wild child when I was younger. Me and my friends used to get up to all kinds of mischief. Nothing too bad, but I got busted a few times for shoplifting stupid little things. It was enough to worry my mother, and she begged Vivian to let me care for Lily after her first nanny kicked the bucket. I hardly counted as an adult myself but caring for that girl gave me a sense of purpose and a focus that I guess I was lacking up until then. I grew up real fast. I had to, for Lily's sake. So I learned how to play the game, how to behave myself and blend in with all these uptown snobs so I could stay in her world. She needed me, and I suppose I needed her too."

It sounded too good to be true to Matt, and it must have registered on his face. She leaned back, arms hanging loosely at her sides. Vulnerable. "You don't understand what a dysfunctional family the Vanderhoffs are. They live almost separate lives, pursuing their own passions. Mr. Vanderhoff has his mistresses and Mrs. Vanderhoff has her pool boys. He grew bored with Vivian ages ago and the only reason why he doesn't divorce her is because of all the money he'd lose if he had to split his assets. They don't spend any time with each other and almost no time at all with Lily. They just trot her out like a prize pony to show off to all their friends at parties. 'Oh, look how beautiful our daughter is, see how smart and funny and talented she is,' then they think they can shove her back into her little display case and forget about her until the next big formal occasion arises. She's not a person to them, she's a prop. It's disgusting! I'm the only one who really cares about her, who sees her! And when I couldn't be around to show her some love, she had Mr. Fluffy. I wouldn't have ever taken that away from her. *I couldn't!*"

Matt's skepticism was crumbling. His gut told him she was telling the truth. But there were still a few things he needed to understand.

"Why do you still live in that awful neighborhood, then? With your money, you could live anywhere in the city!"

She shrugged. "Because it's *home*. Sometimes I lose myself in the role of the uptight nanny, okay? Living there recharges me, reminds me who I really am. Besides, I won't be there forever. Lily's growing up fast. Too fast! They won't need me much longer. I still live at home with my Ma, making smart investments and squirreling away the money I don't have to waste on these costumes." She flicked the lapel of her pressed jacket with a manicured nail. "When Lily is old enough, I'm gonna retire early down to the Jersey shore, and start over. Get away from all this phoniness. Start *really* living."

Her face changed to an odd sort of interest. *At him.* "Hell, maybe I'll even start up a little family of my own down there before it's too late. If I can ever manage to find the right man, of course."

Jesus Christ! Is she flirting with me?

Now he understood why she had been so quick to drop her act with him. There was no mistaking the desperate hunger in her eyes. He really had to hand it to her, she could be cold as ice one minute and hot and bothered the next. She sure was getting him all hot and bothered! She uncrossed her legs like she was Sharon Stone in *Basic Instinct* – and, he noted with a suddenly dry mouth, that wasn't the only thing that she shared with that scene in that movie.

His mind whirled. He didn't imagine that her devotion to Lily left her with much time for herself. He was certainly flattered. She was an attractive woman, but he clung to the hope he could make whatever it was with Sara work somehow. There was also the fact she clearly carried a lot of emotional baggage. Or was it just that it was too like his own? He could relate to her need for financial independence, and her struggle to assert her real identity. But could two people as broken as they were really heal one another?

He didn't think so. Getting more deeply involved with her might be fun at first, but it would be another dead end. Also, he had spent most of his young life dreaming about escaping from the shore. The last thing he wanted was to go back there, even with someone as beautiful as Cathy Knots. With some effort, he managed to look away from the new show she was putting on to entice him.

"Well, I appreciate your *baring your soul*, Ms. Knots. I can definitely cross you off my list of suspects and I wish you well."

She took a more modest posture with a head bob that said *whatever*.

In a more tender tone, he added, "Lily is a special young lady and she's lucky to have someone like you in her life. Take good care of her. I'll be in touch if I come up with anything new." He stiffly walked to the door, then opened and closed it, but not before giving her a last look. She was already back to reading her newspaper.

Have I just been played? he wondered. But, no. There was something too genuine about the entire interaction. He decided his instincts had been correct, up to a point. She did have secrets and she did have a deep-seated hatred for her employers, but her love for Lily was real. He was sure of that.

Still, he shook his head in disappointment. Back at square one with no promising suspects. He'd have to return to the dull task of interviewing more people. Since he was already at the theater, there was no time like the present to get started.

Part Seven: The Canary That Ate The Cat

Matt corralled anyone who could spare a few minutes for him. He made the best of the smoke breaks, as this allowed him to do plenty of smoking himself, but everything felt as tedious and fruitless as it had the day before.

Despair was just beginning to take hold when a balding, middle-aged fellow came through the door and asked to borrow a cigarette. "So, I hear you're the one to talk to if I've got any ideas about what might have happened to that missing kitty," the man said cryptically.

"That's right." Matt said coolly and shook a cig from his pack and offered it to him.

The man took it gratefully, deftly putting it in his mouth and lighting it before shaking out the match and discarding it to the ground. "Well, I might have a suspect for you."

Matt raised a quizzical eyebrow. This was the first time someone approached him to make an accusation. Typically, he had to initiate all the conversations, and when he asked someone if they had any idea who might've stolen Mr. Fluffy, he was met with blank stares.

Matt led the man away from the rest of the group that had congregated around the backdoor. "Tell me more."

"My name's Paul Skinner. I'm in charge of the prop department. We also help maintain the sets, stuff like that. There's a guy who works in my department who's always been a little bit off, if you know what I mean? Ever since that cat went missing, I've had a feeling about him."

Matt was already taking notes. "What makes you suspect him specifically?"

"Lots of things. I'm the one who hired him, you know? He had some interesting things on his resume. Things from his past that weren't relevant to the job, but he kept on there anyway."

"Like what kinds of things? Be specific." Matt was rapidly losing patience with this guy's innuendos.

"Like the fact he went to veterinary school. He came damned close to graduating with a doctorate, too. He was either thrown out or dropped out in his last year."

"Well, which was it? Did he drop out or get tossed out?"

The man shrugged. "Depends on who you ask. He keeps to himself for the most part, but every so often he turns into a real Chatty Cathy and won't shut up. Mostly he likes to brag. He's told different members of my crew different stories about why he left school. When I interviewed him for this job, he just told me he realized he didn't want to spend his life patching up other people's pets, and liked theater. I didn't really care; I was more interested in his theater experience.

He told one of us he got into theater to blow off steam when he left school to take care of his sick mother. He told somebody else he quit school because his ideas were too advanced for his professors, and they were jealous of him."

"Really," Matt said, intrigued by that last comment. "What kind of ideas?"

"He wouldn't say. The guy's a real mystery. We've all been trying to figure him out. He is a good worker though and came highly recommended from the other shows he worked on before. Honestly, the guy is a little too good. A perfectionist and sometimes a pain in my ass. Always wasting time fiddling with minute little details the audience won't ever see or notice. Always messing with his hair and his clothes too, like a prima donna. And he has a weird smell about him all the time. He tries to cover it up with cheap cologne, but every once in a while, you get a whiff of it."

"What does the smell remind you of?"

"Oh, it doesn't 'remind' me of anything, I can tell you what it is. It's unmistakable. It's cat piss."

"Does he own a cat?"

"Probably a whole litter of 'em by the smell of him! He told someone once that his parents used to make a living breeding and selling them somewhere upstate where he grew up. But he's said so many different things about his past, who can know?"

Matt digested the new information. It was certainly interesting. Someone who likely owned several cats and who had a possible background in breeding them did sound like a prime candidate for the thief. He was someone who would know the value of such a rare animal, and possibly have the right connections to sell her.

"Does he have any kind of a criminal history? Did you do a background check when you hired him?"

"Sure, we wouldn't have hired him otherwise. It was clean."

Matt looked him in the eye. "What makes you suspect him then? You mentioned earlier he 'seems a little off.' Can you elaborate on what you mean by that?"

"He keeps to himself, which is almost unheard of in theater. It's like he lives in his own little world. He has this attitude, too, like he's too good for this place and he's better than the rest of us. What can I say, the guy has a creepy vibe about him. Also, the day Miss Lily's cat went missing he said he was feeling sick and left early. This guy's a machine, perfect attendance, he never does that. And he never takes his tools home, but he did that day, in a big duffel bag. If you know what I mean."

Matt chafed at Paul's feeling like he needed it spelled out for him, but it was an important clue. That could explain how he got the cat out of the building unnoticed. If he had a veterinary background, he would have known how to drug Fluffy to keep her quiet.

Everything seemed to fit, but . . . "Why didn't you tell any of this to the cops?"

Paul scoffed. "The police? They never asked me! Also, I'll admit I didn't really put two and two together until a few days ago. And that I don't have any real proof, just my suspicions. So take that as you will."

"It's the closest thing to real evidence I've heard yet," Matt admitted.

Paul shook his head, his voice softening. "Look, I'm not sure I want the guy to get into that much trouble. He's an arrogant weirdo, but he *is* a good worker. That's more than I can say for half these kids I hire. Sure, it's messed up, lord knows Miss Lily loves that kitty, but it's also kinda lame, right? It's not like he killed anyone or anything. He just needs to learn a little humility, and maybe he'll be okay. You're not a cop, maybe you can just get him to return the cat, take care of the whole thing quietly?"

Matt locked eyes with Paul for several seconds, impressed with the man's apparent soul searching. And maybe he could convince his client not to press any charges if he could make this guy see reason. "Sure, I'll try my best. What's this guy's name?"

"Lance Hoagland," Skinner informed him.

Matt thanked Skinner for that and asked for the names of other coworkers he could talk to, especially those whom Hoagland had given conflicting stories to. He wanted to see if there was any way they could be stitched together into something that wasn't as inconsistent as it appeared.

When he interviewed them, their opinions were similar to Skinner's. They found him to be quiet and distant one minute, then an abrasive braggart the next. They found that annoying, but none could deny his talent, attention to detail, and craftsmanship. They all disliked him while being a little in awe of him.

Matt heard at least four different versions of the story of how he left school and drifted into working in theater. The most interesting one concerned his supposedly inventing a new technique for safer organ and limb transplants. This technique was "perfected" without the approval of his professors, and they found his methods unethical and threw him out of school.

Armed with that, Matt decided he had enough information to confront the man himself. He didn't look forward to the conversation, given the man's reputation, and would have to be on game with his people skills and not fire off at him as he sometimes did. There wouldn't be much success in getting the man to confess and return the cat if Matt came at him too hard.

Matt got one of Hoagland's colleagues, a young lady named Ruby, to bring him to the workshop where the man spent most of his time on the job.

"Huh. That's weird!" she remarked when they found the place to be devoid of human life. "He almost never leaves this place. Oh well, maybe he had to use the can? I guess he's human after all! You should just hang around here for a while, I'm sure he'll come back."

Matt hung around a while then decided he must have gone home early again, despite Skinner telling him he rarely did that. The only other time had been the fateful night Mr. Fluffy disappeared. Matt recalled something else Skinner had mentioned, that Hoagland always left his duffel bag of tools here at work. Matt looked around the workshop for it, hoping it was left behind since that was likely how he smuggled the cat out. It was just as absent as its owner.

Matt cursed and slammed a fist on a nearby workbench. Somehow, word must have reached Hoagland that Matt had made inquiries about him, and he hightailed it out of here.

It was suspicious behavior, certainly. But what about Skinner? Wasn't it a little too convenient that the old man had steered him towards Hoagland? As the resident weirdo, Hoagland made a tempting scapegoat. An unpopular guy like that wouldn't have anyone to defend him. Maybe Skinner was trying to cast suspicion on someone else to mask his own involvement? Matt decided it was time to head back home. He wanted to look at Skinner's employment records, which were buried somewhere in the stacks of papers Genevieve had sent him days earlier.

Back in his office, Matt stared into Paul Skinner's application. It was standard stuff. He'd worked in theater both on and off Broadway for over thirty years. Some of the productions listed were ones Matt was familiar with and others were real head scratchers. Either way, there was nothing which jumped out at him as suspicious.

Next, he combed through the papers on his desk for Hoagland's papers. The information on them was just as Skinner had described.

Matt got Hoagland's address from the application and took a ride over there. He wanted to keep an eye on the place, If the man left his apartment, Matt would tail him. He had a pretty good idea what the guy looked like from the coworkers' descriptions, and wasn't too worried he'd miss him leaving the building.

Matt parked across the street from Hoagland's building, and noted with mixed emotions it was in a seedier part of town than Matt's office was. *Hoagland's job must bring him a shit ton of satisfaction if it justifies having to live in this hell hole!* he thought. It also was a strangely good feeling to be reminded that, as poor as his own living conditions were, there was always something worse. He was more grateful for what he had. And at least Matt didn't have to pay for the dump he called home. He shuddered to think how much Hoagland and his neighbors were being overcharged for this place. Matt could practically feel the radon and lead poisoning trying to worm its way inside of him as looked upon the crumbling structure.

Matt waited outside all night, eventually falling asleep behind the wheel of his car. As the first rays of dawn spread their way between the buildings, he was awakened by the sound of a car door slamming. He rubbed his eyes and yawned, tempted to return home for a shower, clean clothes, and a cup of coffee, but he didn't dare leave. What if Hoagland decided to skip town and left before Matt could get back? He might never find him again. Matt had to content himself with a cigarette to get him through the morning instead.

Three cigarettes in, he was rewarded by the sight of a tall, thin man with a ponytail emerging from the building with a duffel bag in hand.

Matt wondered if he owned a car or would use public transportation. If he took a bus or subway, it would be trickier for Matt to avoid being spotted. He let out a sigh of relief as he watched the man open the door of a battered old maroon Volvo. With a whine of protest, Matt's engine sputtered to life and he began his pursuit. Matt was an old pro at tailing cars through the city, having spent too many hours working Alan following cheating spouses

To his surprise, Hoagland's destination was the theater. He was returning to work as if nothing had happened! Either the guy had an impressive set of balls on him, or he really *was* innocent, which darkened Matt's mood. He wondered again if he should be looking more closely at Skinner.

Matt lingered in his car to finish his cigarette before following Hoagland inside.

Once in the building, Matt resolved to squeeze a few more interviews in before trying to confront Hoagland. He didn't want to scare him off again, if indeed that had been what happened the other day. He decided to use it as an opportunity to ask some of the staff about Paul Skinner while he was at it. Somewhat embarrassed by his slept-in clothes, he swallowed his pride and started the process. He spent about an hour talking to three different workers. None of them had anything very interesting to say about Skinner. He seemed like a nice enough old guy to them, and a solid worker.

Matt realized he was just putting off the inevitable. Skinner was just another dead end. It was time to man up and confront Lance Hoagland.

Matt tracked him down in his isolated workshop, where he was busy painting a fake sticker onto the side of a suitcase. He appeared to be about five or six years older than Matt, and about as tall. He was brown-haired but was going prematurely bald, thinning in the middle of his head and the rest swept back into a ponytail. Round frame glasses perched precariously on the ridge of his aquiline nose, almost comically so, threatening to take a dive into oblivion on his paint splattered work desk.

He reminded Matt of John Lennon, if John Lennon was a cold, naked ego and intellect.

Hoagland didn't look up from his work as Matt entered the room, and Matt could already smell him from across the cramped space: a musky aroma that the peddlers of colognes and deodorants wanted us to associate with masculinity, covering something more pungent and inhuman just below it.

"So, the great detective has finally deigned to speak to me," Hoagland said without looking up. He droned in a flat, nasally, world weary tone. "I'm sure you have many questions. Fire away! I've got nothing to hide."

"Okay, sure," Matt said, refusing to be put off. "We'll get right down to it. Do you recall where you were the day Mr. Fluffy disappeared?"

"You're wasting your time talking to me, you know? I was barely even here that day. Sick to my stomach. I have issues with my digestive tract that flare up sometimes. I had the same problem yesterday too. I left hours before that cat was reported missing."

"Really? That's funny. Mr. Skinner recalls you left just before Mr. Fluffy's cage was found empty."

Hoagland's shoulder rose slightly, then fell. "Skinner's a raging alcoholic lucky if he can remember what he did an hour ago. I wouldn't place too much stock in anything he says."

"Okay," Matt said, addressing his notes. "Another one of your colleagues said they remembered you leaving around the same time as Skinner reported. Leaving with a duffel bag. Is it that one?" Matt pointed at a crumpled, featureless black bag lying on the floor near Hoagland's feet.

Hoagland glanced at it, then returned to his work. "Yes, that's my bag. Sometimes I bring my work home with me. Is that a crime? It's how I achieve the superior results that I get. The others are all jealous. Jealous of my dedication to my craft. They'll say anything to try and tear me down. You shouldn't be so gullible as to fall for their lies."

"I'll try to keep that in mind," Matt said mildly, although inside he was fuming. This guy was everything he'd been led to expect that he was, and then some! He knew he'd get nowhere fast by antagonizing him further, but it was a risk he had to take. "Do you mind if I take a look inside it?"

Hoagland barked out a short, humorless laugh. "Why? So you can see if there's any cat hairs inside that match a sample you took from the cage? Do you think you're fucking Sherlock Holmes or something?"

"Is that a 'no'?" Matt asked, keeping his voice neutral.

Hoagland dismissed him with a wave. "Have at it, then. See all the exciting, completely non incriminating contents of my bag! Perhaps then you'll understand that I have far better things to do with my time than run around stealing cats from spoiled little rich kids."

Matt walked the few steps to Hoagland's station and retrieved the bag from the ground. He unzipped it and peered into it. Inside were a few small, random tools and paintbrushes, and no cat hairs that he could identify. Taking the opportunity of being closer to Hoagland, he saw no evidence of hairs on his clothes, despite the undercurrent of feline urine that hung about him like a dark cloud. Matt recalled how Skinner had said he was so meticulous about his appearance. It wasn't too difficult to believe that he'd carefully removed all traces of such things from himself and his bag.

Then, as he was about to zip the bag shut, Matt noticed a series of dozens of small holes punched into the top of the bag on either side of the zipper, too regular in size and position to be from wear and tear. *Airholes.* He placed the bag back on the floor.

Before he'd even straightened, Hoagland spoke up. "See? Nothing! Just like I said. Now perhaps you can stop badgering me and let me get on with my work?"

Matt suppressed a grin. It wasn't like he'd ever really stopped his work since Matt had entered the room. "My apologies," he allowed. "I'm still curious, though. You seem to think that everyone is jealous of you. It's not just your co-workers here, that's how you felt about your professors back in veterinary school too, isn't it? I wonder where that attitude comes from?"

For the first time, Hoagland put down his paintbrush and met Matt's eyes. A cold fury burned from them. "I see you've been doing your research. I congratulate you. However, simply having an interest in veterinary medicine in my youth hardly means I'm a catnapper."

"An *interest*, you say. According to your resume, you nearly graduated with a doctorate and top honors! That's one helluva an 'interest'. Why give up at the eleventh hour like that? Why not just see it through to the end when you've already taken things so far?"

The corner of Hoagland's mouth twitched. "My mother fell ill. She had nobody else to care for her, so I did what any good son would do. Besides, I'd already been questioning if I really wanted to be a veterinarian long before that. It's unfair you're expected to know what you want to do with the rest of your life when you're still little more than a child yourself. Often the reality of what a certain profession demands doesn't match the dream."

"Your mother used to support herself by breeding cats, is that correct?"

Hoagland raised his eyebrows in mock surprise. *He's a terrible actor,* Matt noted, seeing right through the affectation. *No wonder he has to work behind the scenes.*

"I don't know what kind of lies the people around here have been telling you about me, but we never bred cats. We did have our own little farm upstate, but the only cats we ever owned were a few barn cats that kept the vermin out of our stables."

"It's quite a leap to make though, isn't it?" Matt pinched his thumb and forefinger together. "You go from coming *this* close to becoming a veterinarian, to working in the prop department for a play. I'm not sure I understand how you got here from there."

Hoagland's expression didn't change, Matt could give him that. "I enjoy working with my hands. I could have been an excellent surgeon. It's very calming, very peaceful to work with my hands. Zen-like. If you did your homework on me more thoroughly, you would have seen I was quite active in theater at my college. It's not really so unusual of a career leap as it might appear. It's money versus passion. Being a vet would have meant money, but it can't buy the satisfaction my current art brings me. I'm a craftsman. I create beauty – *perfection* – where there wasn't any. You can't put a price tag on that."

He sure can talk a good talk when he wants to, can't he? Matt thought, *But I'm not buying it.*

He decided to give Hoagland a rest for now. "Well, I'd appreciate it if you'd contact me if you recall anything else about the day Mr. Fluffy went missing which might seem significant. Any suspicious activity, or if something was out of place that you might have observed." He handed Hoagland one of his newly minted business cards, which he'd spent his last few dollars getting printed up.

Matt turned away, then turned back. "You know, if you *did* know something significant, I'm sure we could come to some sort of an equitable arrangement. If you cooperated with me fully and helped bring Mr. Fluffy home safely, I might not be able to save your job, but I'm pretty certain that I could convince the Vanderhoffs to not press any charges against you. This doesn't have to ruin your career. It's not too late to salvage something out of this whole ugly situation."

"I don't like what you're implying," Hoagland said acidly while looking down at the card. "Mister *Spike*. I've already told you everything I know, which is nothing. You're barking up the wrong tree by focusing on me. Take a closer look at some of these kids Skinner hires. Half of them are hooked on drugs and willing to do anything to finance their filthy habits."

"Thanks for the tip. And remember, I'm just a phone call away if you change your mind," Matt said as he moved towards the doorway.

"I won't," Hoagland said over the sound of the card being ripped up.

"See ya around," Matt said, offering his own dismissive wave.

Of course, Matt fully intended to see much more of Hoagland. The interview had completely convinced him that, if Hoagland wasn't his man, he was at least hiding something. He decided to shift his investigation from interviewing people to doing surveillance on Hoagland, hoping that, now that Hoagland knew he was onto him, he might take some sort of reckless action.

If he did, Matt had to be there to see it.

He decided it might be time to see what secrets might lie inside of Hoagland's apartment. He knew that Hoagland was going to be busy here at work for the next few hours, so why not take advantage of that fact to look around? He'd be committing a little crime himself, breaking and entering the guy's apartment, but it was hardly the first time he'd had to employ such questionable methods during an investigation. One of the good things about not being a cop was that he didn't have to worry about following procedures and having evidence thrown out because of how it was obtained. So long as he got results for his clients and didn't get caught, he'd be fine. His gut told him he was on the right trail. His primary duty was to find Mr. Fluffy and bring her home, not help the authorities obtain a conviction for her abductor.

Part Eight: Into the Abattoir

Matt returned to Hoagland's building. He pretended to be a pizza delivery person to get someone to buzz him into the building – a cliche, but a cliche for a reason because it always worked. No cameras were present to betray his subterfuge.

He made his way up to Hoagland's apartment, past scuttling cockroaches and flickering hallway lights. As he approached the door, it occurred to Matt that Hoagland might have roommates, but this man didn't seem like the kind of guy who'd be able to deal with roommates. That said, Hoagland's current gig probably didn't pay much, and New York, even in its worst neighborhoods, wasn't a cheap place to live. Even a shithole like this would be out of the price range of many people.

Matt decided not to risk a blind entry. He'd knock on the door and if anyone answered, he'd pretend to be looking for someone who used to live there, and come back when he was sure that the place was unoccupied.

Several unanswered taps satisfied him his caution was unwarranted, and he set to work picking the lock. The lock on the door was an antique and didn't present much of a challenge to his modest lock picking skills. The door swung open on rusty hinges.

The stench hit Matt immediately. It stank like the entire apartment was a litter box that hadn't been changed for far too long. The awful smell probably permeated every rafter and beam in the place.

"Here's one dude who's not getting his security deposit back!" Matt quipped, and choked on the contaminated air. He regretted he'd opened his mouth at all.

With a quick scan he saw that he had a captive audience for his witticisms – a captive audience of the feline variety. In the dim light of the room, only lit by yellowed light streaming in through filthy windows and curtains, he saw dozens of cages, some stacked three or four high and pushed up against the walls of what might have once been the living room. The sum total of the furniture was a long table that stood in the middle of the room, with a single stool and a desk lamp. A long, thin sheet of paper like the kind Matt remembered seeing in a typical doctor's office covered the table along with what Matt guessed were various surgical instruments. If Matt needed any more reason to vomit, smears of what looked like dried blood crisscrossed the white paper like some gruesome abstract painting.

What the fuck is going on here? Matt wondered, this time remembering to keep his speculations inside his head. He looked at the cats in the nearest cages, and fury and pity rose in him. Most of the cats appeared to be asleep, if not in a more permanent condition. A few of the pitiful animals stirred and meowed weakly at him

He could see their ribs clearly. They were all criminally skeletal, malnourished, underfed.

Jiminy Christmas! This place is like a kitty Auschwitz! Matt thought angrily. As his astonished eyes continued to scan the contents of the faintly lit room, he spotted something even more bizarre than what he'd already seen.

In one oversized cage was a cat that was unusually healthy looking and plump compared to his companions in captivity. However, this cat's forepaws didn't match his hind legs. Neither sets of legs matched the rest of the body. Nor did the long, shaggy tail whose fur had a completely different color and pattern from the rest of the body.

Matt looked to the cage beside this cat and saw that in that cage was a cat that also had mismatched front legs. Yet they *did* match those he would've expected to have found on the cat in the adjacent cage. Below that was a cat with mismatched hind legs, again these back legs looked like they originally belonged to the first cat in the big cage. Matt looked closer and could see where the fur had been shaved away and was in process of growing back, revealing rows of stitches.

"It's like a fucking Frankencat monster!" Matt exclaimed with a gasp that triggered a series of hacking coughs in the rancid air.

He recalled hearing Hoagland created a new process for transplanting limbs and organs when he was in veterinary school . . . unethical experiments that had upset the faculty and ruined his budding medical career.

These were more than just stories, and the experiments were still ongoing!

Matt was horrified. He remembered being in his biology class back in high school and seeing a cat that was kept in a Lucite block. This unfortunate feline had been split down the center with its skin pulled open to reveal the interior organs. What had disgusted Matt the most was the expression of pain forever frozen onto the poor animal's face. Later, he would discover that the cats used to make these terrible displays were drowned beforehand. This revelation didn't make him feel any better about it. This whole set up in the apartment was a thousand times worse than that Lucite encased cat. He was sure it would haunt his nightmares for years to come. Mr. Hoagland was one sick piece of work.

Matt didn't know jack shit about cat breeds, but as he forced himself to look upon Hoagland's gruesome handiwork, he could tell that the "Frankencats" were made up of several exotic looking breeds that he wasn't familiar with. As he thought about Hoagland's obsession with perfection, he came to a sickening realization: Hoagland was trying to build whatever his idea of the "perfect" cat was from spare parts!

As sorry as he felt for these cats, Matt was there for a reason. Where was Mr. Fluffy? As far as he could tell, none of the Frankencats had contained parts from her. He checked the cages for her and, to his relief, found Mr. Fluffy in one of the larger ones in the far corner of the room. She looked well fed, healthy, and clean, same as the rest of the few cats in that area. With a chill he realized that probably meant they were next on the chopping block.

Matt sighed in relief. He knew he should call animal control right away to save all of these poor animals, but he hadn't thought up a good story yet to explain how he knew about them without incriminating himself for breaking and entering. He supposed he didn't need one, he could just call in an anonymous tip later. The others would have to wait for now, but there was no way he was going to let Mr. Fluffy stay here one minute longer. Her cage was on the bottom so he gingerly shifted the cages to get hers.

Just as he got to Mr. Fluffy's cage, he froze. *Those rusty hinges – someone is coming in!* Matt whirled to see Lance Hoagland striding into the room towards the table.

With a look of pure rage contorting his face, Hoagland said, "After our 'little talk' I thought you might try coming here! It's the last mistake you'll ever make, detective!"

He lunged for the table, snatching up one of the sharper, nastier looking scalpels and ran toward Matt. Matt frantically grabbed the handle of Mr. Fluffy's cage and, with one big effort, swung the heavy cage at his hard charging assailant. Mr. Fluffy meowed in confusion as the cage struck its mark and threw Hoagland to the ground. Matt's shoulders strained painfully with the effort and the cage flew out of his hands and bounced to the floor. He offered Mr. Fluffy his silent apology.

With the speed and grace of a psychotic, Hoagland was back on his feet and on the offensive within seconds. He swung the blade in his hand wildly through the air. Matt dodged the first few slashes and tried to defend himself with Fluffy's cage, but he couldn't pick it up and Hoagland's gleaming surgical instrument made contact with Matt's side.

Matt didn't feel pain, though. In fact, the knife felt like it had struck something hard, and he stared into Hoagland's face as the man's expression deteriorated from crazed triumph to befuddlement.

Why aren't I dead? Matt wondered, then, in an instant he knew. *My gun! Of course! His knife hit the gun!* In the heat of the moment, Matt had completely forgotten that he was carrying his .9mm pistol concealed under his coat. He went for his weapon but failed, his wrenched shoulder feeling like it was going to pop out of the socket. He quickly switched to using the other arm, but Hoagland guessed what he was up to. He threw his knife at Matt, which missed, but it threw him off long enough for Hoagland to charge and slam Matt's back into the table. Matt grunted as pain bloomed in his spine but proved to himself his back wasn't broken by bringing his knee up and crashing it into Hoagland's chin.

"Get off of me you Frankenstein freak!" Matt howled.

Hoagland stumbled back as a wolfish grin played on his face and spat out a piece of his tongue. "Frankenstein? Frankenstein was a fool! His mistake was using dead tissue!"

He charged at Matt again, and Matt fumbled on the table behind him for the collection of surgical instruments and grabbed one. Just as Hoagland made contact, Matt buried the scalpel deep into Hoagland's shoulder.

"Frankenstein wasn't real!" he shouted.

Hoagland cried out and staggered backwards, blood running between his fingers as he tried to staunch the wound, the knife still buried in his shoulder.

Matt ran back to Mr. Fluffy's cage and tried to drag it toward the door with his good arm, while doing his best to ignore the pain pummeling him as he tried to unholster his gun with his bad arm. Finally, Matt succeeded in freeing the pistol and leveled it in the direction of Hoagland. His hand was shaking.

"Stay back! Do you really wanna die over a goddamned cat?" He warned.

"Mr. Fluffy is no ordinary cat! She's a queen! That spoiled brat couldn't possibly appreciate what a treasure she had! Once I add parts from Mr. Fluffy to my creations, I will have the ultimate animal!" Hoagland screamed back.

Hoagland pulled the knife out of his shoulder, sending an arc of crimson into the air. With the manic speed of a madman, he ran towards Matt again before the startled PI could even process what was happening. He slashed at the unsteady hand that held the pistol. Matt dropped the weapon and it went off, blowing a chunk of plaster out of the ceiling.

Hoagland dove for the spot where the gun lay on the carpet, but Matt stomped on his fingers as they shot out to grab at its handle. Hoagland rocked backwards and screamed. When he made another play for it, he was met by a sudden whirlwind of fur and claws. Mr. Fluffy, free of his damaged cage, savagely tore into her tormentor's face, sending sprays of blood and torn flesh flying into the air. Hoagland howled and pulled the frenetic animal from his face, only to be rewarded by Mr. Fluffy going full fuzzsaw on his already mangled hands.

Matt took advantage of the unusual diversion to snatch up his gun. With one swift motion, he swung the handle, making solid contact with the man's head. The maniac finally went down for the count, a fresh trail of blood trickling from his temple. Mr. Fluffy, covered in Hoagland's blood as if he was Freddy Kreuger's spirit guide, sat nearby cleaning herself.

Matt eyed the cat dubiously and looked around the room for an empty cage. He spied one and set it down near the cat, opening the door. She ignored it, which he expected, but you gotta try, right?

Next, he found a bag of kitty treats sitting on an end table. *That* she seemed interested in. "Yeah, that's right! You want some of this, don't you?" he cajoled, ready to protect his face, but Mr. Fluffy seemed as placid as ever. He dropped a few treats into the cage through the gaps in the bars on the top. *That was easy*, he thought, as Mr. Fluffy shot off like a fuzzy rocket after them and into the cage. He quietly shut the door and locked it, and she seemed none the worse for wear.

"Gotcha!" He exclaimed in triumph. He trained his gun to cover Hoagland just in case the guy got his second wind. He'd seen enough horror movies in his day to expect such a jump scare. But as surreal as this day has turned out, this wasn't the movies. Hoagland continued to lay there spread out on the floor.

The rusty hinges sounded again, and Matt whirled to point his gun at the entrance to the apartment, where a startled neighbor stood framed by the doorway. She threw her hands up over her head.

Matt lowered his weapon with relief. "Don't just stand there, call 911!"

She showed him her hands, which were gripping a cordless phone. "I already did! They'll be here in a few minutes!"

Matt swung his arms back around so he could keep an eye on Hoagland, gun at the ready. But the man was still out cold.

The neighbor joined him a few moments later. "I never did like that man."

"Yeah? Join the club!" Matt said, just glad it was all over.

Epilogue: Only the Beginning

Animal Control took away the cats in Hoagland's apartment. The Frankencats died a few days later of acute tissue rejection, as they were dependent on a special serum only Hoagland knew how to synthesize. He had notes, but they were all written in a cryptic cipher. Out of spite, Hoagland refused to share the secret of how to make the serum even though it had the potential to save countless lives, and even earn him a (positive) place in history books.

He was convicted on multiple counts of animal cruelty, assault with a deadly weapon and attempted murder, not to mention the felony theft of Mr. Fluffy. His lawyers attempted an insanity plea, but it failed. He clearly knew right from wrong; he just chose to ignore it. He was shipped off to Rikers Island, spending several years there only to fall off the radar after he was released. Nobody knows what became of him since.

The Vanderhoffs' legion of lawyers waved their magic wands, and all mention of any possible charges against Matt for illegally entering Hoagland's apartment disappeared. Matt collected a handsome bonus on the case, which he used to pay his emergency room bill as well as restocking his mini fridge,and buying a few more items of used furniture for his office. The greatest reward of all, however, was seeing the look of pure joy on Lily's face when she was reunited with her beloved feline friend. Freshly cleaned of blood, of course

Matt was given a pair of free tickets to the show, which he offered to share with Sara, which she refused. "Sounds too much like a real date, Spike," she said. Matt decided he had seen enough of that theater to last him a lifetime anyway, so gave the tickets to Randy as a thank you for his help on the case. The boy took his aunt to the show. As Randy reported later, a good time was had by all.

New cases trickled into Matt's office as news of the unusual story spread. He no longer worried about having to shut down his office, though his need for a secretary to help him keep everything straight became more urgent than ever. He tried to lure Genevieve away from Vanderhoff Enterprises, and although she found the offer to work for a real detective quite tempting, in the end practicality won out. Matt couldn't come close to matching what she was currently earning.

For a brief period, he became something of a hero amongst the local animal rights community until his fifteen minutes of fame were up and he was forgotten. It didn't matter, he'd never been in it for the glory, all of which had just made him feel uncomfortable.

Before he'd faded from the headlines, his father had caught the story on the news. He called Matt up afterwards.

"It looks like I might owe you an apology, kiddo. I guess you're a real detective after all! Good job on that case. I'll bet you were able to squeeze a nice little reward out of those rich bastards, huh?"

"I made out alright," Matt replied enigmatically.

"Maybe I'm in the wrong line of work and you've got the right idea, eh? Anyway, I don't suppose you might be able to afford to pay a little rent now? You'll still get a special rate of course. You *are* my only child."

Matt laughed, knowing from the beginning where this conversation was going. It was always the same with his money-grubbing Dad. "I'm sure we can work something out. Something fair." He meant it. He wasn't going to be like his Dad. He wasn't going to try to live rent-free when he didn't need to. And besides, he was done being dependent on anyone else's charity ever again.

"Ya know son, I might not say it often enough, but you're a good man, and I'm proud of the way you turned out. I know I can come off like a bit of a hardass sometimes, but it's only because I worry about you. I just wanna know that you'll be able to earn a good living and take care of yourself. I wanna know you're gonna be okay, and that now I see that you've got it all under control, maybe I can relax a little? Maybe we both can, huh?”

“Sure, Dad. That sounds great,” Matt said, his voice cracking.

Matt’s father cleared his throat. “Alright, don’t go getting all mushy on me! I’ll be in touch about the rent. Talk to you again soon.”

“Say hi to Mom for me,” Matt said, his eyes stinging.

“Yeah, yeah! Sure! Of course! Goodbye, son.”

Matt hung up the phone and bawled his eyes out. But afterwards he felt like the weight of the world had just been lifted from his shoulders.

Matt continued to discuss his cases with Randy when they’d bump into each other on the stoop, and the detective came to seek out the kid’s preternaturally on the nose insights. It was almost like the guy was psychic or something.

Sometimes, Matt would think about Lance Hoagland and his strange quest for perfection. *Perfection.* What a subjective concept. Matt knew that it was a fruitless, futile pursuit. Perfection, like beauty, was in the eye of the beholder, and like any other human idea, subject to the ever-changing whims of people’s fancies. There were no absolute ideals, although this didn’t seem to stop people from endlessly chasing after them like a crazed cat chasing its own tail. Or clawing at the face of its captor.

Matt's new life might not be perfect, but that was okay. Perfection was a phantom. He was content with his life, shitty office, lukewarm lady friend and all. It was still better than what a lot of people had. And he finally felt he was the captain of his own destiny for a change, instead of a chunk of wood drifting down the river of life – and hitting every damned rock on the way downstream! He was content.

His budding career as a PI hadn't turned out to be much like the detective stories he'd read as a kid. He loved all those old detective stories, but they were just that, stories, and reality was far scarier. And weirder.

Again, he thought of Hoagland, and how obsessed he was with cats. Clearly, he had a unique appreciation for the animals, but he had stopped seeing them as living, breathing, feeling beings, and they became nothing but disposable objects to be sacrificed on the altar of his own vanity. Matt didn't want to start looking at his career like that, striving for an unattainable ideal to the point where he couldn't find any joy in it. To Matt, the lesson of Hoagland was that you could love something so fiercely that you couldn't help but destroy it, and he never wanted to fall into that kind of trap. Randy's discussions helped keep him honest and on the right path, often speaking about the need to balance the various elements of life, when their discussions on the stoop veered into the philosophical.

These were the kinds of heavy thoughts that were swirling around Matt's mind as he drained the last drop of coffee from a mug at his favorite bagel shop. He'd decided to treat himself to breakfast that morning, grateful that he could afford to do so now without breaking the bank. He left a few crumpled dollars on the table as a tip and prepared to head out the door to face the uncertain promise of the new day.

So lost in his meditations, he barely registered a petite young woman coming the other way. As he pushed the door open to leave, he lingered a moment to hold it open for her.

"And they say that chivalry is dead in this city," said an oddly familiar voice in thanks. He absently tipped the brim of his fedora at her, still lost in thought.

She stopped in mid stride, in his way, and Matt was about to tell her to make up her mind when she spoke again. "Omigod! It's Matt, isn't it? Matt from High School? What the hell are you doing here?" she said in a shocked tone. Matt lifted his eyes to really look at her.

She was even more beautiful than he remembered, if that was possible. "Naomi? Wow, it's been years!" He took a moment to take her *all* in, and chuckled. "You look fantastic!"

She blushed but seemed pleased with the comment. "So, um, what brings you to the neighborhood?"

He spread his hands. "I live here now! Right down the street and around the corner. I'm working as a Private Eye now."

She whistled. "No shit! A real life Sherlock! You always did like all that detective stuff. Congratulations!"

She punched him in his bad shoulder, eliciting a sharp intake of breath from him, but he really didn't mind. "Yeah, I just wrapped up my first big case with my very own agency," he said, rubbing his shoulder. "It got pretty strange. You won't believe how it went!"

She tilted her head in a way that made his heart race. "I'd love to hear all about it. We should totally get together for a coffee and catch up with each other."

I'd walk through coals to make that happen . . . "Are you sure your husband would be okay with that?"

Naomi rolled her eyes. "Who cares what that bum thinks anymore? I dumped his lame ass years ago."

"Oh? I'm sorry that things didn't work out for you two." *Yesss.*

"Don't be sorry, I'm not. I jumped into that marriage too soon. I don't need that asshat in my life anymore, I guess I never really did. The only good thing to come out of it all was my son. I'm living with my mom now and taking classes at night. My life might not be perfect, but I'm content. It's what's right for me now."

Matt nodded knowingly. "Let me get your number. I might just take you up on that offer to catch up. Soon."

Naomi smiled broadly as he wrote her number down in one of the many little spiral notepads he kept in his trench coat. The morning sun caught Naomi's light brown eyes, and they seemed to glitter like gold for one shining moment. Matt was certain it was the most beautiful thing he'd ever seen. The future suddenly looked so bright that he wished he had shades.

What were the odds, Matt wondered, that of all the people in this teeming city of millions, they should happen to find each other again?

This was just the beginning for them all . . .

THE HOUSE ON WEST BAY AVE

The following account happened way back during the sweltering summer of 1994. It is completely nuts that I have never bothered to write this all down before, considering how thoroughly these events shaped the trajectory of my life. Fortunately, I kept a diary, which helped jar loose my memories when it came to recalling the finer details of this story.

Where to begin? With the house, I suppose. Yes, that makes the most sense. The house that always loomed so large in my mind, casting its inescapable shadow over all my days.

Part One: Spectre of the Past

I didn't know back then if the house was really haunted.

All I knew was it sure haunted me. I used to walk past it all the time when I was in high school, on the way to my boyfriend's house.

What might once have been a tightly manicured lawn and well-kept bushes and trees had through years of neglect given way to a chaotic vegetative mess, though the house itself had been spared and no life grew upon it. The house itself was in surprisingly good shape. A stately three-story Victorian home with a pair of red brick chimneys, it was unlike many such buildings from that era as it lacked any turrets. Its siding shone a bright, cheerful yellow, yet there was absolutely nothing cheerful about the aura which radiated from the place. No, that projected an omnipresent, oppressive feeling of gloom even on the brightest days. Four columns supported the roof of a generous covered porch. Dark-stained and heavy-looking doors, each inset with crimson stained-glass windows that somehow had escaped the gentle attentions of the neighborhood's rock-throwing youth, guarded the entrance. On either side of these doors were large, dark windows on the second floor, completing an overall look for the house of a yellowed skull.

Even people who weren't quite as sensitive as I was to such things could feel it. Feel it watching them as they walked by. Conversations would falter then fail altogether as footfalls became more hurried and strident. For me, it was worse. I would sometimes feel a sharp pain in my head like it was ready to explode whenever I got close. Even crossing the street to the opposite side didn't help much.

Despite how crappy it made me feel to be so close, I was always helplessly intrigued. Something in it called to me, I could almost hear it. Braving migraines, I'd tread through the unkempt yard to peer into the windows. Usually I didn't see much inside, just vacant rooms which hinted at some past grandeur now faded. A dusty banister with an accompanying flight of stairs vanished up into the darkness.

There was that one time, though. The one time something stared *back* at me from the other side of the window!

It was a woman. I suppose she must once have been beautiful. It was hard to tell given the top half of her head had been blown off. Tiny eggshell fragments of her skull peppered her long, wavy blonde hair, while rivers of blood streamed down her face, pooling into lakes of gore in the space near her collarbone. She wore a terrible expression on her face, something between shock and terror.

I could relate. Shock and terror were pretty much what I felt as I stood there. We were locked like that for what seemed an eternity, staring at each other. You know that old saying about being so scared you can't move? Well, it's true. Every once in a while, you encounter something so unexpected, so terrifying, something that has absolutely no business existing in your world, that it's such a shock to your system you become completely paralyzed.

Someone crashing through the underbrush broke the spell, and I turned my head in the direction of the racket. My buddy Dennis. Yup, there he was, waddling towards me with a big, silly smile on his face. Good old, reliable Dennis, here to save me from my own folly as usual.

Not having forgotten about my ghostly ghastly companion, I snapped my head back to the window. But she was gone.

Dennis panted lightly with his exertion and smiled gamely. I looked up into his eyes, though that's a stretch . . . he's only slightly taller than me, which is to say of average height. A little thick around the middle, but not fat. Not a gym rat, but maybe he could stand to be a gym mouse a little. Despite that, he was pleasant looking, with an open, boyish face and short cropped sandy blonde hair. He wore his customary tee shirt with some obscure superhero on it. I didn't think he owned one without it, and I'd almost think it was some kind of uniform or saw himself as some kind of avatar for the high moral conduct only found in the racks of comic book stores. He was such an unabashed nerd. But so was I. We spoke the same nerdy language. Comics were just one of the many interests we shared. The fact that he was brave enough to advertise his geekiness was one of the things I admired so much about him. He embraced his inner weirdness. I just wanted to hide it away, afraid it would make me a target for other people's cruelty.

His smile tinged with concern. "You look like you've just seen a ghost!"

"Uh, yeah, Captain Obvious! Maybe because I just fucking have!" It came out far more harshly than I'd ever intended, but I think under the circumstances I was entitled to sound a little bitchy, I was still scared out of my wits!

In truth, I was greatly grateful for his presence. It had shocked me out of the trance I had with that specter, but more than that, he never failed to make me feel safe. Silly, but when Dennis was around I became convinced that nothing could get me. Maybe because he'd always defended me, braving the bullies who liked to torture me by calling me "brace face" and much worse when we were still kids.

He was quite used to my often-abrasive demeanor in those days, so he was unfazed as he placed a warm hand on my shoulder and gave it a squeeze. Even my pounding headache lessened a bit at his touch, which is saying something. I closed my eyes and smiled in relief. I wished his hand would stay there forever, but he only let it linger for a moment.

"Are you ok?" He asked gently, his strikingly blue eyes flooded with concern. "You're shaking."

Was I? I hadn't even registered that fact. I found that I was indeed trembling. With some effort, I got it under control. "Yeah. I'll survive. It's hardly the first ghost I've seen. Although this might just be the most frightening one I've ever witnessed!"

He whistled. "So, you finally saw something in there, huh? We were right! This place really is haunted! I knew it! I just knew it!" he noted triumphantly. He was almost hopping up and down in excitement. I would have found it cute if I wasn't still spooked. If you'll pardon the pun.

He walked to the nearest window and pressed his face against the glass so hard it was comically smooshed looking. "I don't see anything in there but spiders. We've been coming by here for years and I never get to see anything but spiders! It's a shame this place is such a mess. Someone really oughta fix it up, or at least mow the grass and trim these damned bushes!" To punctuate the point, he scratched at some marks on his exposed legs where the thick brambles had snagged him.

I crossed my arms, feeling dismissed. I just told him I just saw the scariest ghost I'd ever seen and now all he just wanted to do was prattle on about real estate and groundskeeping? Why wasn't he paying attention to me anymore? Couldn't he see that I still needed a bit more comforting? I took a deep breath and let it out. "Whew! I guess I *am* still pretty shook up from the look of that terrible *thing* I just saw in the window!"

But instead of giving me the hug I so desperately needed in that moment, he just kicked at nothing with his toe. "I can't help but get a little jealous of the fact that you're psychic enough to see ghosts. I'd love to see something supernatural."

"No, you wouldn't," I said pointedly. "Especially what I just saw. It was hugely gross and scary as hell! Sometimes it makes me feel like I'm losing my mind."

Losing my mind? I probably would have thought that, if I wasn't used to seeing such things pretty much for my entire life. My mom called it a gift and it was something she could do too, though to a lesser extent. To me it was not a gift, but a curse. Just one more thing that made me stand out as being different when all I wanted was to blend in and be normal.

I often wondered if – even *hoped* – we were just a bunch of undiagnosed schizophrenics. On bad days, it was easier for me to believe that than it was to have faith in the idea that I was seeing, and sometimes even conversing, with dead people. The only thing which convinced me I wasn't a total basket case was sometimes the dead told me things I was able to later verify through research, things I otherwise had no business knowing or couldn't have known.

Dennis brightened. "I lost my mind years ago, probably on that field trip to Philly where I left my backpack behind too. It's not so bad!"

I appreciated his clumsy efforts to cheer me up with cheesy jokes, usually it worked. This time it didn't. Nothing could dissipate the feeling of dread soaking into every pore of my being every minute I stayed there. I was half convinced my splitting head would explode if I didn't get away soon. "Let's get out of here," I said glumly. I pointedly kept my gaze away from the house, terrified that if I did, I'd see that horrible, ruined vision of a woman staring back at me, her empty eyes devoid of anything resembling hope. In a way, those eyes had been worse than her bloody face and half blasted off head.

Okay, I thought as we walked away. *Now I know, it's* definitely *haunted. But by who?*

The next day, I got my answers. As it often was, it was a slow day at the library where I worked, so I was able to squeeze in some time for personal research. It was amazing I'd never thought to do this before, looking into the history of that house, considering how many years I'd been low key obsessing over it. Even though the house had been built in 1887, the style of clothing my ghost wore was far more contemporary, so I started my search in the present day and worked my way backwards. Going through some local papers from a little over a decade earlier provided me with the information I needed.

It had been a grisly suicide/murder. The woman's husband, a well-connected local lawyer, flipped out one day and killed his wife, then ate the shotgun too. There had apparently been a long history of domestic abuse, and paranoid accusations of infidelity amongst them. The worst part was the troubled couple's kid had been in the house when it all went down, and worse, had witnessed the entire thing. Today, she'd only be a few years older than I was. It gave me a chill to think we might have even passed in the hallways at elementary school.

How the hell was it that I'd never heard about this? In a town this small, you'd think such a thing would be pretty damned notorious! Nobody had ever mentioned this before in all the past conversations where I'd brought up the house. Everyone who was familiar with the building agreed it gave them the willies, but nobody could ever explain exactly why, and were even less interested in anything to know about its history. I found myself wondering if the husband's family, who came from old money, had used their influence to quash the talk.

For his part, this whole incident with the ghost got Dennis excited. Even more so when I shared what I had learned about its history the next morning when we met at Dunk'n Donuts. For years he'd talked about getting into doing paranormal investigations, ghost hunting and all that. He'd busied himself gobbling up all the books on the subject he could find, or rather, that I could find for him at my library.

Lately he'd graduated into actually stockpiling equipment for it. The guy made a pretty decent living as an HVAC repairman, so even given his high maintenance girlfriend, Stacy, he managed to squirrel away enough for this paranormal stuff, and a little left over for his geeky passion for collecting comics and action figures.

Dennis had barely touched his cinnamon cruller. "This is it! This has got to be the inaugural case for the Jersey Shore Paranormal Society!"

"The say what now?" I asked, blearily fumbling for my cup so I could take another sip of brain-resurrecting coffee.

"The Jersey Shore Paranormal Society. That's us!"

"*Us?*" I asked doubtfully, post-sip, pre-resurrection. "I don't remember signing up."

"Too late, I've already got your t-shirt!" he said. He meant it, too. Laughing, he pulled a poorly folded (really, wadded up) and wrinkled shirt from his backpack. He unfurled it for me with all the solemn dignity of a military funeral. "What do you think?"

Between all the wrinkles, it looked cool, I had to admit. I was gonna have to tumble dry this baby when I got it home. It was black, and in white letters were the words "Jersey Shore Paranormal Society" around a round seal with a ghost, a UFO, and, naturally, the Jersey Devil inside it.

I took it from him, admiring it more closely. "That looks so good! Did you make it?" As far as I knew, though Dennis was a great admirer of art (mostly comic book art, but hey – it counts!), he didn't have an artistic bone in his body.

"The people at the silk-screening place did it for me. Based on my own design, of course," he said, that last said conspiratorially.

"Of course," I replied in the same tone, warming up to this. "*Society*' huh?" I said it in a cheesy English accent that made Dennis laugh. "It sounds so classy, so fancy! Okay I'll join your little ghost hunting club. I ain't 'fraid of no ghosts."

It was true. I wasn't usually all that scared of ghosts, as they were my lifelong companions. Truth be told, it was the living who tended to leave me petrified.

"I knew you wouldn't be able to resist! I mean, we've basically been doing it unofficially for years now anyway. Now we'll just be doing it in matching t-shirts!" His elbow shifting his ignored cruller to totter on the edge of the table as he leaned toward me. "So now you just have to figure out who owns that place to see if we can get permission to get inside it."

"I already know who owns it." I said, deftly rescuing the cruller to the middle of the table. "The township put a lien on it. They've had the deed on it for years, but somebody just bought it at auction a few weeks ago. Now it belongs to a local contractor. I assume they're gonna fix it then flip it."

"Maybe that's what's stirring things up? Maybe they've already been over there working on the place?"

"Yeah, that's what I've been thinking too." I liked that he'd come to the same conclusion. Sometimes we really did complement each other nicely.

"Great, so all we need to do is call up this contractor and see if they'll let us poke around inside. For all we know, they might've had some experiences themselves. Maybe you can call them later today?"

If I'd had coffee in my mouth, it would have ended badly for him. "What? Just call them up out of the blue?"

I had some pretty bad anxieties when it came to dealing with strangers. I could function at work despite that my job involved dealing with the public, because it was like a second home to me and felt safe. However, the idea of speaking to people I didn't even know on the phone made my skin crawl. So much so I was teased for it at work because I was always the last person to answer the phone. I wasn't on any medications for it, not that I didn't believe in science (although science isn't a matter of "belief" really – it just is), but I was skeptical of our pill-for-everything culture and I wanted no part in it.

Especially for *mild* psychiatric conditions, as the "cure" can be worse than the disease, especially when there are unpleasant side effects that make you need to take even more medications, and so on. The next thing you know, you've got a medicine cabinet full of drugs, and you still feel like shit – just about entirely new and different things. No freaking thanks. I wanted to deal with my anxieties in my own ways, and none of that crystal healing New Age bullshit my mom was so into.

Dennis took a bite of his cruller. "Hey, if you're too anxious to give them a call it's no problem. Give me the number and I'll make the call. Don't stress on it, it *is* a little weird to call up someone and ask if you can go hunting for ghosts in their house without them thinking that you're a nut."

"No, no, it's okay," I said, blowing out a breath to make myself relax. "I shouldn't have overreacted like that. I'll do it. Honestly, I'm never gonna get over these anxieties if I just run away from them. I need to confront them head on." This strategy was why I deliberately sought out a job that forced me to work with the public. And it had worked out, mostly, kind of.

He nodded sympathetically. "I appreciate it, I wasn't looking forward to trying to explain all this to them either, but I would've done it. You're a brave lady, Athena Anderson."

Athena Anderson. I asked Dennis once why he likes to say my full name so much. He said he loves my name because it sounds so alliterative, like a superhero's secret identity. More's the better because I have a bona fide "superpower." As far as he was concerned, this made me the most interesting person he knew. God, our town was too small!

Even though kind of a goofball, Dennis was a good friend, I had to say. Always more than supportive and understanding of my personal quirks, of which there were more than a few.

Now might be a good time to clear the air about what was going on between Dennis and me romantically at that time. Basically, there was nothing there to talk about. It was always the great elephant in the room between us. He was attracted to me based on the number of times I'd caught him eyeing my ass like prime rib, I didn't need to be a psychic to understand that! However, I'd convinced myself that the feeling wasn't mutual. I liked his eyes, sure, but otherwise told myself that was the extent of my physical attraction to him. Ideally, I *do* prefer a nice tall man that's in better shape, with rippling muscles. Wasn't that what society was telling me I was supposed to be chasing after? Wasn't settling for anything less than that the same as giving up? With my looks I knew I was certainly capable of landing such a hunk.

I had done it plenty of times in the past. My body's angular lines bloomed into round curves, and once my braces came off and I traded in my glasses for contacts, the same guys who used to make fun of me were paying me a different kind of attention. I should have been more annoyed at how fickle and shallow they were, but I just wanted to be wanted for a change, and on top of that it was empowering being desired by people who only a year or two before had made your life a living hell.

Not all the good-looking guys I managed to snag were such jerks. Quite a few were genuinely sweet. Too bad that my personality inevitably drove them away, or so I believed at the time It takes two to tango and looking back I can see it wasn't *all* my fault that my previous relationships fell apart. I was way too tough on myself in those days.

But I digress. I was talking about Dennis and myself. We had known each other since grade school, and he had always been my rock. My one dependable, constant companion and friend. He stood up for me when everyone else just wanted to spit on me for being the weird dark haired girl who claimed she could see ghosts and always had her face buried in a book. I didn't want to ever risk losing a friendship that was so precious to me, because then I'd *really* be alone. I was sure I would screw it up. Didn't I always? So I convinced myself I didn't have any designs on him in that department. Isn't it amazing the secrets we can keep, even from ourselves? We humans have the most amazing capacity for self-delusion!

And let's not forget he already had a girlfriend, Stacy, though I didn't think much of her. A mooch, just kind of hangs around, and *not* employed. And oddly, she didn't get jealous of the time I spent with Dennis, which might seem like a good thing, but to me that just meant she couldn't care for him very deeply. Worst of all, she was *incredibly* boring.

He didn't seem to mind. He was happy I guess to have such a pretty girl show him that kind of attention for once. The dude had some self-esteem issues, but didn't we all? Anyway, I hoped someday he would find someone nice, a person who really appreciated what made him special. Someone more like me, but, you know, not me, for the above stated reasons.

At that time, I was enjoying a sabbatical from the stresses of dating and relationships. Taking a little time to work on myself. After all, I was convinced that I was the one common denominator in all my spoiled love affairs. Talk about self-esteem issues!

Well, as it turned out, I didn't end up calling the owner of that house that day. We were unusually busy at work and I was too exhausted and stressed out by the end of the day to go ahead and do something else that would add to my stress. I was too ashamed to tell Dennis I'd chickened out.

My luck changed the next morning. I usually went into work much sooner than I had to, and I also drove past that house every day on my way to the Barnegat branch of the Ocean County Library. I was listening to some of my favorite music during my rather short morning commute from the modest ranch style home I shared with my mom in the Pebble Beach section of town. It was weird, but back then I often felt like I could only connect to certain kinds of emotions by listening to music, or by watching a particularly dramatic scene in a movie, or on TV. Or of course, by reading a particularly gripping passage in a good book.

Even though I'd had all kinds of drama in my life, I was often numb to it emotionally. Maybe it

was a defense mechanism? I had even lost people I really cared about and barely been able to shed a tear, even without the reassurance of having seen them as a ghost or having felt their presence around me. When I did grieve it was usually for the benefit of the other people who were grieving.

But if you sat me down in front of a real powerful tear-jerking scene in a good film, I would go to pieces!

Music had the same effect on me, but thankfully, that morning, the music I was listening to was pumping me up with joy rather than making me blubber, because that would have made what was about to come next even more awkward than it already was. Thankfully, my shit is a lot more together these days. It's amazing how much of a difference feeling properly supported emotionally can make you feel. Goddamn it! There I go! Digressing again! Pull it together, Athena!

That morning, as I approached the house, I there were a couple of big white pickup trucks parked in the driveway, and a few workmen outside. For whatever reason, I was feeling bolder than usual. Perhaps it was the music lifting my spirits? But I suspected it was more likely my guilt over not calling the day before. Either way, I found my courage and pulled into the driveway behind the trucks. I recognized the name of the contractor, "E. L. White," painted on the side of the trucks.

The two workmen outside regarded me with curiosity as I exited my car. Calling them men might be generous, as they were barely out of their teens and only a few years younger than myself. Their similar build and facial features marked them undoubtedly as brothers.

"Hi. Excuse me, I was hoping to speak to your boss, is he around?" I inquired, flashing my best smile. My parents had spent a small fortune on orthodontic appliances during my childhood to cultivate them into their current state of perfection.

Hey, if you've got it, flaunt it! It was always a source of ironic pleasure to me that I got so many compliments on my smile, after enduring years of being called "brace face," and worse. People always complained that I didn't smile enough. That was true. It didn't help that I also suffered, so I've been told, from that curious medical condition named "resting bitch face," a condition whose only cure is perpetually walking around grinning like an idiot. I decidedly lacked the energy for that. I found peace with the fact that people tended to mistake my serious, pensive nature for the kind of simmering hostility people reserve for being stuck in traffic.

The boys, err, *young men* gaped at my grinning self for what seemed like an eternity before the taller one finally snapped out of his stupor. "Dad! Someone here to see you!" he called in the direction of the house. He said it *loudly*, and I winced. *The front doors are standing wide open kid, what the hell.* Years of working in the library had made me unusually irritated by loud people.

A man stepped out onto the porch of the house. And I do mean, a *man*. Not a boy like the two pimply dudes in the driveway who probably couldn't muster enough chin fuzz between them to upholster a peach. Still, there was an unmistakable family resemblance there, in the eyes and the set of the jaw. Dad looked like he had a good ten or fifteen years on me, which would put him anywhere from his mid thirties to early forties. I found myself wondering if Mrs. White was still in the picture.

He wiped his hands on a cloth, the muscles in his forearms moving in a way that didn't help my attitude at all. "Are you from the township? We've got all the permits."

God! He thought I was an inspector. Did I really look that official? I mean, I've gotta dress professionally for work, but I didn't think I looked quite that officious.

I tugged at my suit jacket, which felt very polyester all of a sudden. "No, it's nothing like that at all," I said, trying not to gush and getting the most out of that orthodontic smile. He relaxed visibly.

I walked up the steps and extended my hand. "My name is Athena Anderson."

He reached out for a handshake. My hand felt tiny in his, which was rough and calloused, yet warm and nice. I was probably blushing. I fought to get that under control. *C'mon blood, outta my face!* For the first time I wished for the kind of body control practiced by those Tibetan monks my mom idolized.

"Athena? Like the Greek Goddess of wisdom?" he asked. I said nothing, but the confusion and admiration at his knowledge must have been apparent, because he continued. "Don't look so surprised! Just because I spend my days swinging a hammer doesn't mean I'm uneducated." His voice was gentle, not accusing, and accompanied by a playful grin.

My mouth raced ahead of my brain, as it often does. "Of course! I don't mean to imply that you're not an intelligent person," I sputtered, back to my default mode of shy awkwardness, all of my pretensions of smooth confidence crumbling like a sandcastle in a windstorm.

He laughed. Thankfully, it wasn't a cruel laugh. "Relax. If you're not here to harass me about permits, then I think we can be friends. How can I help you today, Mrs. Anderson?"

Mrs. Anderson? Later on, I'd realize this was his flirty way of inquiring if I was married or not. In the heat of the moment, I'm often too flustered to figure shit like that out. Apparently, daddy here was into girls that were only a couple of years older than his own boys. Years later, I might have, probably would have, found that sort of thing to be not a little bit creepy. But at that point in my life, I just wanted to bask in the positive attention of this attractive stranger, and I'd be lying if I said I wasn't feeling an attraction myself. A strong attraction.

"It's Ms.," I corrected, my face even hotter than it was before and totally out of my league to be able to handle a flirtatious verbal dance like this without falling flat on my face.

"Noted," he said without missing a beat. "Now, what brings you out here so early in the morning, *Ms.* Anderson?"

"Well, this might sound a little crazy," I said, for an instant wishing I had a less embarrassing reason for being here, but then decided it was best just to dive right in and embrace the weirdness. "Have you noticed anything *strange* about this house since you started working on it?"

He tilted his head. "Athena? Are you trying to ask me if this house is haunted?"

"Umm. No. Not exactly. I mean, I already *know* it's haunted," I said, my mouth suddenly dry. "I was just wondering if you've noticed that too, like if you're open to such ideas?" Any kind of cool I'd once possessed in this situation was washed out to sea.

He laughed again. It thrummed against my heart. "I *do* believe in those kinds of things. And yes, I've had a few strange experiences since we bought this place. I'll hear footsteps when there's nobody else in the house. Once I heard a loud sound, like a gunshot. I thought it might have been a car backfiring, but there was no traffic on the road outside at that time of night."

"And there's that feeling you get around here, like you're always being watched," one of the boys piped in. The shorter one.

"Like someone really doesn't want you in here!" the taller one added, not to be outdone.

Mr. White nodded. "Athena, my apologies. These are my boys, Eli Jr." – he indicated the taller one – "and Brad." The older boy waved at me with the easy confidence that being the older brother bestowed upon him. Brad, on the other hand, studied his shoes.

I knew the feeling. I often didn't know quite what to do when being introduced. I mean, I knew you are supposed to say "Hi" or something, but I didn't always know quite how much emotion to put into it. How could I tell if I'm really happy to meet someone or not? They could be a secret axe murderer for all I know, or maybe just kind of an asshole. I just didn't like being phony is all. I prized genuineness. Unfortunately, the world seemed to run on endless displays of insincerity. I hated that kind of pretending. It took real effort for me to do it, an effort that frequently left me exhausted and gasping for air.

I attempted a non-awkward smile made awkward by trying not to be awkward, then whirled my head back in the direction of their kind of disconcertingly sexy parental unit. Trying not to focus on the fact of his sexiness and concentrate on why I was there. I nervously played with a crystal amulet given to me by Mom, supposedly to be for protection. I don't believe in that stuff, but it was pretty, so whatever. And good for nervous tugging.

"Wow! So you've all had experiences too, huh? I grew up around here and I used to ride my bike past this place all the time. It's been empty my whole life. It always gave me a bad feeling. I've sort of been fascinated with it, and recently I . . . er . . . saw something inside it."

I could feel their eyes upon me, looking at me expectantly. This was something that normally would have made me feel super nervous. But somehow, I found my groove again, like falling into a slot. Maybe a part of me enjoyed being the center of attention for once?

So, I told them everything. All in one big, long babble, but I made it. The lady with her head blown off. The history behind the house. And, lastly, about the Jersey Shore Paranormal Society, and our desire to investigate there.

Happily, Eli – Mr. White, but he insisted on Eli and I missed it *again* and I was clueless again so sue me – was eager to give us permission to do so.

"Maybe you can even get rid of the ghosts, too? It's gonna be hard enough to sell this place once anyone finds out what happened here, let alone if they think the place is haunted, no matter how good of a job we do restoring her to her former glory."

I put on my most mature voice. "We can try to put whatever souls may be inside to rest." Really I was overjoyed they had not only decided I wasn't a complete nutcase, but were actually really gung ho about our desire to investigate here. Problem: I had no idea how to get rid of a ghost. It's not like I had a proton pack hidden in the trunk of my car.

Mr. White - I mean *Eli* – offered to show me around the house and show off the renovations he had already done. I had to turn him down, telling him that I was on my way to work and didn't want to be late. This was a lie. I would still be early to work if I spent another ten or fifteen minutes there. I just wasn't ready to go inside yet, because I could feel something watching me, and I was spooked. Something that did *not* want me there. That old feeling about the house was coming back, the one that included a migraine.

I thanked him for his time, took his business card and promised to call him soon to set up a time when we could do our investigation. I shook his wonderfully powerful hand one more time, not wanting to let go, and returned to the sanctuary of my car seat.

As I drove away, a heady mix of emotions swirled through my brain. Unease at being so close to the house as well as relief as I got farther away from it, mixed with elation at being given permission to investigate there. And, of course, all the peculiar feelings that come with forming an infatuation on someone. *I am taking a break from dating,* I told myself firmly. *And I am not about to become anyone's stepmother!* All this while I couldn't help but fantasize about rugged dudes with hammers and all the various ways in which they might be *handy*.

Yeah, I wasn't very good at this will power stuff, and focused instead on how happy Dennis would be when I told him our first investigation was a go.

Part Two: An Origami Nightmare

Dennis was indeed overjoyed with the news when I called

him up from work to tell him about it. He came to my home

later that night lugging so much equipment that Mom and I

had to help him bring it in. But as they say, many hands make

light work. It was a host of new equipment he'd purchased

for our investigations, and he wanted me to get familiar with

how it all worked.

Honestly, there wasn't all that much to it. The stuff was

pretty easy to operate, and self-explanatory for the most part.

Of course, technology has always come easily to me. People,

not so much. That said, his joy and enthusiasm with his new

toys was infectious, and I truly had a great time with him.

The equipment consisted of a few camcorders with

tripods, a variety of infrared motion sensors, digital

thermometers and EMF (electromagnetic field) meters. He

also had a few digital voice recorders. All pretty standard

ghost hunting stuff, according to him. Then he asked me

about designing a website for the Jersey Shore Paranormal

Society, which I readily agreed to do. I didn't really need

much persuading, I would have suggested it eventually if he

hadn't brought it up first. I already had a few ideas for it. Web

design was one of my many talents, and a way for me to

occasionally earn a few extra bucks here and there. In this case, As a founding member, I would be offering my services to the JSPS pro bono, of course.

As we sat around my mom's modest living room – yes, I still lived with Mom, don't give me shit about it, it beat the hell out of having to pay rent – I could tell there was something he was eager to tell me, but couldn't quite find a way to say it. It was a problem I had experienced often enough for myself, so I recognized all the signs and didn't need my oh-so-amazing psychic powers to tell me that.

I kept quiet about it at first, trying to give him ample opportunity to get it out, but eventually I lost my patience with this little game. "Alright! Out with it! What is it you *really* wanted to tell me tonight?"

He blinked at me in shock, and I recognized that, too. He was surprised I could see through him so easily, even after all the years we had known each other. We'd known each other over half of our lives. It would be weird if I *couldn't* read him like a book by now. Yet he's always amazed by it, and always mildly irritated.

"I've been doing a little amateur detective work myself," he said cryptically, chewing his lips.

"And?"

"*And*, I've made contact with the lady who used to live in that house," he said with a blooming smile. "The little girl who saw it all happen."

My jaw dropped open and stayed like that for some time. Almost long enough to require a drool cup.

Almost. "What! How? Why?" I asked, when I regained my power of speech.

"It was easy, really. Her name was in that file you left with me with all your research on the house in it." He paused again for the maximum dramatic effect, during which I remembered how the file contained a photocopy of her parents' obituaries. Her name had been in the "survived by" portion: Miranda Drake, daughter of the late Molly and Dean Drake.

"I just looked her up in the phone book. Luckily, she hasn't gotten married or anything, so she still has the same name. And still lives in this area!"

"But why call her up? Do we really want to rub salt in an old wound?"

"I wanted to invite her to participate in our investigation. If the ghost you saw really is her mother, it might stir up some activity if we bring her daughter there."

I bit my lip. "I don't know. It seems a little callous if you ask me, using her like that."

Was getting proof that ghosts really existed worth putting someone through that kind of horrific experience again? Since the existence of ghosts was such a certainty for someone with my particular kind of curse, sometimes it was hard for me to understand why capturing really solid evidence of the phenomenon seemed to matter so much to other people. For me, it was like trying to prove the sky was blue.

Dennis seemed a bit taken aback. "I was thinking more along the lines it maybe would give her a sense of closure," he said slowly. "She agreed, by the way. She doesn't really remember any of it, she blocked out the memory of it all. She is eager to confront it though, to finally put the whole thing to rest. You know. Cathartic."

I supposed that made a twisted kind of sense. There was even a clinical term for it: exposure therapy. Basically what I do all the time, when I force myself into social situations that really make me want to go run and hide under a table as a way of coping with my anxiety issues.

I couldn't imagine how strange that conversation must have been. "Hello, I was wondering if you're the little girl who saw her Daddy murder her Mommy right before he killed himself? You are? Great! I'm planning on looking for proof that the ghost of your mother is haunting your old home. Would you like to tag along?" I wouldn't know how to even *begin* to have such a crazy conversation. I had to hand it to Dennis, he had some really big, brass balls on him when it came to going after something he really wanted. Apparently, brass balls confer more courage on someone than balls made from other metals. Don't ask me why, I didn't come up with the saying.

"Here's the thing," Dennis said in a vaguely embarrassed tone. "The only *slight* problem is I think she might have gotten the impression I could somehow free her mom's spirit from the house, to help her move on."

I leapt up. "Oh, great! And you didn't do much to discourage that idea, did you?"

I was totally aware I was being a hypocrite here. After all, I hadn't told Eli White that such things were beyond my abilities when he'd jumped to similar conclusions this morning either, hadn't I? Oh well, sometimes I just liked to bust Dennis' balls for the hell of it, I guess. Okay, that's the last time I'm going to mention anyone's balls, I promise! No more testicular tales, scrotal sagas or ribald reproductive references from little old me! The rest of this account will be as sexually sanitized as a Disney cartoon.

He scooted back half a scoot. "Not when it seemed like it might discourage her from joining us! Besides, I *have* read a thing or two on the subject, maybe it's enough to wing it? I was also hoping your mom might be able to help out in this department too . . .”

Mom ran a small occult shop located in one of the various strip malls in town that cropped up every few miles like an asphalt oasis in a sea of pine trees. She considered herself to be a witch. Even though I knew ghosts were real, I was more skeptical when it came to the spirituality behind all of this stuff. I knew there must be something to it, but I didn't pretend to understand what it truly was or what any of it meant. I honestly didn't know quite what to believe when it came to religion. All of Mom's spell casting and prayers hadn't been able to bring Dad back when he decided to walk out on us, so you'll excuse me if I'm not exactly sold on the efficacy of such things.

“I'd love to help out in any way I can!” Mom's voice reported from beyond the kitchen.

I had almost forgotten she was there. She was puttering around doing God knows what for the past few minutes, and I was trying my best to ignore her, while she had apparently been innocently eavesdropping on our conversation the whole time. My face flushed red in embarrassment. Okay, so there *are* some definite downsides to still living with your Mom as an adult, and this was one of the biggest ones: the lack of privacy and proper boundaries. Forget about trying to bring a guy back to the house to fool around with . . .

"We just have to burn a little sage, say a few prayers, and we can probably get that poor woman's tortured spirit to move on to the next plane lickity split!" she said, leaning against the door frame. Classic Mom. Was it really that simple? I doubted it. We were discussing how to get a spirit to move on into the White Light, and she was talking about it as casually as someone else's mother might explain how to cook a casserole.

Dennis looked genuinely relieved to have her on our team. I, however, felt the opposite. This was supposed to be a me and Dennis thing. Now suddenly it was also turning into a me, Dennis, Mom, and mysterious, sad orphan lady thing. Talk about there being too many cooks in the kitchen!

"Thanks, Barb. Happy to have you along!" he called back to her. Yeah, he was on a first name basis with her. It always mildly weirds me out whenever I hear someone call her anything other than "Mom," or "Mrs. Anderson," especially when it's someone my own age.

I shot him an ugly look that said, "why did you have to involve her in this?" but he either didn't notice, or studiously chose to ignore it. Instead, he fidgeted with the glass unicorn statue Mom had sitting out on our coffee table. Most of our house was decorated in rainbows, unicorns and plaques with inspirational messages written on them in cursive. It made me wanna puke. My bedroom, which hadn't been redecorated since I was in my high school Goth phase, was the only safe oasis from these saccharinely positive vibes.

I supposed it could be worse. He could be bringing his girlfriend Stacy along too, but thankfully there was virtually no chance of that happening. She was too scared of things like ghosts to ever go near this kind of an investigation. In fact, she thought the whole ghost thing was pretty weird. I guess she was right about that. It was weird. The difference was she saw said weirdness as a bad thing, whereas I didn't.

Not that I had much choice in the matter, due to my "gifts." You either accept this stuff as a normal part of life, or you go barking mad. I preferred to maintain some semblance of sanity, it's the responsible thing to do, isn't it?

I might not see the paranormal as being something so black and white you could categorize it as either being all good or all bad, but a part of me *wasn't* looking forward to our investigation.

For one thing, there was the awful way that being too close to that house made me feel physically. For another, seeing the apparition of a lady with the top of her head blown off was, you know, upsetting. The other spirits I'd seen in my long career hadn't been in such, shall we say, rough shape.

On the other hand, after all these years of obsessing over that house it was exciting to finally be able to to step inside and get to the bottom of the mystery. There was also the fact that Dennis was so adorably excited to finally start doing some proper ghost hunting, I didn't want to let him down or rain on his parade by sharing my trepidations. Who knows? Maybe Mom's bullshit would work, and we really *could* get that spirit to move on like we'd accidentally promised. If we could do some actual good, make a difference, then it would be worth enduring the pounding headache that inevitably awaited me. As usual, I'd just have to stuff my own feelings down and get over myself. Oh, and I'd also have to be sure to bring plenty of extra strength Tylenol with me!

The big day came the following Saturday. Eli had agreed to let us have free run of the place for the weekend. We arranged to meet at the house about an hour before sundown, so we could familiarize ourselves with the layout of the property. When Mom and I pulled into the driveway, Dennis was already there, sitting on the steps and chatting with a pretty lady I'd never seen before. This must be Miranda Drake, the girl who used to live there. She looked like maybe she was a few years older than me and Dennis. Her hair was bleached blonde, by the telltale look of the dark roots in the center of her scalp. She was tall and thin, wispy even, and casually dressed in jeans and a t-shirt. Not just any t-shirt either: she wore the same Jersey Shore Paranormal Society shirt Dennis and I were.

That didn't sit well with me. *Okay, so I guess she's a proper member of the team now?*

But I had to swallow it. In the end, it was Dennis' group, not mine. He could invite anyone he wanted, but it put me in an awkward position. I didn't want to dislike her right from the start. If anything, I thought she was extraordinarily brave for daring to ever come back to this house. The house where her young life had been destroyed. How had life been for her since?

That said . . . she looked fine. Smiling and laughing at some comment Dennis was making. Still, appearances could be deceiving, and nobody knew that better than I did. On the outside, I appeared fine too. Nobody truly understood what a seething, roiling mass of anxieties lies beneath my perfect smile.

With some effort, Dennis got up as Mom and I walked up to them, and Miranda followed his lead.

"Athena, Barb, this is Miranda Drake. She grew up here," Dennis said without flourish, and for my part I thought that was a wildly understated way of describing her relationship to the place.

"Pleased to meet you both," she said, shaking hands with us. The headache, a spike in my brain, had kicked in before I even got out of my car but it subsided as soon as I took her hand. My breath caught and I held her hand a moment longer than I should. And all of my psychic senses were telling me she was a good person, a very good person. So that just made me feel even more guilty about my initial annoyance at seeing her.

I tried to make amends, reaching for the only topic I could think of. "I can't believe you'd ever want to come back to this place, considering what happened here."

Mom put in, "I'm so sorry about what happened here, dear. It must have been horrible."

Several emotions played over Miranda's face, but I would guess the primary one was confusion. "Thank you," she said, "but I really don't remember it. I barely remember anything about living here, or about my parents. The few memories that I do have don't even seem like my on. It's like looking at old home movies and not recognizing yourself. I know that this place is a part of my past because I've been told that it is, but I don't feel any substantial personal connection to it. Not so far, anyway. Maybe that'll change once we get inside. I just don't know."

I nodded. Hers was a classic case of dissociating oneself as a defense mechanism. Sometimes I liked to read about psychology to understand my own personal brand of crazy a little better.

"Well, I think it's really brave of you to join us here," I didn't mind telling her. Seriously, what if she started to have flashbacks while we were inside and had a panic attack? I was genuinely quite worried for her, this person whom I'd only just met. I wasn't sure she fully appreciated how dangerous this could be for her, not because of any literal ghosts that might be lurking inside, but because of the ones that might be loosed from her mind just by coming here, the ghosts of her tragic past. Yet, she radiated a certain inner strength that also made me feel like such fears were unfounded.

"How could I not come back? If my mother is really still trapped inside, I owe it to her, to try and save her. To help her find peace. I might not remember much about her, but she's still my mom, y'know?" She punctuated it with a gaze up into the dark windows above, as if searching for her mother even now.

Your mother might not be the only one trapped here, came a thought that just popped into my head like it had been placed there from the outside. I shivered as it hit me. What if that was true? What if her mother wasn't alone in there? What if her father was here too, constantly re-enacting his terrible dance of death with her?

My headache came back in full force, and just as I felt like I might throw up all over Miranda's rather cute red Chuck Taylor Converse All-Stars, a car drove up, one driven by the very handsome Eli White. Just the distraction my jumpy tummy needed.

Mr. White was as charming as ever, and I tried not to follow after like a lovelorn puppy as he unlocked the front door and led us through the house. He wasn't as flirty as he was when I first met him, or even when I had spoken to him on the phone to arrange all of this. I didn't know if it was due to the presence of my mom, or maybe he assumed Dennis and I were a couple.

Inside, everything was gloomy, with the spreading, purplish shadows of twilight. Even when he turned on the lights, those shadows still lingered, proving to be not so easily banished. Foreboding worry threatened to overcome my feeling of awe from finally standing inside this house I'd spent so many years obsessing about. It temporarily overrode the pounding in my head. I glanced over at Miranda and our eyes locked for a moment. Neither of us could believe we were really there yet both unsure if being there was actually a very good idea.

Eli proudly showed us what he'd done to the house thus far, which mainly seemed to consist of updating the kitchen cabinets and repairing damage done by a family of raccoons. I guess raccoons didn't mind sharing the place with ghosts.

The first floor consisted of a wide foyer, its floor painted a bloody red by the late afternoon light streaming in through the stained glass windows set into those imposing double front doors. The stairs to the second floor cascaded down out of the darkness above into this room. To one side of this foyer there was a parlor with its wallpaper peeling off, and a long dining room on the opposite side. Adjacent to the dining room was a large kitchen with a door that led out to the backyard. The house lacked a basement. Which was just as well, because I didn't relish the idea of spending any time in one with whatever spiders might be lurking down there. Wedged into what had once undoubtedly been a closet was a rather sad little half bathroom under the staircase. Through a door in the parlor was what Eli called a sitting room. Honestly, I wasn't sure what the distinction was supposed to be between these two kinds of rooms. Also, can't you theoretically sit in any room in a house? I'll never understand those Victorians and their wily ways!

On the second floor there were five bedrooms, far too many for the deeply dysfunctional family of three that had last occupied the place. Miranda pointed out the one that had served as her father's study, another as a guest bedroom, and yet another her playroom. Just off of the master bedroom where the massacre had occurred was a proper bathroom, featuring a nice claw foot bathtub. When we entered that bedroom, Miranda swooned, and lost her balance. I shot out a hand to catch her by the arm. She gave me a small half smile in gratitude for my quick reflexes. *Either her memory isn't as spotty as she'd thought, or some of it's coming back*, I thought. I worried about what other things she might recall.

The third story was the attic. The only way to it was up a winding, narrow flight of creaky steps which led to a door that was nailed shut.

"We haven't gotten around to opening it up yet," Eli admitted sheepishly. He looked cute when he was embarrassed. Who am I kidding? He *always* looked cute!

Occasionally, out of the corner of my eye I caught a glimpse of some fluttery, shadowy form darting just out of my field of view. We had gotten their attention already. I could feel them watching us as we moved through the empty rooms.

Them. Plural.

I shuddered as my intuitive flash that we were dealing with more than one spirit was becoming impossible to ignore. I was increasingly convinced that one of these spirits was anything but friendly. I could feel his malevolent energy burning into me. Yes, *him*. It had to be Miranda's father, Dean Drake. I didn't feel particularly inclined to share this knowledge with the others, not quite yet. No need to start a panic.

Besides, in my experience, there was little these spirits could actually do to harm you, aside from scaring the bejesus out of you. Maybe a little push here, a scratch there. I'd never heard of anyone being killed, or even seriously hurt, by a ghost outside of a movie or a horror story. I was far more concerned about the psychological harm that Miranda might come to if she knew her father was here than I was about any of us coming to any great physical harm.

Eli escorted us back down the stairs and into the foyer. He dropped the keys to the house into my hand. "I trust you won't be throwing any wild parties here this weekend, Athena?" he said with a playful wink. "I don't wanna have to clean up a bunch of crushed beer cans when I come back!"

"I dunno, we librarians are universally known for our wild parties!" I joked back, not missing the social cue for a change, probably because I was feeling a bit more comfortable around him now. Also, having my best friend and my mother there helped put me at ease somewhat. Well, as at ease as one *can* be when standing in a haunted house where one of the ghosts might be the spirit of a homicidal maniac, all while suffering from a throbbing headache.

He chuckled. "Just leave the key under the welcome mat on the porch when you've had enough. Be careful, and good luck. I hope you find what you're looking for here."

We all thanked him, and before he was even gone from the driveway, we were hard at work pulling equipment from Dennis' van into the house in the waning sunlight. Between all of us, and Dennis' skilled instruction, it didn't take long to get it set up in the rooms. As I grabbed the last of the cameras from the van, Miranda volunteered to carry its tripod, and I decided to take the opportunity to ask her a little about her life since leaving this house. Normally I wouldn't be so bold, but this was a special circumstance and occasionally my curiosity overrode my anxieties.

"My grandmother on my mother's side took me in. She lived down in Egg Harbor Township," Miranda began with a shuddering sigh. "It was cool for a while, but she passed away when I was sixteen. After that, one of my great aunts on my father's side heard about my situation and took me in until I went off to college." She leaned against the van, looking pensive. "We were never very close. I think she took me in out of guilt. Guilt about how she and the rest of that part of my family wrote me off after what happened here."

There was an unmistakable note of bitterness in her tone. I decided to change the subject.

"So what do you do these days? How do you make a living?"

She chuckled, an ironic little laugh. "I'm in real estate. It's one of the reasons I'm so interested in all this ghost stuff. I've had a few interesting experiences in some of the properties I've shown. You wouldn't believe how many of the houses around here are haunted!"

I'd love to hear some of those stories. I thought but kept that to myself. I had a good feeling about Miranda, like we were going to become friends, especially if she was really a proper member of the JSPS team now. If so, there would be plenty of opportunities to ask her about it later.

If we survive this night, my anxieties whispered.

Her brow furrowed. "The other reason I've had a fascination with it is I've always wondered what would happen if I could talk to my dad somehow? Ask him *why* he did what he did. Not that there's any justification that would ever make sense, but I still can't help but wonder how he'd try to explain himself."

You might just get your chance, sister! I thought, which was very different from what I said next. "It's something you'll probably never really be able to understand. And maybe that's a good thing. If you could understand what drives someone to do something so terrible, then it would mean you'd be capable of doing the same thing. Be grateful that it seems so senseless to you."

She looked at me as if seeing me for the first time, her eyes wet. "Damn! I never thought about it quite like that before! As his daughter I've always been a little scared maybe I had the capacity for that sort of thing. I guess if it's so incomprehensible to me, then perhaps I don't have much to worry about. Thanks, Athena. You've given me a lot to think about.

"Every once in a while, I live up to my name," I beamed back at her, feeling pleased with myself. It made me feel great to know that it was helpful to her. I could only imagine the burden she must have been carrying around, wondering if the same evil that had infected her father had been passed down to her

Once we had that final camera set up, we joined hands as Mom led us all in a short pagan prayer of protection. I always felt a little disingenuous participating in such rituals because I really didn't believe in them, but what the hell, why not? It made Mom happy and we could use a little good luck if it actually did anything.

Next, Dennis passed out flashlights and walkie talkies to everyone, then it was lights out for the rest of the investigation. Our cameras had night vision, so they'd operate just fine in the enveloping oppressive darkness

We turned the lights out because it's a widely held belief in the field of parapsychology that too much electricity interferes with spirits being able to manifest themselves. It's things like that which really irritate me about this field. So many of the ideas that are held up as gospel truth have absolutely nothing resembling actual science to back them up, it's all just half baked theories, yet everyone goes along with the conventional wisdom on these things anyway. Dennis eats up all this stuff unquestioningly, but I pride myself on being a bit more skeptical. I'm the Scully to his Mulder. It's a dirty job, but someone's gotta do it, as they say.

The investigation began uneventfully enough. Before we got started, I made sure to take a few Tylenol to combat my headache. I also made sure to do it in front of Dennis, as my talent for dry swallowing pills never failed to gross him out

"Ugh! I really wish you wouldn't do that in front of me!" he said, looking like he'd bitten into a lemon.

I just smiled back at him innocently, like the supreme smart ass that I can be sometimes. See? I told you I love to bust his balls!

We broke up into two groups. Me and Dennis in one, Mom and Miranda in the other. In addition to our flashlights and walkie talkies, each group had one EMF meter, one digital thermometer, and one voice recorder with them.

"Are you sensing anything yet?" Dennis asked as he took some readings with the EMF meter in the dining room. He meant my psychic sense.

"Nothing like that one time," I said in a whisper, not sure why "But they are certainly aware that we're here, and they're definitely watching us."

"*They?*" He asked and turned to me, all other activity ceased. Gotta hand it to Dennis, nothing gets past him!

Well, the cat was out of the bag now. "Yeah, I'm picking up on a female presence, *and* a male one."

He broke a smile. "Are you sure you're not just picking up on my male presence? It *is* pretty powerful!"

"Don't flatter yourself!" I scoffed. Geez. "But seriously, I think the man I'm picking up on is Miranda's father, and he's not a very happy camper, to put it mildly. Don't say anything about it to her yet. I'm not sure how she'll react to the news."

He nodded. "She's pretty great, isn't she?"

That raised my hackles a little, not sure why. "She's okay, I guess."

"You don't mind her joining the team, do you? I mean beyond this investigation? She seems to be pretty into the whole idea of the JSPS." Through his excitement I felt like he was probing me.

"Sure," I said, not really looking at him. "The more the merrier, I suppose. I mean, ultimately, it's not up to me is it? This is your show, not mine.

That seemed to really disappoint him. "What? No! I don't see it like that. I think of it as a partnership. This group is your baby as much as it is mine."

"Oh? Now we're having babies together, huh?"

Before Dennis could reply, our attention was drawn by a sound above us. "That sounded like a scream!" he said, his eyes searching the decaying ceiling. The flashlight held under his face illuminating his shocked expression reminded me of spooky story time around a campfire.

"That was Mom!" I gasped, taking off at a run from the dining room and up the stairs two at a time until I reached the top. "Mom! Are you okay? Where are you?" I called desperately.

"In here!" Miranda's voice answered.

I flew into the room two doors to the left, and inside, Miranda and Mom stood side by side. Mom was rooted in place pointing with an outstretched arm, which I followed to the window and saw the object of her terror.

Standing in front of the window was my old friend, the woman with half a head, looking as nasty and gory as ever. Maybe even more so in the darkness. *No, that's disrespectful! She has a name, and it's Molly Drake, Miranda's mother. Use it!* I chastised myself.

Miranda's terror-filled eyes flashed to me then my mom then back. "What's going on? Is someone there?"

Miranda couldn't see the ghost, but Mom and I could. "Yeah," I said, swallowing. "Yes. It's your mother. She's standing right there in front of the window."

"My mother?" Miranda blinked in astonishment. "Mommy!" She took a step forward.

Dennis, having reached the room shortly after me, advanced towards the window with his EMF meter held out.

"There's definitely something anomalous in this area!" he said while waving the device inches from the ghost's face.

The spirit, for her part, looked mildly irritated. *There's a human being standing there*, I thought, and all of my fear of the ghost dissipated.

She looked right at me, her hand trying to swat at the meter but passing right through it. It chattered in protest. "Can you hear me as well as see me? Please tell him to stop that. You're all in great danger!"

"Dennis!" I barked. "She wants you to back off!"

Dennis took a couple good steps backwards, like someone had just told him he was three inches from a hornet's nest.

"You can hear her?" Miranda asked incredulously, then turned her attention to what was to her an empty spot by the window. "Mommy! It's me, Mira! I've come back!"

"Oh, love. As happy as I am to see you, you shouldn't have returned. *He's* still here! He won't let me go! And now that he knows you're here too, he's going to want you to join us! You need to leave!" She cocked her head as if listening to something, and somehow turned even whiter. "He's coming back! Go! Go now!" she screamed and disappeared like a dissipating fog.

"What's she saying?" Miranda demanded, tugging on my shoulder.

"She's gone," I said, wishing *I* could disappear. Her ethereal screams still haunted me, no joke.

"Barb? Are *you* alright?" Dennis asked Mom.

Mom seemed to come back from far away. "Uh, yeah. Just a little shaken. They're not usually so . . . *graphic.*" She said it with a glance to Miranda, struggling to find the least upsetting words to describe what she'd just witnessed.

I touched her arm. "I'm glad you're okay. You had me scared there for a second!" She returned an unconvincing smile.

Miranda spun me around to face her, something I normally would have been pissed off about, but compared to what had just been going on I barely registered it.

"What did she say?" she demanded.

"She was warning us," I said numbly. "Warning us we should leave. That he's still here." The words tumbled from me like coins from a piggy bank.

"*Who's* still here?"

"Who do you think? She was talking about your dad!" I said, tired of the grilling.

"My *dad*? Here?" She seemed to get control of herself, took her hand off my shoulder "Geez, I'm sorry Athena. I'm just . . . it's a lot to process!"

"It's okay, I understand. Forget about it," I said, my irritation with her completely forgotten. I saw her for what she truly was in that instant; a frightened and confused little girl. My heart went out to her.

During all this Dennis had crossed to the other side of the room to check the camera, and made a disgusted sound. "The camera didn't get zip!"

"What about her warning?" Mom asked from the center of the room. "Are we just going to ignore it? She said we were in danger!"

Dennis looked at me, his eyebrows raised in question.

"I don't think we're in any physical danger," I said, despite Molly's warning. Maybe *she* was in danger from him, but not us.

Mom looked at me doubtfully but said nothing. She might be the witch in the family but she tended to my judgment on these matters because she knew my "gift" was stronger than hers. Despite this, I could sense her displeasure. She was justified in doing so. I wasn't making this call based on my intuition as I should have, but rather my stubborn conviction ghosts couldn't really hurt you. Standing by it because it's what I *wanted* to be true.

The look on Dennis' face for me was even less pleasant, but he said nothing to me and addressed Miranda instead. "And what about you? Are you comfortable continuing with this investigation? Just say the word and you can sit this one out. Nobody will think less of you if you want to go home now."

She shook her head. Her faux golden locks glinted in the dim light she did so. "No, I can't give up now. I'm not scared."

It was true. Fear wasn't the emotion I could sense radiating from her. It was ruthless determination. *The courage of the girl.*

"Okay. Well, I guess we'll continue then," Dennis said, and thought for a moment. "I suggest we have a psychic in each group. Barb, you're with me. Athena, do you mind pairing up with Miranda?"

That sounded like a good idea, and I said so.

"Cool. All right, let's check out some of the other rooms. Barb and I will go back downstairs, you guys stay up here. Let's try to see if we can capture some EVPs next, okay?"

"EVP," as every ghost hunting TV show these days will tell you *ad nauseum*, stands for "electronic voice phenomenon." It's why we had our digital voice recorders. When we *do* think we've recorded something supernatural, most of the time it's just our brains trying to make sense out of a bunch of chaotic background sounds, but every once in a while, there's one that's unusually clear – or seems to be responding to a question or statement made by the living, and is therefore more difficult to dismiss.

So we split up again. Miranda and I checked out the adjacent room, the one that used to be her playroom. I have to say, I was a little jealous that she had once had a room of this size brimming with toys. I'd never had anything like that in my life. But then again, I remembered how shitty the rest of her life was and I wasn't jealous anymore. *Perspective.*

Once we were alone, Miranda asked, "I'm a rotten daughter, aren't I? Defying my mother like that! She knew it was me though, didn't she?"

I stopped what I was doing and gave her my full attention. "She knew it was you. She could hear and see you, Miranda. Don't ask me how it works, it's not like they have real ears or eyes anymore, or even a brain that can receive that kind of sensory information. They're beings of pure consciousness. They must sense the energy of our being somehow." For some reason I was more comfortable speculating over the murky mechanics of such things than mining the emotional depths she must be experiencing.

She stamped her foot. "It's so frustrating! Knowing that she was right there, but I couldn't see her, or hear her, or – or, wrap my arms around her!"

"So near, and yet so far, huh?" I replied, not knowing what else to say. It *wasn't* fair.

Miranda crossed her arms and began to pace. "It's all so strange! After all these years I never expected to be in her presence again. Or his. Though it's what I hoped for, I didn't *really* believe we'd make any kind of contact with them so soon, or at all." She stopped pacing and looked directly at me. "They're both here together too? My God! What must that be like? After what he did to her?"

I shrugged. "Who knows? A lot of times these spirits don't even realize they're dead. They seem to perceive things like the passage of time differently. It's almost like they're stuck sleepwalking in a dream they can't wake up from." *Ooof!* Maybe I answered that question a little too honestly. I told you I sucked at being comforting!

"Did she seem like that to you?" Mirand asked, biting her lip. "Like she was confused and didn't know what was going on? She knew enough to give us a warning."

"Actually, she did seem remarkably lucid," I had to admit, and I would have said more except for the sound of a door slamming below us. Worse, it was accompanied by an arctic chill in my bones, in a house in the summer with no A/C. *This is new.*

I rubbed my arms. "Do you feel that?" I asked, knowing she couldn't. Also, my headache was back in full force and worse than ever before.

"Yeah, it's like an icebox in here!" she replied, her teeth chattering.

"What? That's impossible!" But I could see my own breath and knew it wasn't. *Uh oh.*

Mom screamed from somewhere right below us. "Christ! What now?" I wondered aloud as I ran from the room and repeated my trick with the stairs, only this time in reverse.

The shouting was coming from the other side of a heavy, cherry wood door that led to the drawing room. This must have been what I heard slam shut. On the other side of the door my mom chanted or prayed, trying to cast some sort of witchy spell against whatever was inside that room with her.

Go Mom! I thought proudly as I tugged on the brass handle of the door. The damned thing wouldn't budge!

Miranda was beside me in a flash. "What's going on? Open the door!"

"Help me!" was all I could say. We both pulled on it, and when that failed, we slammed our bodies against it until I was sure we'd break something – either on the door or ourselves! Finally, it swung open on its own, nearly knocking the pair of us off our feet. Neither one of us was ready for what we found inside.

It would have appeared to Miranda that Dennis was hovering in midair. I knew better. He was held aloft by his neck by the strangest, most frightening spirit I'd ever had the rotten luck of fixing my eyes upon. It was massive and filled the room from floor to ceiling, a huge, black shadow with little resemblance to anything human. For one thing, instead of regular legs, it had a multitude of writhing tentacles. And the entire shadow monster was oddly angular – all right angles and no curves, as if it was made of black construction paper. An origami nightmare.

The worst part was the head, or rather the lack of one. There was a neck and a shattered lower jaw. Some of the teeth were gone but some others were jagged and split into fangs. This must have been what was left after he shoved the shotgun in his mouth. Two malevolent red orbs glared at us, hovering in the air where his eyes should have been.

The upper body was vaguely humanoid, but the arms terminated in crab-like claws rather than hands. One of those claws held Dennis, choking the life from him. The other claw held the agonized and struggling spirit of Molly Drake, crushing her waist. When she'd said that he wouldn't let her go, I hadn't expected her meaning to be quite so literal!

My mother circled the thing, chanting a spell and making arcane gestures. In one hand she held a bundle of burning sage. The smell of the stuff always reminded me of the smell of Marijuana, only more intense. My mother's efforts seemed to have no effect, other than to amuse the thing. That's the feeling I picked up from it. It was laughing at us. Nobody laughed at my mother, goddamnit! Nobody tried to kill my best friend!

I rushed forward, filled with a rage so intense it made my entire body shake. *"You get away from him you gaddamned dead mother fucker, or I'll kill you all over again! Let him go!"*

That only made it laugh harder. I had the presence of mind to recall some of my mother's occult nonsense at that moment: naming a spirit gave you power over it, and I knew this asshole's name. I had his number, and it was up!

"Dean Drake! Release Dennis, I command you!"

The red of the monster's eyes dimmed, and it dropped Dennis to the ground, who landed with a sickening thud that made me question the wisdom of my wording. Maybe I should have told him to gently set him down? Specificity was everything when it came to coding a website, the same thing was true of spell crafting too, I suppose. Both ghosts faded away. I ran to Dennis' side and knelt next to him, praying the fall hadn't killed him.

"Don't die on me, you idiot!" I shouted at him as I cradled him in my arms. Then I did the most extraordinary thing without even thinking. I leaned over and kissed him. A real kiss too. I'm not talking about some lame ass peck on the lips, but the one shared by lovers.

Like Sleeping Beauty (only less hot) he opened his eyes and returned the kiss. To my eternal astonishment, it wasn't weird at all, as I'd always assumed kissing him would be. It was quite nice, in fact. Or maybe it had just been far too long since I'd kissed anyone, and I was making too much out of it?

Was I in love with Dennis Arden? With my childhood friend? Christ! Was I that much of a cliche? Hey, if we got married, I would still have an alliterative name like a superhero – Athena Arden! Our last names both began with "A," and was part of how we'd gotten to know each other so well. We were always stuck standing next to each other in line at school, and later on we were always in the same home rooms. It's funny how your proximity to someone else in the alphabet can dictate who you get to know, isn't it?

Okay, now I was *really* getting ahead of myself wasn't I? Fantasizing about marrying him? It was just one little kiss! No need to take things to such extremes just yet! What had gotten into me?

I didn't know if I had secretly been in love with him all this time – so secretly I had even kept it from myself. Either way, I *did* know I wanted more kisses like that one. A whole bunch more, in fact!

"That was nice," he croaked out through his bruised throat. "Maybe I should let myself get strangled by a ghost more often!"

I narrowed my eyes, hoping for a particular answer. "But what about Stacy?"

"Stacy who?" he said after a moment.

"Right answer!" I said, and leaned in for another one of those divine kisses.

"He's back!" Mom screamed. Screaming really was her forte tonight. I hadn't heard her scream so much since I'd climbed out my window and spent the night at Joe Mitchell's place Sophomore year. Or maybe it was the last time we went to Six Flags Great Adventure, and I convinced her to ride the Lightning Loops? Either way, her vocal chords didn't typically get such a workout.

I whipped my head around. The thing was back, and this time it was going after Miranda, scooping her up with one of those terrible claws. I realized his attack on Dennis had just been to lure us all down here, and Miranda was his true target! He was a crafty bastard, I had to hand it to him.

In my mind, his voice howled like the rustling of dry leaves in a tornado: "Family belongs together! Now we'll be together forever!"

That *was* his game. If he had wanted them all to be together in the great beyond, I wondered why he hadn't just shot Miranda when she was a little girl before doing himself in? Oh well, apparently he'd had a change of heart during the years he had spent prowling around this property – a change for the worse.

Had I really driven him off before, or had he just been messing with us? I didn't know, but I had to try something.

He gripped Miranda around the middle with one claw and choked her with the other. There was no sign of Molly this time, and Miranda's lolling head had turned a ghastly shade of blue.

"Leave her alone, Drake! You leave her alone!" I screamed.

To my utter shock and everyone else's, an intense white light shot from me toward the monster and punched a hole right through it, causing it to howl, and disappear. Miranda landed on her feet and nearly fell over, but thankfully my mom caught her..

Mom and I exchanged a look. Later I learned no one else had seen this aside from my Mom. I had no idea how I'd managed to zap him like that.

"Let's get the fuck out of here!" I shouted.

"You don't have to tell me twice!" Dennis agreed.

Fortunately, the room we were in wasn't far from the front doors. We all hightailed it out of there without incident and I slammed the doors behind us.

"Wait! Aren't you going to lock it?" Dennis' voice had that high pitched tone it took on when he was teetering on the verge of panic.

"Is that really the most important thing right now?" I couldn't believe he wanted to quibble over details like that at a time like this.

"I've got thousands of dollars worth of cameras in there!"

"You think anyone who goes in there is going to get very far?" I said as I dragged him off the front porch and down the steps into the yard where Mom and Miranda had gathered

"Fair point," he conceded when I let him go.

Mom and Miranda were both panting. Mom from the running, Miranda from the throttling.

"Is everyone okay?" I asked.

They nodded like bobbleheads, just numb from all the craziness.

Dennis dusted himself off. "Let's all meet back at my place and figure out what we're going to do from here."

Again, the others just nodded.

Dennis drove Miranda, as he'd picked her up from her home. Mom came with me, and as we climbed in and the engine roared to life, she made sure to catch my eye. "If we're going to come back here, we're going to need more help. Someone who can really kick that thing's ass."

I put the car into reverse, not wanting to stay one second longer than I had to, and started down the driveway. "Who were you thinking of?"

"I know a guy who would be perfect for the job. A real wizard, not like all those poseurs who come into my shop." She nodded like she'd just fixed an election.

I rolled my eyes. As far as I was concerned, there was no such thing as a "real wizard," and I wasn't completely ready to risk my butt or anyone else's for that matter on my mom's flaky belief systems. That thing had laughed at her burning sage! Laughed!

That said, as I drove towards Dennis' house that night, I realized we'd tried everything and I was out of ideas, and by the time we arrived, I couldn't deny I was intrigued to find out what she had in mind.

Part Three: The Final Nightmare

Dennis' house was another ranch style one, like the one Mom and I shared, but bigger and nicer. It had a red brick exterior with an attached garage too crammed with his tools to ever squeeze in a car. It was located on the edge of the sprawling housing development paradoxically called Settler's Landing, even though the place was located far too inland for anyone to land there unless someone tossed them out of an airplane!

The inside was unusually tidy for a bachelor pad, and it had nothing to do with Stacy's "woman's touch." She didn't have one! She was too lazy even to clean up after herself most times and the place had been this clean long before she ever arrived in the picture. Dennis was a little OCD about the place, especially when it came to displaying his impressive collection of action figures, which stared out at us with their painted-on eyes through four stately glass display cases in the corners of his living room. Framed posters from his favorite movies and paintings of dragons decorated the walls.

Dennis made coffee for all of us, and we sat around his dining room table trying to make sense out of what we had just been through.

My mug was shaped in the likeness of Bart Simpson, and as I sipped coffee so deliciously hot I'd already burned my tongue on it, I kept one hand on Dennis' leg under the table next to me. His hand was on top of mine as if it had always been there. He was a real smooth operator when he wanted to be! Sure, this all seemed like some basic high school puppy love shit in some ways, but it was still nice. It felt *right*, and for once, I didn't feel like questioning myself about the wisdom of taking our relationship to this new level. No need to torture and sabotage myself with a thousand self-doubts over it. I was just going to roll with it and enjoy myself for a change. Thankfully, Stacy wasn't around that night. We had all been through enough recently without having to contend with the awkwardness of her learning about my new relationship status with Dennis right now.

We had already established that, physically at least, everyone was okay. Dennis and Miranda both had nasty welts on their necks, but whatever injuries Dennis and Miranda had sustained didn't seem severe enough to warrant a visit to the emergency room. Dennis, being Dennis, had diligently documented this evidence right away, using a small digital camera he'd had in his pocket.

Dennis regarded Miranda sadly, "I'm so sorry about how this turned out, Miranda. It was a mistake to bring you back there. I had no idea how dangerous it would be."

I jumped in. "It's just as much my fault as it is yours! I'm the one who basically said it would be okay to ignore her mom's warnings. I truly believed there wasn't much her father's spirit could do to hurt us. Boy, was I ever wrong about that!" Damn! Listen to me, already dutifully springing to the defense of my man! You'd think we'd already been a couple for a few years.

"You're both being silly. Neither one of you had any idea that things would turn out this way! Even I didn't, and I'm a psychic too! Who could possibly have anticipated something like this? I've never seen such an unusual and powerful entity before." Mom added, who being a mom, naturally had the corner marketed on defending the two of us.

Miranda waved away this guilt like it was a cloud of gnats and swallowed a gulp of coffee. "It's okay, I'm not blaming anyone here. None of us understood what we were getting ourselves into. Seriously. I just want to know what we're going to do about it next now that we *do* know."

Dennis shook his head emphatically. "*What are we gonna do next?* This investigation is obviously too dangerous to continue. When it's daylight, I'm going to go back to the house and get my equipment then lock up the place. We're in over our heads here. That place needs a goddamned exorcism or something!"

"Like I'm letting you go back there alone," I insisted. "You're not gonna risk yourself for a few electronic doodads, I don't care how expensive that shit is! I don't think you realize how close you came to becoming a ghost yourself tonight! I'm coming with you. I'm not sure exactly *how* I did it, but I drove him off before, and I'll bet I could do it again."

Miranda blew out a long breath and looked me straight in the eye. "It was pretty amazing how you stood up to him like that, Athena. You really saved my life tonight, thank you. I'll never forget it, I really owe you one."

"Fuggetaboutit!" I said, sounding like a character out of *Goodfellas* or some other Martin Scorsese mafia epic. "Don't get all mushy on me, it's not like you owe me a Wookiee life debt or anything like that." I heard Dennis snort in laughter at this incredibly nerdy Star Wars reference.

Miranda laughed, too. "Okay, I won't pretend to have any clue what a 'Wookiee life debt' is, but if you ever need a good deal on a house, I'm your woman!"

"I might just take you up on that offer someday, so long as there aren't any ghosts included with the property!"

"It's a deal!" She smiled, then turned serious. "I'm going back there with you guys tomorrow too. I can't just walk away from this investigation. Those might just be a couple of ghosts to you two, but to me, they're my *parents*. I can't just leave them there like that, especially my mother. What's it like for her, trapped in that house for decades with the man who murdered her? We've got to set her free somehow, we've just *got to*! And we have to get *him* out of there too. Nobody can live in that house with him there. It's not safe!"

"Yeah, precisely. It's not safe, especially for you! That's why you're *not* going back there with us. He tried to kill you, in case you hadn't noticed!" Dennis said, his face flushing red as it sometimes did when he got all worked up. It was so cute! Okay, stop. This is getting pathetic now. Every little thing he does isn't going to automatically seem stupidly adorable now is it? Jesus! What is wrong with me? I'm such a loser!

"I haven't forgotten," Miranda said, rubbing the marks on her neck.

I felt sorry for her at that moment. What must it be like to be attacked by the spirit of your own father? Almost being killed by anyone is traumatic enough, but this added a whole new layer of weirdness to it.

"I heard him say he wants you all to be together again as a family. The attack on Dennis was just staged to lure us into the room. You were his real target all along. It's way too dangerous for you to go back there. I don't understand exactly how I was able to hurt him long enough for us to get out like we did. I mean, I *hope* I can pull it off again if I need to, but there's no real guarantee. It's probably okay for me and Dennis to go back, but not you. You're the one he's *really* after. He won't be happy until he's got your spirit trapped there like he has your mom."

"But I won't be happy knowing that my mother is stuck there, stuck in that *hell!*" She shook her head. "I can't just go back to my normal life now. I just can't forget!"

Mom grasped Miranda's hand and gave it a squeeze. "It's going to be alright. I have a possible solution."

"Don't tell me you know an exorcist!" Dennis scoffed light-heartedly.

"Ugh. Catholicism!" Mom exclaimed, making the sort of distasteful face over the notion that only a lapsed Catholic could make. No doubt she was recalling how the nuns at her Catholic school had made her feel when she tried to explain her 'gift' to them. Their response? They told her she had a devil inside of her. The problem was, she'd spent far too many years of her own life believing it, being ashamed of it, and trying to overcompensate for it. But she'd obviously made peace with it now. As hard as she had tried, she couldn't pray away her gifts, or ignore them. As for her aborted Catholicism . . . she liked to say she hadn't given up on mainstream religion, mainstream religion had given up on her first.

She went on, the corners of her mouth playing up mischievously. "No, I'm not talking about an exorcist. I'm talking about something much, much better!"

"Well? Don't keep us in suspense! What are you talking about exactly?" Dennis wanted to know.

"Not what, *who*. Clark Kismet."

"Clark Kismet? Like, Clark Kent? Sounds like a comic book character! I like it!" Dennis said approvingly. Of course he would like it, the guy was drinking out a coffee mug with Spider-Man on it!

"Oh, he's a *character* all right!" I said in a rather significantly less approving way. "Mom, isn't that the name of that loser who's always trying to hit on you? The one you said is a real weirdo?"

"Yes. He may be a little . . . peculiar, but he's also the most powerful wizard I've ever met. He used to be a bigwig of some kind in a secret order of magic users called 'The Temple of the Old Gods,' up until he retired a few years back. At least that's what he told me."

"'The Temple of the Old Gods'? Never heard of them! Sounds like some H.P. Lovecraft bullshit to me," I scoffed. I mean really! Was this guy gonna show up waving around a copy of the *Necronomicon*?

"Of course you haven't heard of them!" Mom replied, a bit too testily for my tastes. "They're called a 'secret order' for a reason. Anyhow, they're the real deal. He did things when he was trying to impress me, things which are quite impossible."

"Probably just some sleight of hand stuff. I mean, 'Clark Kismet.' What kind of name is that? Dude's gotta be a stage magician with a name like that!"

"Don't patronize me, Athena!" Mom reprimanded and slammed her hand down on the table so forcefully everything rattled. "I'm a *witch.* I know the difference between a magic trick and the real thing! These were no mere illusions! When he retired from his order, he started up an occult shop too. I get some of the crystals that I sell in my store from him, that's how I met him. He does some kind of a special blessing on them that makes them into powerful protective amulets. I have one." She dipped two fingers into her generous cleavage and retrieved a crystal set in an elaborate clasp. "And so do you, dear. I saw it light up and blast that evil spirit when he was attacking Miranda. Somehow, my girl, without knowing it, you unlocked its power. And channeled it. Correctly."

"*That's* how that bolt came out of me? It came from *this*?" My fingers found its slick hardness beneath my shirt and pulled it out so I could look at it. "This amulet you gave me came from *him*? You never told me."

She nodded in the affirmative at me as she slurped from her cup.

I was surprised Mom put so much faith in this guy. Whenever she'd talked about him in the past, it was more in a mocking manner. I remember her laughing about his awful mullet. She actually did go on exactly one date with him. She told me all about it afterwards. It was a disaster. The guy showed up dressed so oddly he made them the center of attention at the restaurant. He dressed like that at his store too, but Mom had assumed he'd never go out in public like that, and . . . yeah.

Clark was only one of many losers she'd gone out with since Dad left when I was fourteen. It was something I was still a little bitter about, their divorce. I used to blame myself for their break up, combined with Mom's "spiritual reawakening," when she finally jettisoned Catholicism altogether in favor of all this New Age stuff. Dad was a pretty down to earth guy, and where I got my skeptical mind and devotion to reason. Because of that kinship I have tended to blame everyone for the divorce but Dad for some reason, but that's changing. The older I get, the more I am realizing it takes two to tango, as they say, and he was probably as much to blame for their relationship imploding as she was.

Unfortunately, back then I didn't have this kind of perspective. Even though I was no great fan of the Catholic Church and was a bit relieved when we didn't have to go every Sunday, in the back of my head I resented anything associated with the New Age movement. To me it represented everything that drove Dad away. I always hoped Mom would get bored with it and they would get back together someday, but no such luck.

In fact, Dad moved on with his life fairly quickly and remarried less than a year later. That seemed a bit quick of course and made Mom wonder if he had been cheating all along on top of everything else. But I didn't buy that. Dad had gotten lucky finding my stepmom, and it was a kind of luck thus far that eluded Mom. Mom was still pretty, and smart too, so you would think she would be able to do a little better for herself, but I suppose it could be pretty slim pickings in this neck of the woods when it came to finding available singles her age. Hell, even finding people my own age to date had been a struggle for me. Not that I ever would approve of most of the guys she would go out with anyway. I believed nobody was good enough for her. Only the best for my mom!

"Do you think he'll really want to help us?" Miranda asked hopefully, shaking me out of my reveries.

Mom laughed. "Oh please! I've got that man wrapped around my little finger! I just have to bat my eyelashes at him, and he'll be jumping out of his skin to help out!"

I smiled, but I wasn't quite sold. "I'm going to go with Mom's confidence on this one. He'll help. My worry is, if his help will really be worthwhile. C'mon, Mom! We've both laughed over what a flake he is!"

She nodded. "He's got a terrible haircut, questionable fashion sense and half of what he says doesn't make any damned sense, but despite all of that, I have total faith in his ability to work magic. So much so I was tempted to string him along just to see what magical secrets I could learn from him, but it's not nice to use people like that. He really is a sweet man. But just a little too out there for me."

Mom was hardly a pinnacle of rationality herself, so in my mind that was saying quite a lot. It didn't help with my concern at all, but I dropped the topic. I could tell when I was being outvoted.

Dennis spoke up. "We only have access to the house for one more day. Whatever we do, we have to do it tomorrow. Will he come on such short notice?"

Mom shrugged. "I don't see why not, I don't think his shop is even open on Sundays. I'll give him a call tonight and find out."

"Well, look at us!" Dennis exclaimed, rubbing his hands together. "A real bunch of hardcore motherfuckers! Any normal people who had been through what we've just been through wouldn't go near that place ever again, and here we all are, itching to go back!"

"We're a bunch of badass bitches alright!" I joked, swept up in his mood. Despite my misgivings about Clark Kismet, the idea had cheered up the rest of them, and I was ready to jump in with both feet.

Miranda raised her mug. "I'll drink to that!" I lifted mine and we clinked them together in a toast.

Mom bumped her shoulder to Dennis. "Hey, Dennis! Ya got anything a little harder than coffee on tap?" Mom, let it be known, could drink all of our asses under the table if she really wanted to.

"I think I have some Bailey's," he said conspiratorially, and in a moment returned to give us all a generous helping.

I raised my mug to the room. "Let's drink tonight, my friends, for tomorrow we may die!" I thought I remembered reading it somewhere, and it seemed appropriate. I meant it jokingly, but we all knew horrible death wasn't off the table. We all toasted anyway.

The Jersey Shore Paranormal Society is indeed a bunch of hardcore motherfuckers.

The time came to say goodbye for the night. Mom didn't want to be out too late, as she thought it would be rude to call Clark past a certain hour. I decided I wasn't too tipsy to drive the relatively short distance back home. Miranda's car was parked in front of Dennis' place, and was the first one to leave. Dennis promised to keep her in the loop regarding tomorrow's plan of attack.

"Ya know, you don't *have* to go home," Dennis said, his body wonderfully close as I lingered on his front doorstep. "You're welcome to spend the night here."

I pressed my body closer to his. "Oh, I'm sure you'd *love* that, wouldn't you, Romeo?" I said over my shoulder.

He shrugged, hands thrust in pockets. "You can't blame a man for trying!"

"Try this," I said, and turned to give him a kiss. It was just as good as before, his arms coming about me. I cut it short deliberately though. I could feel Mom's eyes burning into the back of my head. "Don't worry, there'll be plenty more where that came from, but let's take it slow, okay?"

"Some things are worth the wait," he agreed.

"Yes, they are," I replied, with mock-smugness. "Besides, there's still that breaking up with Stacy you have to do!"

"*Who?*" he said with a smile. This was fast becoming his new default answer whenever I brought her up.

"Ha! Very funny," I said, slapping his stomach. "Just make sure you take care of it! I don't want her walking in on us at an inopportune moment, if you know what I mean."

"Hmmm. Maybe that wouldn't be so inopportune, if she joined in . . ." He squeezed me tighter with a goofy look on his face.

"Nah, she's too flat chested for my tastes," I replied, playing the game. But I did press away from him. "Just promise me you'll take care of it, okay?"

"You've got it!" He saluted.

I started down the steps. "See you tomorrow!"

"Definitely! Drive carefully!"

"Not all that smashedthh yet!" I replied, slurring my speech on purpose and staggering towards the car. "But it was just one little drinkie winkie, officer!" Yeah, my corny-ass drunk driving comedy routine was fucking fantastic. I should take that shit out on the road. I'll be selling out every comedy club from here to Vegas. God, I'm such a dork! He laughed at my bad jokes anyway, which is really the most important requirement of any romantic partner isn't it?

As I got into the car, Mom looked at me pointedly. I, of course, pretended not to notice. We hadn't made it down the block before she asked, "Well?"

"Well what?" I replied, innocently.

"You and Dennis, huh?"

"Me and Dennis what?" I replied, deadpan.

Mom harrumphed. "Well, for what it's worth. I'm happy for you. It's about time. He's a nice boy. I've always liked him. Just treat him right, okay? I know how you can get sometimes."

There wasn't even any conflict yet in our fledgling relationship and already she was taking his side! If things weren't going to work out for the best, it was automatically my fault. It was preordained! I mean, I tended to blame myself enough for the string of broken hearts I'd left behind, I didn't need anyone else adding to my relationship anxieties. I couldn't believe it!

Actually, I *could* believe it. This was some classic Mom shit right here. She was always interfering in my love life, trying to protect me like I was still a little girl and not a grown ass woman. I thought nobody was good enough for her, and she obviously felt the same way about my choices in romantic partners. Although in retrospect, I can see that she was usually right. Most of those other guys I'd dated were pretty bad. You'd think I'd be happy that she approved of my choice for once, but I had my head stuffed too far up my own ass back then to be able to see any silver lining in her criticisms.

I decided to take the high road and ignore her comments. We drove home in silence the rest of the way home. I mean, I'd *never* consent to go out on even a single date with a guy with a mullet and a silly name. Who was she to tell me how to run my love life?

In a big surprise to no one, Mom was successful in convincing Clark Kismet to join in our fun little plan to revisit the house where a homicidal ghost lived. Or didn't live. Hell! You know what I mean!

We gathered at Dennis' house in the morning, and in a big surprise to everyone, he cooked breakfast. Eggs, bacon, pork roll and pancakes. All the classic, artery clogging components of a good American breakfast. My man could cook! Although admittedly it was hard to fuck up such a basic breakfast.

So, he wasted no time dumping Stacy. Which was good, though the time honored "we need to talk" telephone conversation had been his preferred method of assassination. My feelings on that matter were mixed. I had no love for Stacy, but she deserved better than being broken up with over the phone – although, truth to tell, yeah, I'd done it myself once or twice. I would hope he'd be a bit classier about it if he ever ditched me. All in all though, I was just glad she wouldn't be around to complicate things between us any longer. We were free to smooch and stuff in a more relatively guilt-free way, so huzzah for that!

Clark Kismet was late and arrived in a serial killer van, one of those old conversion vans from the 1970's. And it was *purple* and complete with a picture of a wizard, I kid you not, riding on a unicorn that was galloping on a rainbow, all airbrushed by a barely competent third grader as far as I could tell. Rainbows and unicorns – no wonder Mom had consented to give this guy a date! If he ever got a makeover, he'd probably be her ideal man! But I digress, yet again. "7th Heaven Occult Shoppe" was emblazoned above this charming iconography.

The location of the "Shoppe" – God, how I hated it when people tried to make a business seem more quaint by spelling it like that – was listed too, in some town farther down the shore that had an even sillier sounding name than Barnegat did. I didn't have to see inside the van to know it was filled with shag carpeting from floor to walls to ceiling.

Clark himself was every bit as strange as I imagined him to be. We all watched this odd, lanky guy through Dennis' front window as he exited his vehicle and walked up to the front door. I wondered what kind of an idiot dressed like that in the middle of July.

He dressed in a sharp business suit perfectly tailored to his body, and it was the same shade of violent violet as his van. And sewn into it were yellow sickle shaped moons, five pointed stars, and one planet Saturn. It reminded me of the way the Riddler sometimes dressed in Batman movies. Also like the Riddler, he wore a purple derby hat, but with a single yellow sickle moon emblazoned in the center. And his necktie, purple with a single yellow sickle moon. The hat was far too big for his head and was only stopped in its gravityward advance by the bridge of his nose. It looked permanently pulled down over his eyes in preparation for a nap and I seriously wondered how he could possibly avoid bumping into everything around him.

The only part of this ensemble that I liked were the yellow Chuck Taylor Converse All-Stars he wore. They were just like the red ones Miranda was wearing. It made me want to dig out a pair from wherever they were hiding in my closet and join the fun. Just as Mom had described, he had an unfashionable mullet of wavy brown hair spilling out of his hat and down his neck. I could totally see why Mom had been too mortified to be seen out in public with this man.

"Are you *sure* he's not a stage magician?" Dennis asked Mom, with a sense of awe.

"We're doomed, aren't we?" I said, stepping away from the window. "It's been nice knowing you guys."

"Oh ye of little faith!" Mom chided, falling back into Catholic mode in pinch as she sometimes did.

"Here goes," Dennis said as the doorbell rang. He invited Clark inside with a friendly-if-stiff smile, and we all shared that smile as we pretended poorly that we hadn't been gaping at him through the window for the past few minutes.

Mom greeted him as he entered the house. "Hello, Clark! Thanks for coming!

I stiffened as she gave him a hug. Even after all these years, such displays of affection between my mother and someone other than Dad still made me *very* uncomfortable.

Yes, I was overreacting. It was a short, innocent hug. Nobody was copping a feel or anything. I couldn't help being overprotective of my mom, I guess.

She introduced everyone, and in turn, Clark would shake a hand and raise his hat over his head in greeting. Have I mentioned how much I *loathed* shaking hands? It was because, right or not, I was convinced my hands were continually cold and clammy and I feared people would judge me on that. Not to mention it often turns into a strange contest of how much pressure to apply. Apply too little and people will assume that you're a spineless pushover, apply too much and it seems like you're some kind of a domineering alpha out to crush all the competition in your path. Finding that sweet Goldilocks spot of normalcy in the middle is an art unto itself, and an elusive one when one is already too preoccupied with how cold and clammy your hands are to calculate the correct amount of pressure to apply.

When it came time to meet me, he said, "Ah yes, Athena! The one with all the potential. I've been wanting to meet you for some time. Your mother tells me that you handled that ghost quite handily last night, most impressive!"

"Err, thanks," was all I could say.

His hands weren't so bad. Soft like an elderly person's, though he appeared to be in his forties.

The brief psychic impression I got from touching him was also generally positive. I hated him for being so genuinely nice to me when I was *desperate* to hate him.

He dropped the hat back onto his head before I could really get much of a good look at his eyes, then whirled around to face Dennis and Miranda. He dug into his pants pockets and pulled out a pair of crystal amulets like the kind Mom and I already wore. "I brought these! Better put them on. They'll help protect you, but they're no substitute for caution. They're not foolproof. If you see something scary, just visualize a bubble of bright light surrounding you while holding it. Go on, try it!"

Dennis and Miranda exchanged puzzled glances, but they accepted his gift gratefully. To his instruction, they took hold of their crystals and concentrated as Clark watched. In moments a bubble of light formed around each of them. From the satisfied expressions on Mom and Clark's faces, I could tell they could see it too.

Miranda and Dennis couldn't, though, and Dennis' skepticism made his bubble flicker and dim. Miranda soldiered through.

"Not bad," Clark said appreciatively, "not bad at all! Okay, you two can stop."

Mom gave me a "see, I told you so," look, to which I rolled my eyes, unwilling to give her the satisfaction.

"Now, what was the name of this demon again?" The wizard asked nobody in particular.

"Dean Drake." Mom answered.

"Ah! Dean Drake! What a delightfully alliterative name! Just like a superhero, eh?" He tipped his ludicrous hat back and winked at Dennis. I did a double take. He seemed to know Dennis loved names like that for exactly that reason. Was this joker reading our minds somehow?

". . . or in this instance, a super villain," Clark went on. "Yes, a name like that shouldn't be too hard to recall, even for someone as forgetful as I can sometimes be. Oh, how I miss superheroes. The supervillains, not so much." He said this with an enigmatic smile.

Yeah this guy was definitely off his rocker. Didn't he know that there were no such things in real life?

His head swung toward me like he'd heard my thoughts, and my breath caught in my throat. *"Athena Anderson!"* he said, trying my name out in his mouth like he was tasting the words. "Another alliteration! My, how the air is thick with synchronicities this morning, isn't it?"

Geez! This cornball just loves to hear the sound of his own voice doesn't he? I thought, relieved but annoyed. Who was he trying to impress here? Was he still carrying a torch for Mom? I felt like he was putting on a show, which always rubs me the wrong way. I prefer it when people can be real with each other.

"You were quite right to use his true name when confronting him, Athena. Yes, very well played indeed! There is great power in names." The compliment did little to improve my impression of him, in fact it made it worse since it made me suspect that he was just saying it as part of an attempt to kiss my ass.

Buttering up the daughter so you can get into the mother's pants? Is that your game, you freakazoid? I thought bitterly. I was a bit paranoid in my younger days, wasn't I? So desperate to find fault with others! I'm happy to report that I've mellowed out a little. It's amazing what having the support of the right partner can do for you.

Miranda broke in bitterly. "He's not a demon. He's no fallen angel or anything like that. He was my 'father,' though I'd say 'sperm donor' is more appropriate."

Clark took a gentler tone. "Yes of course, my dear. You must forgive me. When I use the term 'demon,' I apply it more broadly than Christians tend to. I use it to mean any negative spirit, which feeds off of misery, fear and suffering. A human can become a kind of demon after death – if they're enough of a jerk."

"Is that what he's doing? Feeding?"

"I rather think so," he said, pursing his lips. "I can find no other explanation for how he's become so powerful. You see, all human spirits living or dead give off a kind of potent psychic energy that my people call Ambrosia–"

"The food of the Gods," I said, interrupting him to show off the sort of useless information I specialized in. The kind of stuff my head was full of, which made me so dangerous at games of Trivial Pursuit or Jeopardy!, yet unable to change my own tires. Hey, could I help it if most kinds of truly practical knowledge bored me to tears?

"The food of the Gods," Clark agreed. "Yes, quite literally! Prayers are one of the most effective ways of concentrating it. Any spirit can absorb it to make themselves stronger. It doesn't have to be a God. I fear it is that which he has been doing to your poor mother, Miranda. Terrorizing her, then extracting her Ambrosia to make himself more powerful. Powerful enough to keep her trapped there. It is imperative we stop him before he can hurt anyone else. If someone else moves in there, he would begin feeding off them too. If he gets too strong there's no telling what might happen."

Miranda shuddered and crossed her arms. "Is that what he wanted to do to me? Feed off of me? Is that why he was trying to kill me?"

"Yes. He's become something of a psychic vampire now. Addicted to eating the fear he causes, and he wants more spirits that he can feed from." He put his hand on Miranda's shoulder. "Don't worry, my dear. We'll free your mother and make sure your father can't hurt anyone ever again. I personally guarantee it!"

"Thank you," Miranda said, seeming to genuinely relax.

At least his act comforted one of us, I thought, as I remained filled with misgivings about him.

Dennis coughed. "Well, let's get this show on the road, shall we?" His motivation wasn't just eagerness to get on with it. I knew Stacy planned to come over to his place later on today, hopefully for the last time ever, to pick up the stuff she'd left here.

Isn't it funny how much of one's stuff spreads, virus-like, to your partner's residence when you've been dating someone for a while? I wondered at first how long it would take for this pattern to repeat itself with Dennis, then realized with a start I already had quite a few of my belongings scattered around his house. Mostly in the form of various books he'd borrowed over the years. Would these books soon be joined by a spare toothbrush? By sundry personal hygiene items, and perhaps even a few unmentionables? Time would tell.

But I also intended to be present when Stacy showed up, no matter Dennis' preference. No matter how uncomfortable it might be for us all.

Not to rub it in her face. I'm far too classy for that. No, I just wanted to make sure it was really over between them. I guess a part of me was still afraid to trust Dennis' word on that. I didn't think he'd burn me like that, and I didn't want to believe that, but I also had been screwed over too many times to be humiliated like that again. Trust but verify, as they say.

Clark offered to drive us to the house in his obnoxiously tacky van, which he assured us had more than enough room for us all, and Dennis' equipment too, when we retrieved it.

Dennis accepted, perhaps as curious to see what the inside was like as the rest of us were. The van was stunningly roomy. Like, almost bigger on the inside than the outside, but that's impossible of course. And yes, shag carpeted the floor, *and* the walls, *and* the ceiling of the van's interior. I was right, in full challenge of my gag reflex. *Purple* shag carpeting.

I marveled that Clark could see well enough to drive with that stupid hat drooping over his line of vision, and happy to report he managed to get us all to the house in one piece.

The headache returned with a vengeance as soon as we neared the place. And that familiar, all-consuming feeling of dread. Of being watched. It was the same feeling I felt when I was in the presence of Dean Drake's bizarre looking ghost.

In a way, seeing that monster was like meeting an old friend again for the first time. How many times had I passed this house in my life? It had to be in the thousands! There was an almost comforting familiarity in the feeling, as awful as it was. An intimacy borne of repetition. It just goes to show that you can get used to just about *anything*. Would I miss this feeling if we were successful? A twisted part of me knew I would. How fucked up is that? It was as if I was trapped in an abusive relationship with that house!

"Ah yes, the headaches." Clark tsked, noticing my pained expression. "Barbara mentioned that. Do you normally experience such a sensation when using your gifts?"

"No, it's only when I'm around this place," I replied, digging in my purse for my bottle of Tylenol. Was it my imagination, or was it even worse than usual today?

"You're tuning into the pain of Miranda's mother," he said simply. "It's a wonder you're able to function at all. Good on you."

So, this is what it feels like to have the top of your head blown off? Well now I know. And knowing is half the battle. I produced my bottle of ShopRite brand Tylenol and fought to get the top off. Goddamned child proof lids! Sometimes, they were adult proof too!

"You won't need that," Clark said. "Whatever relief they provide is temporary and the drug will dull your gifts. You will need to be at a hundred percent if we're going to defeat the thing in there. Please, allow me."

He twisted around in his seat to face me and placed his slender, bony fingers to my temples while muttering some gibberish just under his breath. And just like that, the headache was gone.

"How did you do that?" I stammered.

"I cleared up some energy blockages," he said in that matter-of-fact way I was getting used to. "It should become easier to focus your talents more broadly, rather than focusing so intensely on the pain of the poor woman inside."

"Thanks," I said reluctantly, not really wanting to acknowledge any debt to this person. But how could I not? Whatever he had just done *did* seem to actually help me. It was the decent thing to do. Maybe this guy really did know his stuff, maybe we really were going to be okay. I started to regret all my harsh thoughts about him.

"Don't mention it!" he said, beaming. Then his face fell pensive, and he shifted to Miranda. "I can't go around calling your mother 'that poor woman' forever, Miranda! What was your mother's name?"

"Molly. Molly Drake," she answered from her seat beside mine.

"Molly! What a name! You know, I once knew a girl named Molly. She was a troubled young lady, our Molly. She also created the universe. Well, *that* universe, not this one, mind you."

I sighed. Maybe we *wouldn't* be okay. This latest outburst of utter nonsense demolished whatever fledgling confidence I had started to feel regarding Clark. I was beginning to see what Mom meant when she said only about half of what he said ever made any sense. Maybe a splitting headache was preferable to listening to Clark prattle on like this?

Clark looked from one to the other of all our blank stares and cleared his throat. "Well then, just remember to try and control your fears. Don't deny them, simply move *through* them to the peace of mind that lies beyond. It feeds on fear, and we don't want to make it any stronger than it already is. I imagine it had rather a nice little feast off the raw emotions you were haphazardly slinging around last night." With that, he opened his door to step down out of the vehicle.

Easy for you to say buster! Half of us almost got killed last night and you don't expect us to be scared of coming back here?

As we walked towards the house, we were startled by a deafening sound from within.

It sounded for all the world like a gunshot. We all heard it.

"What the hell was that?" Dennis shouted in alarm.

I turned my head in the direction it came from and was greeted by a sickening sight. I could make out a mass of blood and brains slowly sliding down the window, painting crimson trails of grey matter on the glass. I could also see a hint of the hair of Molly Drake at the bottom of the window.

"My God, it's happening again, isn't it?" I said. Against all reason I was running towards the window where the gruesome scene had just played out. My headache returned, but this time was only a vague throbbing at the edge of my awareness.

Clark ran beside me. We both reached the window at the same time and peered inside, where we witnessed Dean Drake stalking forward, holding a smoking shotgun in one hand. He was in a far more human form than he had been the last time I'd seen him. His entire head was intact this time. He was actually quite handsome. And most disturbingly of all, his face was almost exactly the same as Miranda's. He locked eyes with me and made the most of having a functional mouth again by smiling at us, obviously pleased at having an audience. It was a smug smile that was creepy as fuck. I suppose it was meant to terrify me, but it only succeeded in making me mad. I wanted nothing more than to wipe that nasty, predatory grin right off his face.

"Steady on, Athena," Clark instructed in a whisper. "You can draw strength from your anger, but it can also feed him just as surely as fear can. Don't dwell on your feelings for too long."

I was annoyed at the wizard for intruding into my mind like that, but I was too spellbound by what I was watching through the window to redirect my anger at him.

Dean Drake tossed aside his gun and lifted Molly up by her hair, proudly showing off her exposed brain to us. As a ghost she was still "alive," gripping his arm and whipping about, struggling to get free.

Without breaking eye contact with us, he leaned forward and opened his mouth wide, sucking some sort of black oily substance which shot out of Molly's nose and mouth and into his. Molly flailed and spasmed about as this was going on, and it was one of the worst things I'd ever seen. Dean's form twisted, darkened and grew in size. His ever-staring eyes became two brilliantly glowing balls of red as he regained his "origami nightmare" form.

"Holy shit! What's he doing?" I breathed.

"Absorbing her negative Ambrosia, exactly as I suspected," Clark observed, in his customary flat voice like he was discussing the weather. "And trying to freak us the hell out while he's at it! Don't let him win. I suggest we stop watching this ghastly spectacle."

I was unable to tear my eyes off it. Clark had to grab me by the shoulders and turn me away, then he took my hand and led me back to where the others had gathered in the yard.

"Are you okay?" Dennis asked as he jogged up to me and threw an arm around me. Apparently, I was looking even paler than usual and was shaking.

"It was horrible," I said numbly.

"I felt it too," Mom said and put an arm around me as well, turning it into a group hug.

"Do you still think this is a good idea?" Dennis demanded of Clark.

"Yes. I'm sure I can handle him. He's an arrogant bastard, that's for sure! He's trying to rattle us before we even get through the door. We mustn't fall for his tricks! Besides, I made a promise to Miranda and I intend to keep it."

We walked up the steps and onto the porch, Clark leading the way. When he reached the door, he slowly turned the knob and stuck his head inside. He then lifted one arm and wrapped his hand around his head and pulled it towards the door, creating the illusion that he was being pulled inside.

"Ahh! Ahh!" He cried unconvincingly.

We all just looked at him and shook our heads. He stopped his little act, smoothing out his suit jacket as he faced us. "Just trying to lighten the mood with a little humor. I thought we might need it after that last experience. No?"

We continued to stare at him in mute disapproval.

"No. Okay, point taken." He pushed the doors open wider and stepped inside.

The first thing I noticed was that it was freezing inside. This was made even worse by the fact that I had dressed lightly in a pair of shorts and a tank top because it had been so damned hot in there the day before. It was almost as cold as it had been right before Dean had attacked us before. I looked at Clark jealously as I rubbed my arms. Clark's three-piece suit wasn't so stupid after all.

The second thing I noticed was that even with the bright morning sunlight streaming in through the various windows, the place was still dark as a tomb. It became apparent to me that many of the shadows inside weren't natural. They were part of *him.* He was *everywhere.* All around us. He practically *was* the house.

I wasn't sure how to communicate this information to the others without creating a panic, but I tried. "Be really careful, guys. He's all around us, watching us. Don't split up this time like those idiots in horror movies do."

Dennis didn't listen very well. As soon as he spotted one of his cameras in the next room he scampered off to check on it by himself. I frowned at his impulsiveness and led the others in his direction.

He knelt on the ground in the room where the attack had happened last night. His camera had been knocked over, and the videotape was out and unspooled into long brown coils that were snaked around his legs.

He looked up at us as we entered the room. "The ghost did a number on this camera! I think it still works, but that tape is ruined. Doesn't matter anyway. It looks like the battery died before it had a chance to capture much. I wonder if the rest of them are like this?" He stood the camera up on its tripod, then tried to get up himself, but was stopped by strips of videotape which wrapped themselves around his legs with alarming speed. In no time at all, the tape covered his lower torso too and had started on his arms.

"Holy shit! What the hell?" He shouted, his beautiful eyes wide with terror.

"Dennis! Quickly! Use your crystal!" Clark urged.

Dennis fumbled to pull the amulet from beneath his shirt and hold it in his hands to form the protective bubble of light around himself, but he was too frightened to concentrate enough to activate the crystal. I looked on in despair as the tape worked its way up his body and started to curl and tighten mercilessly around his neck.

"*No!*" I shouted. My crystal shot out a beam of light like it did the night before, and not just mine, but *all* of them. Somehow, I was controlling all of them. The five beams struck him, causing the tape to shrivel and split, falling from his body in ashes. Once the tape was off him, the beams disappeared. He shot to his feet faster than I'd ever seen him move before.

I moved to Dennis' side to comfort him, but before I could say a word our attention was drawn to a strange sound nearby. It sounded like something being dragged, something that didn't weigh very much, scraping and sliding across the naked hardwood floors towards us. Everyone exchanged worried looks.

"What's that sound?" Miranda asked, her voice quavering.

"Try to stay calm," Clark reminded us. "Use your crystals. He wants our fear."

It wasn't long before we saw the source of the strange sounds. Shambling towards us through the two doors to the room were a pair of vaguely human shapes that appeared to be made completely out of ripped up videotape. They slowly moved towards us, arms outstretched like the Mummy.

"Well, now we know what happened to the rest of our tapes. He's using anything he can find inside the house against us. It's a good thing Mr. White didn't leave his tools lying around in here, huh?" I commented.

"Video tape monsters?" Mom said in a voice that sounded more amused than terrified. I was happy that she'd found her groove, as just last night she'd had the irritating tendency to want to scream at every little thing. "He gets points for originality."

"Enough of this!" Clark said angrily. He then chanted in some language which sounded strangely familiar to me even though I was sure I'd never heard it before. As he did so, his hands glowed, and from his hands shot out a beam of yellow energy to each of the approaching creatures, vaporizing them instantly.

We *all* saw him do it. Whatever kind of magic he just used, it was visible to non-sensitives! I'd never seen anything like it before.

"How, how did you just–" Dennis stammered.

"I *told* you I was a wizard, duh! Now, let's put an end to this," Clark said as he stood up straight, tugging on the lapels of his jacket as if he was getting ready. He produced a small cloth bag from one of his coat pockets, which looked as if it was too big to have fit inside it, especially since there had been no corresponding bulge in that spot a moment earlier. The bag was made of a blue, velvety material and fastened at the top by a golden rope. It reminded me of the little bags they package Crown Royal whiskey into, in a vain attempt to make it seem classier than it is.

He shook a white powdery material onto the floor, drawing a circle on the floor with it, then a star inside the circle – a pentagram. Once, when I was small, and Mom was still in the thrall of her old religion, I would have found such a sign terrifying, as I associated it with Satanism and evil. But it wasn't evil at all, as I absorbed later second hand from

Mom's knowledge of Wicca. When he was done he disappeared the back bag into one of his impossible pockets.

He wasn't done. Next, he pulled a long and impressively bejeweled dagger from somewhere, using it to slash open the palms of his hands and dripping a drop of blood into each of the points of the star.

He then raised the dagger above his head and said in a loud, commanding voice, *"Dean Cain! I command you to appear within my circle!"*

Nothing happened.

Dennis stifled a laugh. "Clark, Dean Cain is the guy who plays Superman on TV. I think you mean Dean Drake."

"Ah! Yes, of course! Alliteration! DD! For Dean Drake! Or Doctor Doom!" Clark chuckled at his mistake.

Before he could begin his spell again, I watched in horror as the camcorder flew across the room and slammed into Miranda's head, knocking her to the floor.

"Miranda!" I called out, and ran toward her, but before I could reach her, more objects sailed into the room from elsewhere within the house. Mostly they were camcorders and IR sensors that we had placed the previous night. They pelted us mercilessly. We covered our heads with our arms to try to protect ourselves.

"These crystals aren't helping now!" Dennis complained. He had his shield up but it apparently only worked against ghostly energy, because those real objects being thrown at him had no trouble bouncing off him again and again.

"Working on it!" Clark cried and hastily chanted a new spell. A U-shaped glowing wall of green energy curled itself around us. This did stop the objects, but it had an open top, and Clark had to constantly move it up or down with hand gestures to block objects that tried to fly around it. One of those things was an actual porcelain sink! It shattered against the barrier, the shards spraying everywhere. Fortunately, it was the old sink that had been torn out when they put the new one in, so maybe we wouldn't get in too much trouble for this . . .

"This is getting tedious!" Clark griped. He held aloft his dazzling dagger once more.

"Dean Drake! I command you to appear within my circle!" he shouted. Then again chanted some mysterious words in his nonsense language, causing a great whooshing wind that knocked off Clark's hat and made a mess of my hair.

Then silence. The constant rain of objects being flung at us stopped, and everything that had been hanging in the air ready to attack us dropped to the floor.

In the circle was trapped Dean Drake, randomly flickering back and forth from human to origami nightmare form, glaring at us with hate. *All* of us could see him. Dennis gaped in fascination.

Clark exhaled heavily and dismissed his green energy shield with a deft flick of the wrist. "He's safely contained now. He can do us no further harm." I could no longer see my breath, so the temperature was returning to normal.

"Are you sure about that?" Dennis asked nervously.

"Quite. He's bound by a very old, very reliable kind of magic. The old magic is the best. Magic Classic, that's what I like to call it! It never goes out of style!"

"Omigod! Miranda!" I cried, jumping to her side. Blood trailed from her temple as she lay senseless at our feet. I took her wrist. Her pulse was strong. Clark joined me next to her. He scooped up his hat and plopped it back down on his head by first rolling it down his shoulder and into his hand. What a cornball! Always putting on a damned show! Even at a time like this!

"An ugly bit of head trauma for such a pretty girl. Can't have that can we?" He pressed two of his bony fingers to the spot she was bleeding from, closed his eyes and whispered something inaudible. A soft glow suffused the area around her wound and it disappeared.

Miranda's eyes fluttered open, and she smiled as if waking from a deep sleep. "Where am I?" she asked, then remembered where she was. "Did we win?"

"Of course we did! I made you a promise, didn't I?" Clark said as he pulled her to her feet.

She saw the circle and what was inside, and flinched. "Is that him?" She asked, unable to take her eyes off the apparition.

"In the etheric flesh," Clark muttered, then stalked to just outside the circle. " A nasty bit of work, aren't you? Trying to kill your own daughter? What would ever make you do such a wicked thing?"

We didn't really expect an answer, but we got one. "Benjamin Crooke's been whispering to me, always whispering! He convinced me to do it all, right from the beginning!"

"Who the hell is Benjamin Crooke?" I asked.

"Hm, no idea. Never heard of him," Clark said, and rubbed his chin. I didn't have to be psychic to know he knew more than he was letting on. He had a shitty poker face.

"The man's mind is completely gone," Clark went on. "It's best not to listen to his nonsense. I should go ahead and get him out of here already. Then perhaps even a soul as twisted as his can actually heal? Stranger things have happened."

He looked over at Miranda and spoke gently. "Before I send him through the portal, is there anything you'd like to say to him?"

She recoiled at first, but then changed her mind. "Yes. Yes, as a matter of fact there is."

Clark gestured for her to step forward and pointed to where she could safely stand.

She stared into the entity's face, unblinking. "I used to worship you. You were my Daddy. You were my everything, even though you terrified me sometimes when you fought with Mom. Then you took her away from me, and you didn't even have the courage to face the consequences. You're not my daddy anymore. Maybe that person never really existed at all outside of my mind. What you really are is a bully and a coward! For a long time, I felt like you'd taken my life too, as surely as if you'd turned that gun on me that day. But I want you to know that you no longer have any power over me. I'm better now. I'm taking my life back. I've got a good job now." She glanced at me, Dennis and Mom. "And I've got some good new friends too. You're nothing to me. You're pathetic. You're not even worth hating anymore. I'm letting go of my hate, my anger, and I'm letting go of you. Forever! I will no longer allow myself to be defined by what happened in this house."

She stepped back and turned to Clark. "Get rid of that thing."

With that, I became certain of one thing beyond a shadow of a doubt: she had been lying to us this entire time. She remembered *everything*.

I suppose I should have been mad at her for lying to us, for using us to come here and confront her personal demons. But we had used her too, hadn't we? Anyway, how could I be mad at her? She was Miranda, she was my friend. She was fucking awesome and I loved her.

Clark grinned approvingly. "Well said, Miranda, well said!" With that, Clark began to chant, and waved his arms and hands around until a bright funnel of light appeared in the ceiling above the circle. Clark chanted a few more words, and the form of Dean Drake elongated, then got sucked up into the portal of light. Clark barked out another word and snapped his fingers and the portal disappeared.

"Where's he gone to?" I inquired, still gazing at the spot where the portal had been. I also noticed that all traces of my headache had mercifully disappeared.

"I hope he goes straight to Hell!" Miranda swore. Apparently still holding onto some of her hate. It's not like you can get rid of it as easily as Clark dealt with the portal. It's a long process, and one she was just embarking upon.

"That's a distinct possibility. Who knows? He'll wind up wherever he thinks he's supposed to be," Clark answered enigmatically. "But he can't trouble us any longer, that's the important thing."

"And what about my mom?" Miranda asked.

"Oh, I can still feel her hiding around here somewhere. I'm sure if we ask very nicely she'll pop out and say hello." Then Clark cupped his hands and called out loudly, *"Molly! Molly Drake! Come out and say hello. It's safe!"*

I winced, as I always did when people were excessively loud, and also because he was right next to my ear when he started shouting. *This* was his idea of asking nicely?

It didn't take her long to appear. "There she is!" I said, as I pointed. She floated towards us through the wall, looking much better in that special way that having the top of one's head properly attached typically improves one's appearance. In fact, she was positively radiant, and what Dennis would have called "a really hot momma." I wondered why she looked so different now? Had Dean also been preventing her from making herself look decent somehow? I still had so many questions about how all this shit works.

"I can't see her," Miranda said, deeply disappointed.

"I can help with that," Clark said gently, and placed one hand on her shoulder.

She teared up, her hands going to her mouth. "Oh, she's right there! Right in front of me!"

"That's right," Clark said softly. "As long as you maintain physical contact with me, you'll be able to see her and hear her. Even feel her."

The two, mother and daughter, embraced. Since her mother hadn't aged, they looked more like sisters than mother and daughter. They held each other for a long time, crying.

Ghosts can cry? Do they have functional tear ducts? Or maybe they're just mimicking the appearance of crying, based on their memories of what such things were like? See? So many questions!

I couldn't make out what they were saying, and I never asked later. It was deeply personal, so I respected that. Whatever it was, the important thing was it gave Miranda the closure she needed.

The two separated, and with a smile to Miranda, Molly turned to Clark. "I'm ready."

Again, he summoned the portal.

Poor Dennis was the only one who couldn't see it, being the only non-psychic not touching Clark. "What's going on?" he asked.

"Shhh," I replied with the practiced ease that came from years of working in the library. "I'll explain it later!"

Molly's form elongated and was sucked up into the portal. Clark made it disappear as effortlessly as he had before.

Mom moved to embrace Miranda, her natural mommy instincts triggered by the scene. Even I worked up the courage to give her an awkward hug and promised that everything would be all right now, which I only ever half believed anytime I told someone something like that. I mean honestly! Who knows what the future really holds for any of us? Or how much control do we really have over it? But people like to hear it, so I say it even though it always makes me feel like a liar whenever I do.

Once we all calmed down a little, we set about cleaning up the room as best we could. Dennis bemoaned that much of his equipment might not have survived being used as weapons against us, but decided we should load it all up into Clark's van anyway so he could test it all later to be sure. The advantage of having the literal sink thrown at us by a malevolent ghost bent on killing us with our own stuff was that everything we needed to take was already in the room with us. And so was, as it happened, a broom and dustpan. Which really came in handy when cleaning up all the pieces of that aforementioned shattered sink. I can laugh that he actually threw a sink at us, although it was anything but funny at the time.

I was disappointed Clark didn't pull some Mary Poppinsesque magical shit to help us clean up faster, and I said as much. He told me such a thing would be an ostentatious abuse of power, not to mention he had a terrible singing voice and we should consider ourselves lucky to have gotten out of hearing him reenact such a scene.

That said, with five people working together, it didn't take long to get the room cleaned up, even without the aid of magic.

I locked up the house and hid the key under the mat, as Eli White had instructed. We were all silent on the drive back to Dennis' house, trying to process what we had seen and done.

And all before lunch too! Which Dennis offered to cook. Clark declined, saying he was needed elsewhere, he wanted to talk to me personally before he went.

"Yes?" I said, intrigued. What can I say? His manner was completely different from that of the goofball I'd seen him as earlier, so I was caught off-guard.

He looked me in the eye, his eyes completely lucid. "You have amazing talent. That ghost was more powerful than I had anticipated. It's a testament to your raw ability that you were able to get yourself and the others out of there alive last night. I would be honored to teach you how to control your powers better. In time, I believe you could even become one of the most powerful witches in my entire order, the Temple of the Old Gods. While it is true one doesn't have to be a psychic to become a great witch, it certainly adds spice to the sauce. What do you say?"

Dennis practically bounced off his heels. "You mean she could learn how to do some of that crazy stuff you were doing? Shoot energy out of her hands, and shit like that?"

Clark chuckled. "Yes, in time."

Dennis looked like he'd hit the freaking lottery. "Shit! Athena Anderson, Congrats!" he enthused, happy for me. Then, "my girlfriend's going to be a superhero!" We all laughed.

Mom's attitude was more reverent . . . no, it was awe. "You're offering her a position inside the Temple of the Old Gods?"

He nodded. "Once she completes her training, yes."

She gasped. "Oh honey! This is an amazing opportunity! They're a very exclusive group!" There may have been a tinge of jealousy, but, mostly happy for me!

I crossed my arms. "Yeah, well maybe I don't want to learn the ways of the Force and become a Jedi," I said flatly, and watched all their jaws drop open in unison. *Screw them all*, I thought.

This is *my* life, not theirs and I wanted to keep it that way. "I'm grateful for all you did today, Clark, really I am. But the truth is, I'm just not that into all this magic stuff. I never asked to be born with this 'gift.' I don't want it to take over my life. Just like how Miranda doesn't want to be defined by her past, I don't want to be defined by my powers."

I turned to Clark and took a deep breath. "So, I don't think I'm going to take you up on that offer. I like to keep one foot firmly planted in reality, thank you very much." I gestured at his outfit. "If I join your group, I might start to think that walking around dressed like that is a good idea!"

Clark sniffed. "I think perhaps you're concentrating too much on meaningless external appearances."

"Says the guy who's always telling my mom how beautiful she is!"

"I was referring to her aura, which is a direct reflection of one's own inner beauty!" He protested.

"Uh huh, sure."

He pulled himself up straight. "You really should reconsider. There are many benefits to membership, including a generous salary."

"Trying to bribe me now? You can't afford my price."

"I'm not trying to bribe anyone!" he said, losing his cool for a moment, but regaining it. "I just hate to see someone with your extraordinary talents wasting them chasing around ghosts."

"*Wasting?*" Dennis protested. "Hey man, don't insult the JSPS like that!"

Clark took a half step toward him. "Dennis, I didn't mean to insult you, but can't you see how pointless it all is? Even if you obtain concrete evidence of the supernatural during one of your investigations, do you really think you'll ever be allowed to share it with the world? There are people out there whose entire job is to prevent such a thing! I should know, I used to work hand in hand with them."

"Excuse me," Miranda said angrily, "but I don't think what we did here today was 'pointless' at all! We freed my mother from decades of torment, and now this house is finally safe to serve as a good home for someone."

"Yeah! The JSPS is about more than just getting evidence of the paranormal, it's about helping people and giving them peace of mind," Dennis said.

I smiled at Dennis for saying that. I was so proud of him. I made a mental note to tell him as much later on. In my previous relationships, a frequent complaint was that I wasn't very communicative when it came to displaying such feelings. If I thought something, instead of just saying it aloud, I just kind of expected them to know somehow. It was like I expected my partners to be able to read my mind like they were psychic too. This time, I wanted to make sure I got it right. I resolved to make more of an effort to actually verbalize what I was feeling. Someone as special as Dennis deserved my best effort.

Clark sighed and his shoulders slumped. "Very well. I can see you have made up your mind. Please, at least take my card and give me a call if you ever decide differently or should require my assistance again."

He produced a business card from nowhere, but I managed to catch him pulling it from his shirt sleeve. What do you know, he was using sleight of hand rather than real magic this time. I briefly wondered why he thought it was necessary to know both disciplines as I took the offered card, but then it hit me: Clark was all about reveling in such corny theatrics. Like he was always putting on an act, always trying to impress someone. Probably part of why I had such a hard time trusting him.

I glanced at the card, and It read: "Clark W. Kismet – Representing the Ancient Order of the Temple of the Old Gods to the Inner Council of the International Conference of Guilds"

I flipped the card front to back, confused. "There's no number or address on here!"

He shrugged. "It's an old card, but it will work. Hold it in your hand like you are now and speak my name. I'll hear you, and come running, always. That's a promise, Athena."

"Thanks," I said, actively suppressing an eye roll, and stuffed the yellowed rectangle of paper into my purse.

He sighed. "Do think about it. You'll never reach your full potential doing this."

God! This guy doesn't know when to give up, does he?

"Maybe I don't want to reach my full potential. Maybe I just want to be comfortable? Maybe I just want to be happy?" I protested.

What was this obsession people apparently had in our society that reaching your 'full potential' as defined by them was automatically the key to happiness for everyone? The idea seemed insane to me. It just looked like a ticket to more responsibility, pressure, and stress. Not everyone wants the same things out of life. Why did everyone always assume that they did? Not all of us want to be superheroes, some of us are content enough just to read about them.

Clark raised his arms in defeat. "Certainly. Take all the time you need." He turned to face all of us. "I wish all of you well, and it's been lovely getting to know all of you and working with you." He raised his hat one final time and took a deep, theatrical bow before stepping into his van.

Dennis slipped his arm around my waist as we watched Clark pull out of the driveway and roll down the road. The warmth of his arm pressed up against my side felt good.

It felt right.

This all happened many years ago. Nowadays, I'm almost as old as Mom was when this took place, which blows my mind to think about, so I don't. Dennis and I have been happily (more or less) married for ages now. You know how it is when you've been with someone for a long time? They drive you crazy, and yet you can't – and don't – want to imagine life without them.

We are the proud parents of a pack of furbabies, as you're now obligated to call your pets these days. Not having children was a deliberate choice, so don't feel sorry for us. My womb works just fine and as far as we know Dennis' little spermies are in great shape too. No, kids just aren't compatible with our rock n' roll lifestyle, much to Mom's chagrin. So instead, we spoil Dennis' sister's kids rotten, filling them with sugar and sending them home to torment their parents. It's like having all the fun of having kids but with eighty percent less hassle and expense!

The JSPS is still going strong (with chapters in Monmouth, Atlantic, and even Burlington counties too), and Miranda became one of our closest and dearest friends.

In many ways, not much has changed around here. Barnegat made the national news for a few seconds when Rosie O'Donnell's daughter disappeared and was later found holed up in Settler's Landing with some skeevy dude she met on the internet. The town has grown in some ways, and shrunk in others . . . it finally has its own high school and a McDonalds.

So maybe we're not as rinky dink as we once were, but the tradeoff is we're also a bit more generic anytown USA now, as much of the local color has drained away. On a personal note, I'm not quite as foolish or anxious as I once was, but I'm also not as pretty – though Dennis, bless him, would disagree.

I still have Clark Kismet's calling card. It is even yellower now than it was then. I have never had occasion to use it. We've seen some weird shit over the years in the JSPS, but nothing ever quite as weird as what we saw that summer in the house on West Bay Ave. I don't regret never taking Clark up on his offer. My life is my own, and my life is pretty damned good! I do regret being so hard on him though. As I reflect on it now, I can see that he was just trying to help me, and he really did save our bacon.

I still drive past that house every day on my way to work. I still work at the library, and in fact I run the damned place these days. The house is a lawyers' office again, if you can believe that? I guess some things were just meant to be.

The house still haunts me, but strictly in a good way, and I smile whenever I drive by it. When I pass it, I think of how our little adventure there first brought us all together, and the peace it ultimately brought to Miranda and to Molly.

Athena and the Jersey Shore Paranormal Society Will Return in *Jersey Devils*

QUEEN OF THE SHADOWMEN

I am a living weapon

Not a person

My mental condition seems to worsen
Bah!

Does the blade that kills

Ever stop to question whose blood it spills?

Nor shall I, as I sharpen my will

Remind myself that I am naught but an instrument of wrath

Drown now in my bloodbath!

Falling in love, having children

Those are dreams for those who walk a different path

I must not dream I am no longer human

A fact I must accept so I am not constantly fuming

Over the kind of life I have forsaken

If only away my choices hadn't been taken

Bah!

Self pity is for the weak

Joyous release in killing is what I seek

A feeling of ultimate power

When I see my enemies cower

Can't you see?

It's the only pleasure still left to me?

THERE'S ALWAYS A BIGGER FISH

Dimitri almost swallowed his cigarette in shock when a black living shadow landed soundlessly on the asphalt before him.

It was a mistake to go out without his bodyguards, he knew, but was so tired of having them up his ass. *What would it hurt*, he thought, *to just step out around the corner for a smoke and a bit of the fresh night air?*

As it turned out, it just might hurt a great deal.

The thing studied its prey with black hole eyes, the merest ghost of a smile playing across an otherwise impenetrable face, which seemed chiseled from obsidian.

He instinctively reached for the gun hidden under his jacket. *I'll give you something to grin about, you sorry son of a bitch!*

The monster exploded forward just as his fingers made contact with the pistol. Long, mean looking blades swung out of the thing's forearms and whistled through the brisk Chicago air, before slicing into his neck.

Dmitri bore hapless witness to jets of his own blood painting sidewalk and the dirty locked metal gates of the nearby convenience store. He tried to scream, but only slick, gurgling sounds escaped what was left of his ripped throat.

"Hush now, it will all soon be over," his assailant promised him in a husky voice as the other blade speared his rib cage to shishkabob his heart.

Angus allowed himself a surge of satisfaction over this latest kill. Dmitri had not been a very good man, to put it mildly. He had been deeply involved in smuggling all sorts of unsavory things, not to mention human trafficking. Angus had ample opportunity to observe all of this during the past few days he had spent stalking him.

Angus didn't question the morality of his assignments. It wasn't in the job description. He owed everything to the organization he worked for. His job was only to obey, and leave the details of who deserved to live – and die – to the people he served. He did of course develop his own opinions on the matter from time to time. And in this case, in his qualified opinion, Dmitri got off easy, but time was at a premium right he didn't have the luxury of drawing this out.

The satisfaction was qualified, too, as he had every reason to believe that whoever had paid his employers to carry out this hit were as unsavory of a bunch of characters as Dmitri. Indeed, probably worse, since they could afford to meet the exorbitant prices the Shadowmen charged. All above *his* pay level. It was exactly for these kinds of reasons that he tried not to bother thinking too deeply about the relative rights and wrongs of his chosen occupation.

What was *right* was this job allowed him and his wife to have a very nice, comfortable life, and the possible repercussions of his activities beyond that were beyond his concern.

And of course, this job made him feel alive! *Truly* alive, something ironic for dealing out death, but there it was. *Exhilarating*, there was simply no other word for it. He loved how powerful it made him feel: an apex predator, a force to be reckoned with, an unstoppable angel of death.

Now, the task became tedious. The hunt over, it was time for cleanup.

Dropping a device from his belt with a *slop* into Dmitri's liquid leavings, he slung the corpse over his shoulder, took a deep breath, and rocketed up to the nearest fire escape, hopping up from one level to another until he reached the rooftop.

The device was filled with "the Powder," a chemical dreamed up by the Order's tech boys. Once scattered, it instantly dissolved all traces of identifiable DNA in the area around it. His instructions had been to make his target disappear and leave as few traces behind as possible.

He watched as, without sound, a meters-wide cloud formed below, and as quickly disappeared. The device itself imploded into tinfoil with a tiny flash.

Finding the opportune moment for the kill had been the hard part. The guy was constantly surrounded by his guards, girlfriends, or other business associates. Not that killing them too would have posed much of a challenge. It simply wasn't part of the contract. Despite the more practical matter of having more bodies to dispose of, of course.

After mind-numbing days of stalking, Angus couldn't believe his luck when Dmitiri walked out by himself to smoke. And in a dark, empty alleyway in the dead of night, no less. It would have been easier to just shoot him from the rooftop but he preferred the intimacy of an up close kill. It was so indescribably gratifying to watch the light go out of someone's eyes. To feel the last hot breath escape their lips to tickle your cheek.

He sighed. These sorts of thoughts he couldn't share with his wife, who knew nothing of his double life. They were some things only another Shadowman could understand, and he had precious little contact with other members of his own kind these days. Aside from that idiot Mike, who barely counted.

If Celine was around, she'd understand. She wouldn't judge me for my … bloodlust … I suppose you'd have to call it.

He sighed again, more heavily this time. He'd probably never see Celine again. Her father had made sure of that, and she was in his thoughts more than he cared to admit, especially to his wife, whom he loved. Celine had been his first real love, and she'd always hold a special place in his heart. *Was it possible to love two women*, he wondered? He didn't see why not.

Enough of this! No good can come of dwelling on the past! Not when I still have so much work left to do.

On the rooftop, Angus stuffed Dmitri's body into the Case, whose purpose was to process the body and eventually vent out a fine mist of human remains. Dmitri was rather a large man, so Angus had to break the long bones to fit him in there, snapping them in his hands like twigs. Even so, the Case bulged with its "meal."

Case sealed, Angus pressed a button, and that was it. A little red light came on, meaning meat soup. Yellow meant venting. Green meant done. He guessed the tech guys didn't think much of the brain power of the people who used their toys, and that was okay by him. Like most of the tech he used, he had no idea how it worked, and didn't care to know.

With a grunt, he swung the Case onto his back, and leapt from rooftop to rooftop, enjoying the sensation of the crisp March air on his skin. He had to savor every minute spent outside of his "skin suit," the full body human-form costume which concealed his inhumanly inky features. The outfit was a marvel of science, a disguise so complete even his wife couldn't see through it during their most intimate moments. Yet it was also unfathomably hot and uncomfortable at times.

The price of being a Shadowman was you were almost never comfortable in your own skin.

He had parked only a few blocks away, and soon reached the alley where he had (illegally) parked the cab of his semi truck. His cover job was that of a long haul trucker, enabling him to disappear for long periods of time and travel all over the country without arousing suspicion. He humped to the ground with a heavy thud and removed the Case from his back and checked the light, gratified it was already blinking yellow with a mist of atomized Dmitri emanating from its edges. He held it up to what passed for his nose and drew in a deep breath: earthy and pleasant smelling, it gave him a rush like smelling freshly ground coffee.

He pressed his thumb to the handle of the truck, automatically unlocking it, and stepped in. He placed the Case on the passenger seat and lowered the window next to it.

Slipping Into the back section of the truck to change, Angus removed the human-form suit from the small, cube shaped device that stored, cleaned and sanitized it. He got completely undressed and put the durable, yet paper thin, shell on. Once it sensed it was completely on, it adhered to his body using a series of minuscule magnets that were embedded in his body. Then he pulled his clothes on. Once fully dressed, he returned to the front seat and started up the engine, satisfied with the deep, reassuring rumble under his feet. He'd always loved big engines. There were perks to his cover job.

He steered the cab-over truck onto the streets, which were mercifully empty of most traffic this time of night. He had stashed the trailer at a warehouse by the waterfront owned by Silhouette Shipping. It was no ordinary trailer, and concealing beneath hidden panels the wide array of weapons and equipment he employed in his profession.

The sooner he got on the road, the sooner he would be back home and in the loving arms of his wife, Mary. This assignment had lasted longer than he had anticipated when he'd left, and he was eager to put the experience behind him and get back to his normal, mundane routine.

In the seat beside him, the Case made a sharp *ding!* Sound only Shadowmen could hear, meaning Dmitri's remains were completely disintegrated. He glanced over as the light flashed green, then solid green. It would go dark in two minutes.

He smiled as he hit the button to roll up the window. *The scientists at Buhler Industries are truly wizards at their craft!*

Dexter Sinister, the wizard, would no doubt be insulted by the comparison. Scientists could indeed do some remarkable things these days, but in Dexter's estimation, it was nothing compared to the power that could be wielded by a skilled practitioner of High Magick.

Dexter sat cross legged atop the roof of the warehouse, and . shielded his eyes from the intense light of the truck's headlights as it turned into the empty parking lot. He had been using astral projection to trail the Shadowman since he'd arrived in Chicago some hours earlier, and had watched him successfully execute his mission.

Then he hurried back here to his body to await his own victim, at the speed of thought. Dexter figured he'd let the Shadowman retrieve his trailer, and ambush him once he was out of the city and out on the highway. Dexter hated driving in the city.

A spell kept his body nice and toasty warm despite the night's chill. He looked forward to taking Angus' life – literally. The body Dexter currently inhabited had once been quite powerful, but no more. It was the body of a person who had been entrusted with protecting the life of the leader of his own Great House of Magic, but it had atrophied during Dexter's long years of imprisonment, and grown weak.

Dexter had never been in the body of a Shadowman before, and he awaited this opportunity excitedly. To be able to combine his mastery of the mystical arts with such a magnificent, super humanly powerful body. He would be unstoppable!

It was more than a mere lust for power which excited Dexter. A deeper, more primal desire seized him as well. Angus had a pretty wife waiting for him at home, and Dexter itched to meet her. He had spent far too many years alone, in prison. A man had certain . . . needs. Needs that he fully intended to satisfy!

Yes, becoming Angus Chavez would indeed be a most interesting and pleasurable experience, despite having to go by such a ridiculous name. It lacked the flair and style of "Dexter Sinister," a notorious name spoken only in hushed whispers by those who knew it, but it would have to do.

Some time later, the truck-with-trailer pulled out of the warehouse. Dexter launched himself into the sky, following with levitation and high enough to remain hidden in the shadow of any streetlights. He rode the wind currents, grateful for the enchantments which kept the chill out his bones. Without them he would surely freeze to death on a night like this.

The bright city lights gave way to the rural dim of the open road. Dexter felt a sense of exhilaration as he hovered through the starry sky, reveling in his freedom. After years of confinement in a small chamber, it was almost overwhelming to be hanging there suspended above the surface of the earth like this. He felt like he was sailing through the vastness of space. The former jailbird was now suddenly as free as a bird! He smiled at the pun, cheesy as it was.

Not much longer now, Dexter promised himself, as traffic thinned to only two or three cars visible in either direction. When the lights of the nearest car were hidden beyond the next curve and hill, he would strike.

Angus sang along to the radio, doing his best to make his mouth work around the garbled lyrics of Pearl Jam's Eddie Vedder. And mostly failing of course, but melodic fidelity didn't matter! No one was around to judge his performance, nothing but himself and the wide open road ahead of him.

His spirits were high. Another successfully completed mission was well behind him, and he looked forward to the expected few weeks of downtime before the next assignment. Maybe he'd visit his siblings? It had been awhile since he'd seen them in person. He missed them. He missed Mary. Hell, he even kind of missed Mike, the largely incompetent Shadowman who maintained and guarded his truck when he wasn't away on a mission.

He was about to belt out the next chorus of Pearl Jam when the radio went silent, and he was thrown forward as the engine cut out. The road disappeared from suddenly dark headlights, and the dashboard lights went out.

"What the fuck?" Angus yelled as he fought to maintain control, no mean feat with the loss of power steering, even with his super strength. His only guide to avoid ditching into a culvert was a white picket fence on its opposite side. He frantically judged his distance to that as he pumped the brakes to a stop, cursing, sweating and in shock.

How could this happen? The battery couldn't go completely dead like that in an instant! And this was no ordinary truck, it had been tricked out by the finest minds at Buhler Industries with tech that was decades ahead of anything else on the road. There were backup systems upon backup systems, or so he'd been told ad infinitum. This should be impossible.

Muttering another curse, he popped his policeman's flashlight from its velcro under the dash . . . handy for illumination and for use as a weapon, though his natural weapons were defense enough against any ordinary human. Anyway, his superhuman night vision only got him so far and this was an overcast, moonless night. He pressed the flashlight button as soon as his boots hit the ground.

Nothing.

He looked at it incredulously, wanting to pound it to bits on the pavement, but smacked the bottom of it and tried again.

Still nothing.

Shaking his head, Angus threw the useless flashlight back into the truck and took a moment to think, after taking a moment to curse out Mike. The guy had obviously failed to keep up some vital system in the truck, and now he was stuck here in the middle of nowhere as a result.

He was about to climb back into the truck to try his cell phone when something heavy landed on the pavement ahead . . . sounded like about fifty feet away, but he couldn't be sure, and froze. For the first time in his life, fear frosted the edges of his soul. He turned toward the sound to find a hooded figure in dark robes standing in front of him.

Where did he come from? Angus idly wondered, relaxing. What did he have to fear from this refugee from a monastery? But the fear returned again when Angus heard the voice. Low at first, then rising to a deep crescendo as he chanted what sounded like so many nonsense words.

All the Shadowmen knew of the two Great Houses of Magic: the Temple of the Old Gods, and the Ancient Order of the Golden Path. They'd had some nominal training in fighting against them, most of which involved disabling the magic-user's vocal cords, or cutting off their hands. But the incantation had begun, and the wizard was fifty feet away.

Too late. Too far, he thought dismally.

Wind whipped up between the two as a burning began inside Angus. A burning which suffused not only every fiber in his body, but his very spirit. An agony which wasn't merely physical, it was *existential.*

With expanding dread he realized his life and future were being stolen. He couldn't quite explain this feeling, yet it filled him with the same conviction any other well known fact would. With equal unexplainable certainty he knew there was nothing for him beyond this moment. If ever a life beyond this one had been a possibility – with everything he'd done, all the lives he'd taken, that window was shut now, *permanently.* No Heaven for him, not even a Hell, just nothing but endless nothingness. Nothingness and more nothingness for eternity. He supposed it wasn't really *that* bad. If you couldn't even contemplate such emptiness, then you couldn't get very depressed about it, could you?

Then he realized he would never see his Mary again, or Celine for that matter. He had always clung to some kind of a vague hope that if they couldn't be together in this life, then perhaps they could be in some other one. Now he knew with a soul crushing lack of doubt that it would never happen, and that's what hurt most of all – the complete loss of all hope. He wanted to cry, but even that was denied to him as his tear ducts had been surgically removed as part of the process that had turned him into a Shadowman all those years ago.

"I'm sorry, Mary. I'm sorry Celine!" he stammered miserably as the robes of his murderer flapped ever more loosely against the thinning figure within.

The hooded figure collapsed into a heap as the body within the robes evaporated. Dexter Sinister looked down upon his new hands with a childlike astonishment. He'd never quite get used to this part, the moment of transition.

He exhilarated in the wonderful, unfamiliar power contained in these new limbs, as well as in the foreign memories and skills which – so real for a moment – departed like the last vestiges of a lucid dream. He snatched at them like dollars in a carnival tornado machine, wanting at least to remember how to drive a big, ungainly thing like this if he was going to make it all the way back to New York. With relief, that particular dollar he managed to catch as the last vestiges of the previous occupant of this body drained away into complete non-existence. That memory, and a few other tidbits he would need to be able to maintain this charade.

This loose collection of stolen memories was all which remained of Angus Chavez now: a stolen body and a dry, characterless collection of certain facts which Dexter had found worth saving. The apex predator had finally met his match, and hadn't even put up a fight.

A cruel smirk twisted itself onto Dexter's new face as he recalled his latest victim's last words. How ironic that his last thoughts had been of Celine! Who did the fool think had sent him? How did he think he'd been so easily found for the culling? Celine had never *really* forgiven him for breaking her heart all those years ago, and it was true what they said: Hell hath no fury like a woman scorned! In Angus' memory trove, Dexter found the breakup had been something forced upon him by Celine's powerful father, who was the master of his Order – and how it had hurt Angus as much as it had hurt her. The tragedy of it all was to Dexter as Ambrosia was to a God.

He scooped up the robe, not bearing to discard it. He became attached to things easily. People not so much. *Things* didn't betray you.

With a wave of his hand and a simple incantation, power was restored to the truck. The headlights burst into life, shining into the darkness ahead just as an oncoming passenger car crested the curve and drove past. He waved to it.

Dexter climbed into the truck and noticed the flashlight on the passenger seat. *That could really crack a skull,* he thought, hefting it while switching it off. He caressed the Case as a thing beloved, a thing which consumed men.

He maneuvered the truck back onto the road with a practiced ease that was not his. He had places to be and things to do. Oh, so many great things! Impersonating this Shadowman was merely the beginning of his ambitious schemes. It opened the door for the greater plans he'd dreamed of during his long, dull years of incarceration.

He sped down the highway eagerly. Mary waited for him back home. It would be rude to keep her waiting, would it not?

THE GOLDEN INQUISITION

"The Celestial Empress commands you to appear in the throne room immediately," the face in the stone said.

"As She commands," the Grand Inquisitor gave as the standard reply. The face faded from the fist-sized polished jade sphere which floated in the air in front of him. As the message ended, the sphere fell and he caught it without thought, returning it to its place in a pouch dangling from the belt on his armor. He had anticipated this, of course. He had heard all the rumors already. It was his job to know these things. He had known it would be only a matter of time before She summoned him for an audience.

Minutes later, he was kneeling before the Celestial Throne. True to its name, it seemed to be made from the night sky itself. A massive black chair, it was framed by a pair of large, thick bodied golden Asian dragons whose heads lay at the foot of it, their serpentine bodies winding up the sides and meeting at the top. Its obsidian center was studded with millions of jewels that constantly twinkled like stars and nebulae.

Atop the throne sat the Empress, as She had for hundreds of years. Even now, after so much of his life given in Her service, he felt a twinge of fear and awe in her presence. The two of them were related, as most of the members of the Ancient Order of the Golden Path were. In his case, not quite so distantly as the others. He was part of the storied Dragonrider Clan, one of the few lines which could draw a direct line of descent from the Empress. This made him special, but he didn't always enjoy the elevated status this afforded him. The burden of it weighed upon him more heavily than the elaborate ceremonial armor he was required to wear inside the confines of the Eternal Palace.

The Empress Herself was an impressive sight. She appeared to be in Her early thirties despite centuries of magically extended life. Slender and delicate, it wasn't difficult to imagine she could be carried off in a strong breeze but for Her layers of robes and magnificent golden headdress. The headdress was said to contain lifetimes of memories her ancient brain could no longer hold.

"Arise, my Inquisitor. No doubt by now you suspect why I have summoned you here." Her voice had the quality of fluttering leaves.

He did indeed. Although he didn't quite know how much of the rumors were true. He had yet to complete the preliminary investigation he had already begun as a precaution.

"You wish me to investigate the false accusations made against our Order by the Queen of the Shadowmen, my Empress?"

She smiled Her crisp smile. "I should have known you would be aware of the situation. As usual, you do not disappoint me, kinsman."

He blushed beneath his armored mask, made in the likeness of a stylized Asian lion. It was a rare honor indeed for the Empress to acknowledge their shared familial ties.

She continued. "These are troubling times. The Shadowman Queen has challenged your cousin, Arjun Dragonrider, to a trial by combat in order to 'prove' her scandalous claims, and the proud fool accepted. If he should lose, under ancient Guild law, her lies will be enshrined as truth, and we will lose all that we have. Everything and everyone within this organization will become her property. She accuses us of the destruction of her own people, and we all know that mercy is an alien concept to the Shadowmen. If she wins, her revenge upon us will be brutal indeed."

"Surely, a sorcerer of Arjun's skill can defeat a mere assassin?" he replied without falterning. "Then our counterclaim will become the official 'truth' and her vast fortune will be ours. Perhaps there is nothing to be concerned about, my Empress?"

Her hand rose in a sweeping motion as if turning a page, then fell like a leaf. "The Shadowmen are no mere assassins, and Celine is the deadliest of them all! She is no ordinary soul, but an Avatar of Kali Herself! Arjun is indeed a great sorcerer, but he's also an arrogant fool who will surely underestimate his opponent to his own detriment." She looked down, then returned her gaze to him. "I had hoped that appointing him to represent us on the Inner Council of the Guilds would teach him humility by forcing him to learn how to work with others, but it seems to have only inflated his ego all the more. What an idiot I was to allow such a reckless infant to speak for us all!"

The Inquisitor gasped. He had never heard such an earnest admission of shortcomings from the Goddess-like Empress in front of Her subjects. It was unheard of!

Her voice grew stronger. "But the die has been cast, and now all we can do is deal with the fallout. Even if he should succeed, we still have a large problem ahead of us. Before the Shadowmen's Citadel was destroyed, The Orb of Thoth was stolen from it. It is now in unknown hands, which makes *all* magic users vulnerable to attack at any moment. We face an unknown enemy who could use the Orb to plunge this world back into chaos by destroying the Great Houses of Magic. THAT is why I need you to learn who our true enemy is. Find who was really behind the attack on the Shadowmen and the theft of the Orb. Bring me indisputable proof! With this information, the Guilds will have no choice but to listen, no matter the outcome of this ill-advised trial!"

His mind reeled at these new revelations. The satellite photos he'd studied during his preliminary investigation had confirmed the destruction of the Shadowmen's Citadel headquarters, but he hadn't known that the Orb of Thoth had been stolen! He cursed himself. *The Shadowmen's assailants had used magic.* It should have been obvious.

Thousands of years earlier, when the world's first global civilization had been destroyed by a war between rival groups of magic users, the Orb had been created to avert humanity's sure extinction. The Orb prevented spells from being cast for miles around it, rendering magic users helpless. It was entrusted to a clan of assassins who used it to kill the leaders of the magic users. They also left a warning, that unless the new leaders ended the war and used their powers to rebuild the world they'd shattered, the same fate would befall them as well. Thus, the Guilds were born, the secret societies that brought about the modern world. To prevent another apocalyptic Magic War, the use of magic was limited to the two Great Houses of Magic, the Temple of the Old Gods, and his own people, the Order of the Golden Path. In time, the Assassins evolved into the Shadowmen, surgically and technologically enhanced killers that were barely human anymore.

With the Orb no longer in the hands of the Shadowmen, the delicate balance of power that kept the different factions in check was upset. Anything could happen now. Perhaps even another Magic War. The very thought made the Inquisitor physically ill. The last Magic War had so thoroughly devastated the world that there was barely any trace left of that first civilization. In fact, the Eternal Palace, the very structure in which they stood, was the only building to survive intact from that era.

Something else bothered him. "My Empress, if Arjun loses his trial by combat, will we submit to the verdict of the Guilds? Even though it may mean our extinction?"

Her face drew up in disgust. "Certainly not! We will not go meek, as lambs to the slaughter! The other members of our delegation to Guild Headquarters have instructions to withdraw our Order from the Guilds should that happen, even if it will almost certainly mean war to defy them. We've already prepared for the defense of this island, conjuring up a shield and forbidden beasts from the Long Ago Before Times. It is my hope such defenses will be needed only to buy enough time for you to successfully complete your investigation. Once we are armed with the truth, they must listen to reason, and there will be no need for further bloodshed."

Beneath his lion-mask, the Inquisitor frowned. His armor felt heavier than ever. How could she place such responsibility upon him? But of course, he already knew the answer: She was the Celestial Empress, the closest thing there was on earth to a God. She could ask anything of him she damn well pleased and he would happily obey.

He bowed. "I will leave immediately to begin my inquiries, my Empress."

"See that you do. You have the full resources of our organization at your disposal. I am sure I don't have to remind you that the fate of our people, not least the world, now rests in your hands."

"I will not fail you, Eternal One," he swore.

She smiled radiantly down upon him "I know that you won't. You never have before.".

How he could bask for eternity in the glow of that smile, the smile of his Goddess. Her favor made heart rejoiceful, his armor light. Yet he couldn't bask in that glow forever, and bade his retreat, which she granted. He had work to do.

Once he left the audience chamber, the Grand Inquisitor ordered a transport jet be readied for him. He needed to travel to the ruins of the Shadowmen's Citadel, to see for himself what clues he might pry from the rubble. By use of magic, he could teleport there, but the distance was too great to reach in a single jump. It would take at least three, and he needed an hour's rest between each, or he'd be disabled with nausea. The jet was more practical for such distances. Besides, he enjoyed piloting such vehicles himself.

According to the stories he had heard, the Citadel had been deliberately destroyed by its defenders when it became apparent that defeat was imminent. If he could find an intact enough corpse of even one of those attackers in the ruins, he could engage Necromancy to learn what he needed. This art and use of magic to revive the dead, considered an 'Infernal Craft,' was normally forbidden by an ancient agreement between the Great Houses of Magic. However, as the Celestial Empress' Grand Inquisitor, he was accorded special dispensation.

He had his own suspicions about who was behind the attack. The rumors said that the attackers had used magic to penetrate the Shadowmen's defenses and overcome them. This meant that either their enemies were most likely from the Temple of the Old Gods, or perhaps a rogue faction from within the Empress' own ranks.

The latter possibility was one nobody else within the Golden Path seemed very willing to entertain, but one which he could not afford to overlook. Just because nobody liked her, or the possibility of traitors within their own organization, it didn't automatically mean the Queen of the Shadowmen was lying. One had to keep an open mind when seeking the truth.

There was a third possibility, that perhaps there existed a group from outside of the Guilds that had unlocked the secrets of High Magick. He doubted it. Much of his time was spent monitoring the half of the globe which fell under the influence of the Golden Path for such activities. Once detected, such groups or individuals were either recruited into the organization, monitored more thoroughly, or in rare cases eliminated if they proved to be too dangerous.

However, he knew it was his own pride which made him so reluctant to believe in this scenario. He was only human, and it could not be ruled out that despite his diligence such a group could have escaped his notice. What was even more possible was that his counterparts in the Temple of the Old Gods had failed in their duty to keep the unregulated magic users in check on their side of the planet. He often suspected they were not as dedicated as he was in this most sacred of duties.

Yes, if he could just coax the dead to give up their secrets, perhaps he could get to the bottom of this matter before war ravaged the planet once more.

Looking down upon the world from the windows of a jet always gave him a blissful feeling of serenity. Even at a time of great crisis such as this, the billowing expanse of silver clouds, here and there pierced by the tops of mountains, gave him peace of mind. *The natural world goes on,* he thought, *unaware and indifferent to the petty squabbles of mankind.* It was a comforting idea.

He set the jet down at a private airstrip owned by one of the Order's many shell companies. The car to take him to his hotel in Bern awaited him, where he would check in under his favorite alias, "Vihaan Patel." Since a state of war between the Golden Path and the rest of the Guilds was almost a certainty, using such an alias would be necessary should his Order's enemies decide to preemptively hunt down and eliminate known members of the Golden Path. He used the time on the road to study the local map. Having a firm idea of the Citadel's precise location relative to the hotel would facilitate teleporting to the Citadel from there.

The Citadel had been perched atop a high cliff in the Alps, a cliff which no longer existed. He would have to teleport to its new location at the bottom of that mountain and sift through its remaining tons of rock and masonry for corpses. Finding a human body that hadn't been completely pulverized in that mess seemed like a fool's errand. But with magic and a little bit of luck, all things were possible.

When he arrived, he felt as devastated as the ruined fortress that lay at his feet. Its blasted remnants lay strewn for miles, much of it unrecognizable as ever having been hewn by human hands. He did a quick meditation to clear his mind and help him focus, then pierced his thumb with his ceremonial dagger, making a small blood offering to one of the Gods to help guide him towards what he required: an intact human brain, specifically not one that belonged to a Shadowman, but to one of their attackers.

He stretched out his awareness and came to fixate upon a mound of rubble about a quarter mile from where he stood. Something told him that what he sought would be in that vicinity. He chanted a levitation spell to overpass the treacherous field of boulders and floated to the spot that had caught his attention. He cast another spell to one-by-one lift the wreckage around him into the air as well, soon being surrounded by a lazily floating thick cloud of twisted metal and chipped stone. Not a few of them hung red and brown with useless crushed flesh and bone.

The first few otherwise reasonably intact corpses he found were Shadowmen, their bodies preserved by a combination of where they had fallen, the armor they wore, and their unusually resilient biology. These were useless to him too, and he tossed them back to the ground with a gesture.

After two hours of searching, in the body of a black robed woman, he believed he had finally found what he was looking for. Anyone here who was not a Shadowman had to be an attacker as only Shadowmen were allowed inside its walls. While it was true his sources had reported that Director McDowell, the Chairman of the Inner Council of the International Conference of Guilds, had been there too – invited to witness the coronation ceremony for the new Queen, which had been interrupted by the attack – he was the rare exception, and in any event had escaped destruction along with the Queen.

His heart sank as he brought the shattered body closer. Half the skull was crushed. But it wasn't a total loss: he noted with great interest that the woman was Caucasian. Virtually every member of the Golden Path was of Asian descent, so this might help point the finger of blame away from them. He took a holographic photograph of the body before discarding it like the others he'd found. He also noted the body didn't have a pendant around its neck. The key piece of evidence Celine, the Shadowmen's Queen, had used against the Golden Path was a pendant she claimed to have torn off of one of her attackers which bore the insignia of his Order.

However, the Grand Inquisitor was too objective to think that the ethnicity of the woman he'd just unearthed, or her lack of a pendant linking her to the Golden Path, completely absolved his people of any involvement. The group of magic users who attacked the Shadowmen could easily be made up of a coalition of dissidents or radicals from both Great Houses of Magic.

With a sigh, he continued his grim search.

Another hour passed before he found another black robed body with an intact head. With excitement tempered by the need for care, he sent probing tendrils of energy into the skull and into the brain.

Yes, this one will do, he thought with relief, and gently dropped half a town's worth of rock and rubble from the air as he whispered a brief prayer of thanks to the God who had helped guide him to this body.

Then he began probing the man's brain for information.

The brain was almost entirely unspoiled. The cool temperature at this altitude, even in the middle of July, had helped preserve it, and the man had only been dead for a few hours.

That said, he couldn't resurrect the corpse. The spirits of magic users of this caliber automatically ascended to a level of the afterlife from which their spirits could not be recalled. However, he could still pull information directly from the flesh itself, like reconstructing data from a damaged computer hard drive. It was a delicate process, known only to a few.

He discovered names. "Knights of the New Order," that's what they called themselves, but he couldn't discern their goals or ideology. One name kept coming up repeatedly, though: "Justinian Long." Apparently this was the wizard who had recruited this dead man into that rogue order, a man named Clifford Brown. Both men were members of the Temple of the Old Gods, but it was unclear to the Inquisitor if they had acted with the official sanction of that group, or represented a splinter faction.

Justinian seemed to be one of the masterminds behind this group. Even more interestingly, according to Clifford's recent memories, Justinian was not himself present at the attack. And that meant he was almost certainly still alive.

The Inquisitor would have to pay him a visit.

He searched the pockets of the corpse's robes for other clues, but the only other artifact was a spherical stone used to communicate over long distances. He took it with him, it could prove useful. It might even be "primed" to call one that belonged to Justinian.

The Inquisitor recorded the body like he had the first one. Then he used a spell to sever the head and placed it inside an enchanted bag for preservation. He might be asked to present the information stored inside as evidence later.

Upon teleporting back to his room, his first act was to open his laptop and connect the modem to the phone line. Since Justinian Long was a member of the Temple of the Old Gods, he should be in the Guild personnel records the Inquisitor had access to.

He was wrong.

Access Denied to Unauthorized Personnel

He cursed a curse older than the Sphinx of Egypt. He had a bad feeling that he knew what this meant. He pulled out his own jade communications stone so he could be sure. He concentrated on the name of the person he wished to contact. Within moments the face of his aide, a young Chinese woman named Xian, appeared within the stone ball.

"Grand Inquisitor? How may I serve you?" she greeted him in M'bogish, the ancient common tongue.

"I can't get into the Guild Personnel files! Have they cut us off?"

"Yes. The trial by combat did not go well, and we have seceded from the Conference, as have most of our closest allies. The Guilds are now split along east/west lines," she reported as calmly as she could manage. "War is imminent. Our spies show that the rest of the Guilds are already assembling an army against us. For their own safety, everyone has been recalled back to the Eternal Palace, except for you. Your work has been deemed too important to interrupt."

The Inquisitor's mind reeled. This was exactly what he had feared was happening when he'd found himself locked out of the Guild records. The Inquisitor also wasn't convinced that recalling everyone in the Order (and presumably their allies and their immediate families) to the Eternal Palace was the soundest of strategies. Gathering all into a single place was dangerous, as the Shadowmen's fate proved. With a chill he realized this could be exactly what the unseen enemy was planning. He rejected the notion of sharing his worries, as it wouldn't be wise to question the wisdom of the Celestial Empress. He must have faith she had chosen the correct course of action.

"Is Arjun dead?" he asked haltingly. Arjun Dragonrider was a pompous ass and a womanizer, but he was still his cousin and he cared about his well-being.

"The Guilds think so, but the truth is he survived. Barely. The Shadowman Queen really tore into him. Magic is the only thing keeping him from dying. The Great Healer has been working on him for hours now. The Empress hopes she can use his survival as a legal loophole in later negotiations. Since it was supposed to be a fight to the death, we might be able to make an argument that while we didn't win, we also didn't lose. Our legal people are looking into that now."

"Thank the Gods he's alive!" The Inquisitor said. He usually didn't allow himself to show such emotion to his subordinates, but under the circumstances he didn't think it was too unwarranted.

"What about you? What progress have you made? Your mission is more important than ever now."

"I have the names of two of the terrorists behind the attack. One of them should still be alive and I'm hoping that the Orb is with him. That's why I was trying to get into the personnel files, so I could get more information on these people."

Her face brightened, and she signed with relief. "So good to finally get some good news!"

"Is the Red Spiral still allied with us?" The Red Spiral was a minor Guild made up of accomplished computer hackers based out of South Korea.

"Yes, they stand firm with the Golden Path."

"Good. Some time ago I had them install a backdoor into the Guild computer networks in case something like this should ever happen. I need you to let them know the time has come to use it."

Xian's eyes widened. "You anticipated this conflict?" She knew the Grand Inquisitor was legendary for his thoroughness, yet this seemed beyond even his abilities.

"Not the specifics. Yet the idea that the Guilds might split into Eastern and Western factions isn't without historical precedent, and remember, it almost happened as recently as during the last World War. You know how I feel about being prepared for any eventuality."

"I do indeed," she agreed with pride at being his assistant.

He went on. "The Red Spiral needs to get me the files on a man named Justinian Long, and another named Clifford Brown. Both are members of the Temple of the Old Gods. Also, have them scour the database for any references to a group called the Knights of the New Order. Xian, I need this information right away."

"I will pass along your request and get you the information as soon as possible, Grand Inquisitor."

He thanked her, and her face faded from the polished jade surface of the sphere as it dropped into his hand.

What followed next was a tense few hours as he waited for word from the Red Spiral. He ordered room service after carefully hiding the bag holding the severed head he'd brought back with him. Shortly after finishing his dinner, the sphere in his pocket grew warm.

He pulled it out and saw Xian's face again. "They found the information you wanted. Check your email," she told him.

He thanked her and severed the connection. He was pleased to see the files were indeed there. Unfortunately, the name "Knights of the New Order" had turned up no results, but he had known it was a long shot they would have been so stupid as to refer to themselves in any official computer files. However, it had been his hope that his counterparts in the

Temple of the Old Gods might have been aware of their existence and been keeping tabs on them

Either this was not the case, or they had already infiltrated high into that organization's power structure.

He opened the file on Clifford Brown but didn't find anything there of much note. He had been an unremarkable wizard leading an unremarkable life. What might have radicalized him was difficult to ascertain. He did note with some interest that his occupation was listed as being a junior associate to a midlevel assistant of the leader of the Temple of the Old Gods, the Pontifex Maximus.

Next he opened the file on Justinian Long. This file he found to be far more interesting. Some of the reasons for this had nothing to do with his investigation per se. The Grand Inquisitor had an interest in history. It was his firm belief that events moved in patterns, and one could discern the shape of future events if one trained their mind to recognize the patterns of the past. What was so interesting about Justinian was his family history. His clan claimed to be descended from Longinus, the ancient Roman soldier who was said to have pierced the side of Christ with a spear while he was on the cross.

In some Christian traditions, Longinus was revered as a saint, as it was said he had poor eyesight which was cured when stray drops of Christ's blood landed in his eyes. This miracle made him the first convert to Christianity.

The Inquisitor knew the true history, however. The man remembered by history as "Longinus," which wasn't even his actual name, was no saint. Far from it. At that time, the Roman Empire was dominated by the Temple of the Old Gods. Upon occasion their members openly reigned as Emperor, but they preferred to work behind the scenes, exerting influence from the shadows. Although they would later figure out a way to use Christ's ministry to their advantage, at the time when he was actually alive they considered him to be a troublemaker and a threat. "Longinus" had been sent by them to make sure Jesus died before his followers could remove him from where he'd been crucified while he was still alive. Later on, when some Christians venerated Longinus as a saint, his descendants adopted the surname "Longinus" to cement their connection to him since it was now politically advantageous for them to do so. In time, this name had been shortened simply to "Long."

According to the file, Justinian and his family were particularly proud of their ancient Roman lineage. *Does this pride extend to a longing for the days when the Temple of the Old Gods had openly dominated the Western world?* the Inquisitor wondered.

He knew some within the Temple had harbored such sentiments. Only a few years earlier, there had been those who argued for the organization to tighten its waning control over the mundane world. The most notorious amongst them was a radical named Dexter Sinister who had gone so far as to try and assassinate the then Pontifex Maximus and take his place using dark magic. His plot had been discovered and foiled just in time, and as far as the Inquisitor knew he was still rotting in a prison cell somewhere. It had always been suspected that Sinister had co-conspirators, but none were ever found.

Which of course didn't mean that they didn't exist.

A few other things in Justinian's file jumped out. He tested unusually high in psychic aptitude tests and was particularly gifted in reading minds. Also, up until a few months ago, he had been attached to the Temple of the Old Gods' delegation to Guild HQ, serving under Wendy Sommardahl. She was a witch the Inquisitor knew personally from when she lived inside the Eternal Palace as part of a cultural exchange program between the Great Houses of Magic. It was difficult for him to imagine she might be mixed up in all of this.

Justinian's current assignment was also as an aide to the current Pontifex Maximus, Gareth Grimwade. This was how he'd been able to recruit Brown. The idea of two terrorists working so closely with the leader of the Temple of the Old

Gods was troubling, especially given Justinian's talent for reading minds.

Even if Grimwade himself was not part of this conspiracy, the terrorists would be privy to all kinds of sensitive information they shouldn't have access to. The government of the Temple wouldn't be able to do anything without them knowing about it beforehand. Even if they were aware of their existence, they certainly wouldn't be able to move against them without tipping them off.

The more he thought about it, the more convinced he became that this entire incident was a power grab by these Knights of the New Order. They framed the Golden Path for the destruction of the Shadowmen and the theft of the Orb so the Western Guilds would eliminate the Golden Path and its allies for them. He wouldn't be surprised if the Western Guilds conveniently "found" the Orb so they could use it against them in the upcoming battle. In the aftermath of such a war, there would be only one Great House of Magic left: the Temple of the Old Gods. And if they got control of the Orb again, the other remaining Guilds would be powerless to stop them if they decided to exert their dominance over the planet once again.

It all made a twisted kind of sense, but it was just a theory. He needed more evidence to confirm such potentially explosive revelations before he could present his findings.

That meant tracking down Justinian and taking him prisoner if possible.

The records listed his current address as his family estate on Elysium, the Aegean island that was the homeland of the Temple of the Old Gods.

That meant the inquisitor could not reach him there, at least not *physically*. The place would be protected by an energy shield, given the current crisis, but it would serve as no barrier to his astral self. Other magic users could see astral bodies, but he had a little known spell which would conceal him. He could spy on Justinian and perhaps learn where he could obtain more solid evidence, maybe even discover where the Orb was hidden away. Getting control of it was the only thing that could protect his people in the coming war.

The Inquisitor placed himself in a deep trance. His spirit rose from his physical body, attached by a golden umbilical cord. Then he performed the spell that rendered the cord, and his astral form, invisible to all.

He sailed through the wall of his hotel room and into the spreading cloak of the night. It was possible to travel quickly in astral form if you knew your destination well enough, and he knew Elysium. It was not on any nautical charts, and thick cloud banks perpetually obscured it from view, but he knew how to find it. He had been there several times in the past for diplomatic purposes. In his astral body, he'd be there soon enough, even though it was hundreds of miles away from his hotel room.

As he'd expected, the entire island was indeed surrounded by a glowing green magical force field. A field of such immense size was difficult to maintain. There had to be a host of magic users scattered around the island all working in unison to keep it up. In either case, such barriers only kept out physical objects, and he passed through it effortlessly.

Elysium was a hilly island dominated by a large, ancient castle at its center. It was the executive palace of the Pontifex Maximus, and the seat of government.

An airfield stretched beside the castle, and small fishing villages sprung up here and there along the jagged coastline. Many wide, rolling fields served as vineyards, which were in turn dotted with farm buildings and dominated by impressive villas where the oldest and most elite families in the Temple of the Old Gods held court.

The Inquisitor hoped he would find Justinian in one of these villas, and had the address memorized, but was hardly familiar enough with the residential areas of the island for it to be of much use to him.

It took far too long to find the correct home, hours wasted flitting through the walls of the large mansions looking for his target or listening out for some mention of him. When he finally found him, it was in a home deliberately designed to look like it had been built in ancient Rome.

From what he'd read in Justinian's file, it was the man's grandfather who had become particularly obsessed with this aspect of the family's long history and built this place to reflect his tastes. It was a fixation which he had obviously passed onto the successive generations, as Justinian's bedroom was adorned with a large painting of the handsome, blonde-haired man dressed in the purple finery of a Roman Emperor which dominated the whole room. The Inquisitor found it to be a particularly tacky piece of artwork, and it did nothing to dissipate his suspicions about the man and his ambitions.

It wasn't the only thing the Grand Inquisitor found to be distasteful. The man was passed out in a huge bed, naked, empty bottles of the native wine lying about him.

He wasn't alone, either. A pair of attractive young ladies were bound up with him in the satiny sheets. The Inquisitor shook his head at the decadence these Western magic users often displayed. Justinian had been celebrating something tonight, and it angered the Inquisitor to think it was because he believed all of his plans for the Knights of the New Order were coming to fruition.

Still, it was fortunate that he'd found him in this state. A man with Justinian's psychic gifts might have been difficult to pry any information out of while he was conscious. Indeed, despite the precautions the Inquisitor had taken to conceal his presence, Justinian might have detected him and overwhelmed his own mental defenses.

In his present state, however, he was exquisitely vulnerable, and the alcohol might also work to dull his abilities. The Inquisitor could slip into the man's dreams and try to extract the information he needed, and he formulated a plan to do so. The man had a great deal of vanity and weakness for the ladies, and the Inquisitor endeavored to turn both characteristics to his advantage.

The Inquisitor plunged into the head of Justinian and disappeared inside, finding himself on a marble balcony. Justinian, a carbon copy of the gaudy painting, was smiling while waving to a massive crowd in the streets below. "Hail Justinian! Imperious Rex!" they howled up at him in mindless adulation.

He really does take all this Roman stuff far too seriously, doesn't he? the Inquisitor thought with some bemusement.

Insinuating oneself into someone else's dreams always incurred some risk. People eventually tended to pick up on the fact you weren't a product of their own psyche. On the positive side, magic users knew that Gods, as well as spirits of ancestors, often used this method as a way of communicating and were more accommodating as a result.

In any event, It was the Inquisitor's fervent hope the wine had dulled his target's perception to the point he wouldn't figure out the Inquisitor didn't belong until it was too late.

The Inquisitor remade himself to appear to be a beautiful TV reporter, accompanied by a cameraman. That should do for the man's vanity.

"Most impressive, your Imperial Majesty!" the reporter said, while presenting the microphone to the man of the hour. "Would you care to share the story of your remarkable rise to power with our audience? The people are simply clamoring to know all the details of your brilliant plans."

Justinian flinched and turned. A shocked, suspicious look darkened his face, but it rapidly beamed into an indulgent smile as he took in the camera's lens and drank in her curvaceous features.

"I would be happy to!" he replied and turned to the people with his arms spread magnanimously. "Let it never be said that I am not a man of the people! The people will get what the people want! What they deserve! What they *need* under my benevolent reign!"

The people below roared back their approval.

Justinian turned back the Inquisitor, taking the microphone into his hands and running a few fingertips through his hair. "I suppose I must give some of the credit to Grimwade. It was his vision to begin with, him and Dexter

Sinister. They saw what a mess of things everything had become in the centuries since we gave up so much control over the world. Pollution, global warming. The threat of nuclear war. Our ancestors gave these people everything! *We* built the civilization they enjoy, and once we set them off the leash, they used their freedom to create a hundred different ways to destroy it! Too much freedom inevitably leads to chaos. They have proven they are unfit to master their own destiny. Too many voices rending the world in countless different directions. No, what the people truly need is a singular vision, a firm hand to guide them and keep them safe. What better hand than ours? We have done it before and we can do it again! Sinister was too impulsive and it got him caught. But Grimwade was smarter. He pretended to be one of them, and got elected to office. Then he surrounded himself with people who shared his vision. People like me."

The Inquisitor nodded and thrust her chest out. "Yes, the Knights of the New Order. But how exactly did they take control? What was the plan?"

Justinian's eyes drooped then returned as he licked his lips. "There's a man Grimwade made friends with, a boorish American idiot that calls himself Father Steve. He looks like Jesus, and used that superficial resemblance to create a cult around himself. Grimwade realized we could use our magic to make it appear that he was Christ reborn, to trick the world into bowing down to him, and rule it in his name. It's a brilliant idea. Remember the story of Abraham and Issac? A man was willing to kill his own son because God commanded it! People can commit the most monstrous atrocities if they believe they are doing the will of God and serving the greater good. With the right justification, the means always justify the ends. Give them a God they can see, hear and touch! Blind faith can never trump blind loyalty. Those who did not believe would come around in time, would be unable to deny the proof of his divinity that we would create for them."

"Yes, brilliant!" The Inquisitor said, parting her lips and toying with her hair over her shoulder.

"The plan required that we eliminate the other Guilds, since they would never let us get away with it. We couldn't do that without first getting control of the Orb that the Shadowmen guard. It was my job to recruit a Shadowman to aid us, to use my telepathic skills to probe the minds of the members of their delegation at Guild HQ to find someone we could tempt into helping us. What luck that Celine, the very heir to their throne, proved to be our best candidate!"

If the Inquisitor had been holding the mic, he would have dropped it. *The Shadowman Queen herself was part of this conspiracy? She willingly participated in the destruction of her own people?*

"Why would she want to help you?"

Justinian flashed a predatory smile. "She's a miserable creature. I've been inside her mind, it's most unpleasant. Filled with nothing but regrets and self-loathing. She hates what her father has turned her into, a barely human, freakish killing machine. She wants revenge on them all, and most of all, she wants to be human again. We promised her we could do that for her with our magic."

"She helped you to steal the Orb?"

"Yes. We broke Sinister out of prison, and he used his peculiar talent for possessing people's bodies to steal the identity of a Shadowman. Some old boyfriend Celine had a grudge against. In any event, in that guise Sinister infiltrated the Citadel and took the Orb. Once it was safely out of the fortress, my best men swooped in to kill the Shadowmen. I was in charge of that entire operation. I recruited and hand-picked the entire team." For a moment, his eyes became distant. "Unfortunately, we lost all of them when the Shadowmen blew up their own Citadel. Though it made covering our tracks that much easier."

That's what you think, monster! the Inquisitor thought angrily. This man could have no honor, no loyalty whatever save to his own ego, if he could throw lives away so casually.

Justinian wasn't done bragging yet. "Then we had Celine escape and accuse the Golden Path with cleverly manufactured evidence. They would deny everything of course, and Celine would force them to settle the matter by trial by combat. They'd lose, and their insufferable pride would prevent them from accepting the verdict, bringing about the civil war within the Guilds we desired."

The Inquisitor couldn't keep up the flirty act, and Justinian, couldn't seem to care. "Weren't you taking an awful risk with the trial by combat? A Shadowman against a magic user? What if she lost?"

Justinian laughed. "Have you *seen* her in action? She's unstoppable, even for someone with my talents. But we left nothing to chance. We had people hidden among the spectators ready to tilt things in her favor if necessary. As it turned out, it was an unnecessary precaution."

Nakedly pumping him for information, the Inquisitor asked, "This is all so very fascinating, your Imperial Excellency! Please, tell us what happened next?"

"The Guilds attacked the Eternal Palace with their army of mercenaries. They had the Orb with them, to ensure the Golden Path couldn't use their magic to defend themselves. We made sure it was conveniently "found" right before the battle, Sinister hid it with enough clues to lead them to it. Then, once the armies of the Guilds and the Golden Path were all in one place – once the Eternal Palace was breached – *Wham!* We destroyed them all with a *single* missile launched from a nearby submarine. Then we did the same thing to

Guild HQ too, and launched the damned Orb into outer space so it could never be used against us!"

The Inquisitor fought to conceal his anger, wanting to throttle this vile man more than every foul creature ever encountered in his entire life. Even though he wasn't physically there, he could still do it. There were ways he could shut down this man's body from where he was inside of his mind.

He wouldn't do it though. There were still things he needed to understand.

For one, how much of this had already come to pass? Justinian was speaking in the past tense, like it had all already happened. He'd certainly been partying as if he'd already achieved all of his goals, but surely in this dream world he was just picturing himself in the future . . .

"But how did you become Emperor? Surely, Grimwade saw himself in that role?" he asked.

"Grimwade! The fool wants to rule from behind the scenes, denying himself the glory of ruling openly! When the time is right, I will – I mean, I *did* take control from him. I recruited most of the Knights, with my ability to read their hearts - I alone knew who could be trusted. They owe their loyalty to me, not him! Steve is an idiot and easy to control. I will – I *did* – have him declare me Emperor of the World, his chosen representative here on Earth, to rule in his stead. In time, I will eliminate him too. When a public appearance cannot be avoided, I'll masquerade as him. It's a trivial thing to use magic to make myself look like him. There is no need to suffer his foolishness forever!"

The fact Justinian was sounding more confused and mixing up his tenses confirmed for the Inquisitor what he feared most. The only part of the plan that had likely not yet come to pass was this final part, where Justinian betrays the Pontifex Maximus and replaces him.

But if that was true, did that mean he, the Inquisitor, had already failed in his task? Had the Golden Path *already* been destroyed? Being in astral form distorted the passage of time, but surely not enough time had passed for all these things to have already come to pass?

He was seized with a consuming need to get out of here, to see for himself. True, he had no real evidence aside from the testimony he could give of what Justinian had told him, but it would have to do for now. He knew who the enemy was and what their plans were. He had to get this vital information to his people before it was too late! If it wasn't too late already. Not only for his people, but the other Guilds too. They'd all been manipulated, and this entire war was a sham to trick them into destroying one another.

But there was the problem of Justinian. Surely, he should kill the man now, this man whose ambitions made him far too dangerous to be allowed to live. And he already had so much blood on his hands! This warred with the possibility of capturing him later and getting him to confess everything in front of the proper authorities. If he killed him now, he'd destroy the very evidence he needed. Justinian also likely knew the names of all the other conspirators and could be made to give them up.

No, he'd let him live for now, but promised himself there would be a day of reckoning, a day when this man was dragged before the authorities and forced to pay for his crimes.

That's assuming there will be any authorities left when that day comes . . .

"Well? Nothing to say? No more questions? I suppose you must be so overwhelmed by the genius of my schemes that you've been left completely speechless, eh?"

"Oh, shut up!" the Inquisitor replied, no longer able to hide his contempt. The last thing he saw of Justinian was the man's shocked face as he left the man's nasty little mind and rose up through the ceiling out of the house.

In his astral form, the Grand Inquisitor flew as quickly as he could in the direction of the Eternal Palace. Once there, he would reveal himself and tell them everything he knew. He had to stop this war. If it wasn't already too late!

It *was* too late.

Devastated, the Inquisitor hung above the crater which once was the Eternal Palace. Fires still burned, belching thick ebon columns of smoke into the sky which stretched for miles. Millennia of history, all destroyed in mere moments! It was too much to bear.

This must have happened only hours before in real time, which for him was minutes. Rescue and recovery crews were still searching through the wreckage, based upon ships anchored offshore and assisted by the black, featureless helicopters favored by the Guilds.

Desolately, he scanned the devastation hoping for survivors, but knew there would be none.

It did nevertheless buoy his spirits that something of the Guilds seemed to have survived. For a moment he considered going to them, to warn them of what was coming, but then thought better of it. His home was gone now. His entire life, his entire world. He could care about nothing, much less those who considered him an enemy.

He screamed. A great, primal howl rising from the depths of his being. Yet, in his astral form, no one could hear it.

He had failed. His people were gone. The Celestial Empress, a Goddess to him, was gone. Xian, his loyal assistant, was ashes. His entire family, everyone he had ever known or cared for, all gone. He had found the truth, but he'd found it too late, so what value did it have? None, it was all meaningless. Everything was meaningless.

This was the only truth which mattered: death. *Death* was the only thing that was real. It surrounded him. How he longed for it to take him away too, to erase all his pain, to make him not care about what had happened or about anyone or anything ever again.

He considered joining his brethren, but it was never really an option, he knew that. *No.* He still had one duty left to perform.

The last of the Golden Path, as long as he drew breath it was not truly extinct. They could live again someday through him.

As far as he knew he was all which remained of the sacred bloodline of the Celestial Empress, it was his highest priority to ensure that it didn't die out. He'd never taken a wife, or even enjoyed the comfort of a woman. He had been too married to his duty. Now however it *was* his duty to create a family, to pass on what he knew of the history and traditions of his people. In time, perhaps he would search for other possible survivors, and to recruit new members.

But he would have to sacrifice a piece of his honor to survive. He of all people knew there existed a thriving black market for magic users like him, as after all it had once been his job to suppress it. Now, he would turn mercenary and sell his skills to the highest bidder to build a secure financial future for the new family and reborn Order he planned to create.

In time the Golden Path would return, and when they did, they would tear down this rotten new order that was being planned for the world! But that was then, this was now. Vengeance would come in its own time. Today, his only duty was to live.

He set aside his grief and rose towards the first brilliant rays of dawn, to return to his physical body. There was much he needed to do.

The Golden Path *would* rise again. He would make sure of it!

ODIN'S BACKSCRATCHER

Part One: Astral Mapping

*R*andy's *late again*, thought Wendy Sommardahl.

Her astral body sat perched upon the capstone of one of the many megalithic stones which jutted from the ground in regular intervals at Carnac. She wasn't particularly upset by the lack of punctuality displayed by her apprentice, though she mused someone else in her position might find it nigh on a crime to keep the Pontifex Maximus of the Temple of the Old Gods waiting. It was, after all, one of the oldest and most powerful organizations on Earth, but Wendy wasn't your typical Pontifex Maximus. She was more laid back and less hung up on formalities than her predecessors. Just as well, considering the last person to hold her job had turned out to be an evil mastermind with plans to take over the world.

She was quite happy to break with most of their traditions.

Besides, her apprentice had much farther to travel than she did. It was unfortunate there was no convenient halfway point for them to meet . . . unless they were going to try and find each other in the middle of the Atlantic Ocean, which would be rather challenging, considering the lack of available landmarks. Or land, for that matter.

She did love this place though, so contented herself with relaxing and watching the view from atop the dolmen. It was the reason she had chosen this for their meetings in the first place.

Soon enough, Randy's ghostly astral form flew toward her from the horizon. As he came closer, she shook her head, bemused. He had taken to customizing the appearance of his astral body so he was dressed like someone named "Tuxedo Mask," a character he was fond of in some cartoon from Japan. As far as Wendy was concerned, it made him look like some cheesy stage magician. But it made him happy, and was perfectly harmless, so she allowed it.

She lifted off her perch and flew up to meet him.

"Apprentice," she greeted.

"Mistress," he said reverently.

"You're late again," she teased. "Don't you know it's not nice to keep a lady waiting?"

"I'm sorry!" he replied quickly, his face flushed. "Penny had a really cool idea for a new song. I was helping her with it, and I guess I lost track of time."

Penny was Randy's girlfriend, and also his partner in the band currently called "Lung Collapse." *Currently*, because the name seemed to change every other day. Wendy wasn't terribly surprised Penny had been distracting her apprentice this way. She was a prolific songwriter if not a particularly skilled one, in Wendy's opinion. The girl was forever jotting down lyrics in notebooks, or composing bits of music on a small Casio keyboard she carried around with her. The band had only been together for a few months, and already they had enough material for several albums.

Wendy regarded her apprentice. She considered herself lucky to have him as her student, truly, and not only because his high intellect and natural aptitude for magic made him more skilled than more experienced wizards. Nor was it that he was the reincarnation of one of the planet's greatest ancient philosophers – something Wendy divined given her rare skill to see into the past lives of anyone she met. Yet, for all that, he remained charmingly unaware of how important this all made him.

No, what she prized the most about Randy was his earnestness. The boy wore his heart on his sleeve, and even after almost two years as her apprentice, he still wanted so desperately to please her.

"Oh relax! I'm just messing with you!" she said with a slap on his shoulder. "I'm in no particular rush. I could be happy just hanging out here all day, it's so beautiful. And so full of the power of Mother Gaia. Can you feel it?" She gave him a beatific smile. A sincere one.

He returned it, shyly. "Of course I can. But you can't just hang out here all day! You're the Pontifex Maximus, and you have so many official duties. Plus you're a wife now, and a mother. I don't know how you manage it all! It was rude of me to waste your time like that."

She did have many duties. It wasn't easy trying to rebuild her organization into something kinder and gentler than what it had once been, but she had built a great team of aides to help with all that, and honestly, they were the ones who did most of the work. She provided them with direction when needed, and put her official stamp of approval on things. It gave her time to see to her new family, and to train her apprentice.

"Forget it," she said with an indulgent shrug. "You're never a waste of my time. Nor is coming here, for a matter of fact. It keeps me grounded and connected to the world outside the Temple." She pulled something from her beaded purse and tossed it casually in his direction. "Here. Catch!"

He caught the thin, flat, oval-shaped stone handily. Arcane symbols ringed the edges of its polished surface. A Wayfinder Stone (or, more accurately, an astral copy of the physical one held in Wendy's real purse), it was a device used in ancient times to display maps that were magically stored inside. In other words, a prehistoric GPS. Such artifacts were rare nowadays, but as Pontifex Maximus, Wendy had access to many such treasures.

This Wayfinder Stone was special. It could not only display maps, but *record* them, and whatever was recorded by the astral version of the stone would automatically be transmitted to its real-world equivalent once the two were reunited.

This was the purpose of their meeting, to make maps. But not maps of just any old places – rather, maps of the Afterlife.

Two years earlier, Wendy's mind had been telepathically linked with that of her friend Autumn, when Autumn was murdered. In her horror and confusion, Autumn's mind had instinctively called out to Wendy for help. With a shiver, Wendy recalled what it had been like. She'd seen it, *felt* it all, through Autumn's eyes, experiencing the pain and terror of her death as if it had been her own.

Unbidden, the memory replayed in her mind as if it had happened yesterday. Autumn's blood flowed between cold cobblestones. The awful sound of her labored and ragged breaths, awful until the silence of their terrible end.

Wendy pulled herself together long enough to help Autumn recite the mantra that would usher her soul to the mysterious part of the Afterlife their people called "the Summerlands," or "the Next Level." As Autumn's soul ascended, Wendy lost all sense of her body. She unexpectedly was carried along for the journey and, filled with equal parts panic and wonder, she couldn't let go.

If their minds had continued to remain connected much longer, Wendy would have perished too. Thankfully, a newly apprenticed Randy had been present and sensed something was wrong. He saved her by severing the mental connection just in time. But the incident had forever left its mark upon her, not only psychologically, but physically as well – leaving a long shock of silver hairs permanently flowing through her otherwise flame red locks.

Since that time, Wendy had become obsessed with exploring the Afterlife realms. A large variety of them existed, one for virtually every kind of spiritual belief system held by humanity. They were created and shaped by the collective psychic power of all the people who believed in the existence of these places, as were the Gods who presided over them. Magic users could travel to these places while still alive, and had been for millennia, usually in order to cut deals with the Gods who resided there. Yet in all that time no comprehensive attempt had been made to map out these astral realms.

So Wendy had taken it upon herself to do so, and she and Randy had been doing this for the past year and a half. She believed having Randy follow along on such adventures would be a good way for him to master the skills that would someday help him grow into an accomplished wizard.

Of course, this is what Wendy told herself, and how she rationalized it all. The truth of it was she was looking for a way back into the Summerlands. Souls that ascended to this part of the Afterlife upon death could remain there or choose someday to reincarnate.

So it was said, anyway. Very little was truly known about it. Most magic users trained their entire lives so they would go there when they died, instead of to the lower realms where various Gods fed off the prayers of followers like psychic vampires. However, death was the only known way to reach this level. Real death. It was not enough to project astrally into the Aether, which was the universe of psychic energy where the Afterlife realms existed.

Wendy experienced a taste of the Summerlands when she piggybacked there on Autumn's mind, a dizzying jumble of such disparate sounds and images her conscious mind couldn't process. It didn't make any logical sense to her, but it had left a clear impression of such peace and joy that yearning to return there bordered on obsession.

She couldn't shake it despite knowing that such an obsession, like most obsessions, was not healthy. While her position as Pontifex Maximus, her love for her wife April and her daughter Celine, and her mentorship to Randy were all quite fulfilling, they weren't *enough*. She needed something *more*. Something she couldn't quite *define*. Something which she had finally found, ever so momentarily, when her mind had been in the Summerlands.

She also wondered if there was something more to it. After all, *she'd* ordered her friend into the danger that had gotten her killed, and every day she wrestled with the consequences of that decision. And she missed her. Her sharp intelligence, her kindness and courage. She even missed her awful temper. Autumn never had been one to be trifled with.

Could that be what this was all about? To see her friend again, maybe even to apologize for getting her killed? How does one begin to even do that?

Yes, Wendy realized she wasn't being completely honest with herself, but went forward anyway, powerless before her desires. All she could do was follow through on them, to see this through to the end, wherever it might lead.

Randy's voice broke her from her reverie. "Are you okay, Mistress?"

"Huh?" she bobbled, but recovered quickly. "Oh yeah, sure! Just lost in my own head for a minute. You know how it is." She gave a laugh that came out like a snort. "We'd better get a move on."

Randy smiled in his ready earnestness. "Where are we headed to this time?"

She shrugged. "I was thinking maybe Asgard."

"Wow! Really?" he gushed, his face glowing pink with enthusiasm. "I've always wanted to go there, ever since I read my first Thor comic!"

She chuckled. "Don't get too excited. From what I'm told, those comics aren't particularly accurate. Some of the Norse Gods can be a bit crude at times, and the place isn't nearly as clean or pretty as you might expect." Many magic users had found the reality of Asgard to be quite underwhelming when compared to the comic book version. In fact, it was a common complaint amongst her people.

"I know that," Randy retorted without a trace of boastfulness. "I've read translations of some of the original sagas."

Wendy smiled to herself. *Of course you have!*

Though scarcely eighteen years old, Randy was well-read on an eclectic variety of subjects, even before he began training as a wizard. And it was something which never ceased to impress her. He chalked it up to being something of an insomniac, staying up all night reading whatever he could get his hands on.

"Then let's try and steer clear of the Gods if we can, although Balder *is* quite pleasant," she said. "This is strictly a reconnaissance expedition."

They always tried to steer clear of Gods on these trips, who tended to get annoyed whenever living souls strayed into their realms and weren't there to exchange a bit of worship for a favor from one of them. Pissing off a God was generally a bad idea, since they could extend their influence into the material world and tilt probabilities in or out of your favor.

Indeed, just the prior week the pair were unceremoniously ejected from Tlālōcān, the Aztec paradise, with strict orders never to return. This had come about because he had earned the ire of the rain God Tlaloc with an offhand comment, and the wrath of the rain God didn't end there. Whenever Randy stepped outside, it rained torrentially on him alone, for an entire week.

Whereas once the power to make it rain would have been seen as a blessing, apparently this God was savvy enough to realize what an inconvenience this was outside of an agrarian society. Tlaloc eventually grew bored with the game and stopped his persecution of the young wizard, for which Randy was eminently grateful, as the usual remedy was to pull out someone's heart.

"Shall I do the honors, then?" Randy asked her. They would open the magical portal that would take them into the Aether, known to non-magic-users as the famous tunnel of white light mentioned in so many near death experiences.

She nodded. "Go ahead. It's good practice for you."

Randy chanted the spell, and seconds later the vortex of white light appeared above them. For a moment their etheric bodies elongated like something out of a funhouse mirror before being sucked up inside.

When they emerged from the other side, Wendy looked about in annoyance. "Maybe I should have created the portal after all. You've dumped us out near the bottom of Yggdrasil!"

Yggdrasil, also called the World Tree, was an immense ash tree which connects all of the nine worlds of Norse mythology together. From now on, we're just going to call it the World Tree, because Yggdrasil is really quite difficult to say, isn't it? Wendy and Randy now hovered to the side of the great World Tree like a pair of gnats. Below them, three immense roots twisted off into unknown, dark depths.

Randy shrugged, not looking her in the eye. "Sorry. I guess I just wanted to see it for myself, after reading about it so much. Besides, I wasn't sure if you wanted to map the other 8 worlds too, or just Asgard."

She regretted snapping at him like she had and took a deep breath. She couldn't blame him for wanting to check it out. It *was* a truly awesome sight. This kind of curiosity was generally a good thing, she reminded herself, and not something she wanted to discourage. "It's okay. But remember, we're here just to map Afterlife realms, not the entire Norse cosmology! All well and good, I suppose. There's no harm in taking the scenic route. Follow me!"

Wendy launched her astral self up the side of the great tree's trunk at a fantastic speed, and Randy soon joined her. As they flew along, Randy realized with awe that what he took to be its bark was actually the scales of a dragon whose body wound tightly around the tree. A dragon so huge it made Godzilla seem like an amoeba! When they reached its head, it appeared to be sleeping, but stirred from its dreaming long enough to open one lazy, yellow eye. It was the size of an entire world and gazed emptily out at them. To the great serpent they would appear as dust motes if they were perceptible to it at all.

They flew on. Occasionally, they'd meet a continent-sized branch and have to fly around it. At the other ends of these branches, the planets hung like pieces of fruit. Wendy veered in the direction of the blue-jeweled one that was the astral representation of Earth. She slowed reverently to a stop above their world and pointed up to where a rainbow flowed to the planet from far above, connecting it with a distant point far in the distance.

With a smile, she said, "Let's take the short cut!" and shot off towards the rainbow.

"Is that really what I think it is?" Randy asked in astonishment, but Wendy was too far ahead to hear. *Could this be the Bifröst, the famous rainbow bridge to Asgard?*

When Randy caught up with her, landing beside her, he found the surface of the bridge propelled them forwards like a moving escalator. With a goofy grin he got down on his hands and knees and licked it. Then licked it again, looking thoughtful as he did so.

"What do you think you're doing?" she asked with one eyebrow raised.

Randy stood up. "Trying to see if I can taste the rainbow," he replied with a goofy grin.

Wendy shook her head. "You really are too much sometimes!"

"I know it's the first thing Penny will ask me when I tell her about all of this. I just want to be able to provide an accurate report."

"Sure, blame your weirdness on poor Penny who isn't even here to defend herself!" Wendy snorted out another laugh. "Well? How was it? What does it taste like?"

"Photons, I guess," Randy replied simply. Wendy wasn't quite sure how to respond to this, so she didn't.

They stood in silence as the *Bifröst* conveyed them forward at impossible speeds, and soon a new world loomed ahead. It looked very much like the Earth, but with different land masses, and cartoonishly large mountains.

Wendy leaned in. "We won't stay on the *Bifröst* much longer. When we get closer, we'll have to jump off and fly the rest of the way. Otherwise Heimdall might spot us."

Randy nodded. "I've been worried about him."

"Relax, he's not really that hard to get past. My own teacher used to sneak in here all the time."

"Have you ever been here before?"

"He brought me here once, a long time ago," she answered wistfully. "You'd better prime the Wayfinder Stone. We're almost there."

Randy retrieved the stone from his jacket pocket and chanted over it, waving his hands in a particular pattern, then touched some of the arcane symbols carved around its edges. They glowed as he touched each one.

Soon, it was done. "It's ready," he reported. From now until he stopped it, the Wayfinder Stone would record the environment all around them for a radius of several miles.

Ahead, near the base of a massive mountain, was the end of the *Bifröst*. Here it appeared as an expansive bridge. Next to that sat the huge gleaming golden building named Himinbjörg, the great hall of the God who guarded it, Heimdall.

"Now!" Wendy cried and lifted off into the sky. She veered off to the left of the bridge, climbing very high above it. Randy struggled to keep up with his more experienced mentor.

Wendy landed to one side of the bridge's terminus, into a wide-open meadow of tall gently swaying grasses. Animals grazed nearby.

Her brow furrowed. "Where did all these animals come from? They weren't around the last time I was here. Sheesh! Heimdall's really slipping!" She spread her hands, indicating for Randy the unbelievable variety of animals which milled about. Mostly dogs and cats, but also every variety of horses and birds, and – most odd of all – fish which swam through the very air itself. One brightly colored thumb-sized fish passed tranquilly past her nose.

Randy scratched his head for a moment, then snapped his fingers. "I think I've got it! All these animals are pets!"

"Uh, yeah. So?" Wendy replied. "I still don't understand."

"Haven't you ever heard anyone say something about how their pet has 'crossed over the rainbow bridge' when they died?"

She stared at him blankly. "Really? Is that a thing now?"

"Totally!"

"Even with Christians?" This seemed like a very Pagan kind of thing to her.

Randy nodded.

"Jews too?"

"My Aunt Bernice said it when her iguana passed away," he affirmed.

"Wow!" Wendy didn't know which aspect of this she found more baffling: that Randy's beloved aunt had owned an iguana, or that this distinctly Pagan idea had recently been embraced by the adherents of different religions.

"You've really never heard this saying before?" Randy said, still a bit incredulous

"Not applied to pets, no."

Randy should not have been surprised. Wendy had spent so much time doing the work of the Temple of the Old Gods during her life that she had many unusual gaps in her knowledge of the mundane world. In fact, Randy was one of her few strong links to the regular world. As such, he often spent as much time educating her on how normal people lived as she did teaching him how to use magic.

"Well, these can't possibly be these people's *real* pets. Those animals' spirits would go on evolving, so they wouldn't get stuck here. These are obviously just astral copies created and placed here by the expectations of their owners."

Wendy had already explained to him how – unlike the spirits of most humans, whose faith beliefs often caused them to get trapped in the Afterlife realms that corresponded to those beliefs – the spirits of animals automatically reincarnated, their consciousnesses becoming more sophisticated with each new incarnation.

"I suppose so," Randy said, filing this for later. "So where to now?"

"If memory serves me correctly, there are three distinct areas of Asgard where the dead can go. Hel is one. Odin's hall, Valhalla, is another. Then there's Fólkvangr." She tapped her chin pensively when saying each one.

"*Fólkvangr?* I don't remember that one!"

"Don't feel so bad, almost nobody ever does who isn't an expert or an adherent of the old Norse religion. Yet, it's where fully half of the Norse who died in battle go. I guess it doesn't get remembered so much because it's presided over by the Goddess Freyja, who tends to get overshadowed by Odin."

"It's the damned patriarchy at work again!" Randy said, outraged. Wendy chuckled. He had just started taking classes at Rutgers University, and one of them was a Women's Studies course. He had been quick to embrace what he was learning in this class, which Wendy *did* suppose was a good thing, but in her opinion, he could overdo it a bit when it came to showing off what a strong ally he was.

"Yeah, probably," she agreed. "Anyhow, my thought was to check out Fólkvangr first. It shouldn't be very far from here."

"Sounds like a plan. Lead the–*hey*! Lead the way," he said, distracted by a chinchilla scampering over his foot.

"Try to keep up!" Wendy smiled as she blasted off into the air again, knocking several colorful fish aside as she did so.

"You mean like this?" Randy replied as he appeared in front of her in the blink of an eye.

"No fair moving at the speed of thought! You're cheating!"

Wendy laughed. Secretly, she was impressed and pleased to see Randy had mastered this skill. It was possible for someone in the Aether to be able to immediately move to a particular point ahead of themselves so long as they could see it, or picture it clearly enough in their mind at the instant they conceived of the notion of doing so.

"Cheating? No such thing! I prefer to think of it as "creative problem solving!"

"Oh! I like that! I need to write that one down for later." Wendy always threatened to write down new phrases or slang terms she found to be clever and use them to spice up her future dialogue. She never actually did, though sometimes some of them found their way out of her mouth anyway.

Wendy was quite correct; they had been close to Fólkvangr. In no time at all, they found themselves soaring above another wide-open meadow which stretched for countless miles. It was inhabited with large tents erected throughout the fields, and bright banners fluttered nearby. Between the tents people engaged in all manner of games: mock combats, or simply lounging about. It had the feel of being like one immense army camp from the Dark Ages.

It wasn't always easy to tell what was happening below since they always flew so high above the clouds to evade detection. Randy held the Wayfinder Stone out in front of him towards the ground as they moved over the realm.

"Seems pleasant enough down there," Wendy said, as she floated along beside him on her back, her hands cupped behind her head.

"And dull!" Randy complained.

"There is that," she allowed. "We'll head to Valhalla next. There's usually something interesting going on in there."

And so it was, when they had passed over the entirety of Fólkvangr, Wendy led them over a steep range of jagged mountains. Every so often Randy spotted a giant or two milling around as they made their way through the range. On the other side of the mountains sat a city of long, low buildings encircled by a high wall, and in the center had been erected a huge fortress atop a hill. Its pristine white stones gleamed in the evening sun.

It reminded Randy of art by Jack Kirby, the artist who co-created the most infamous comic book version of Thor and his world. *Maybe not as awesome as a Jack Kirby drawing, but still pretty impressive!* Randy found himself thinking.

The two descended toward the city and touched down in a muddy alleyway between two long houses.

Randy, holding his nose, discovered something else impressive about this city. "What is that terrible smell?"

"Poop, mostly," Wendy replied, not seeming bothered by it at all. "The past was a very stinky place, Randy. Livestock and beasts of burden running all over the place, relieving themselves on everything. Humans too, since there was a lack of plumbing in many eras. Regular bathing wasn't always in vogue for the same reasons. Don't worry, your nose will adjust, or you can just shut down your astral body's sense of smell if it's too much for you. I have."

"Yeah, but we're not in the past, so why does it stink?"

"Most of the dead people who reside here came from the past, so they imagined a world that would be familiar to them."

Randy blew out a breath as if to try to clear out his nose, but, if the look on his face was any guide, it only made things worse. "So, they made their idea of Heaven reek? What kind of people do that?"

"These people. Most people. People like what they're used to. It's comforting to them. They freak out if things are too alien." She sniffed. "I *did* warn you that it wasn't going to be what you expected."

"Some of the other places we've visited have been a little, um, *fragrant*, too, but nothing like this! Why is this place so much worse?"

"Vikings like to party a little hardier than most. And remember, these are warriors. There's a generous helping of blood and vomit mixed in there too. Other than that, they were surprisingly clean compared to many other peoples of the era. They had outhouses in cities like this and actually bathed at least once a week." Her eyes flashed and her voice hardened. "Seriously, just turn off your nose already! I'm getting tired of hearing you whine about it."

Randy drew back and apologized. "Sorry, Mistress."

He turned off his nose and felt better immediately. The ability to dull or completely turn off a particular sense was a nice perk of being in an astral body as opposed to a physical one. An astral body was really nothing more than a collection of ideas about yourself, and thus could be controlled more precisely.

With one more annoyed glance cast at him, Wendy moved past him to peer around the corner of the building, her feet squelching with each muddy step. Randy followed close behind, and looked too. Down the street was the entrance to

Valhalla, and a pair of armored Valkyries brandishing spears stood before the hefty wooden doors.

"There are guards. How will we get in?" he whispered.

"Technically we don't have to go in. At this range, the Wayfinder Stone can map it from out here. But even though it's a little risky, I thought you might like to take a quick peek inside, since we've come all this way?"

His eyes danced. "Definitely!"

"I thought so," she said with a bright smile. "But getting in will be easier than you might imagine. Think *astrally*. These aren't real walls, but instead are the *idea* of walls, remember? We'll first disguise ourselves with a glamour spell, and then walk in through one of the walls."

His brow furrowed. "If anyone can just walk through the walls, why bother with posting guards?"

"As I said, these people live in the world they're used to. Most here don't realize the same physical laws they're used to no longer apply, so they keep doing what they've always done. Think of it as a deficit of imagination. Are you ready to go into Viking mode?"

"Sure," he replied, with a mixture of excitement and skepticism.

With that, Wendy performed a "glamour," a low-level spell to temporarily alter one's appearance. Since they were in their astral forms, they could alter their appearance with a thought, but such a spell would be necessary to fool a God in case they ran into one while in Valhalla. When she was done, Randy examined himself with a mirror that he imagined into existence. He sported a thick beard and his build had become broader and more muscular, and he was dressed in a long, shimmering shirt of silvery scale mail armor. A broadsword in a scabbard hung from his side on a belt. His black hair had grown and spilled all the way down his back. His characteristic glasses were missing.

"Nice! You can call me 'Sven the Skullcrusher!'" He laughed. He loved doing these kinds of spells, they were always so much fun.

"You look marvelous! Now you do me!" Wendy laughed back.

Randy performed the spell, and gone was the tall, willowy redhead she was. In her place stood a coppery-haired hulk of a man dressed in a dark leather jerkin with green leggings and brandishing a mean looking battle axe. Her purse became a roughly stitched backpack.

Randy offered her his mirror.

"Badass! You can call me 'Oyvind of Osterhagen,'" she said in a particularly terrible attempt at a Scandinavian accent and snorted as she giggled.

He shook his head, smiling. "I think we'll be okay so long as you don't try to use that accent with anyone we happen to run into."

She screwed up her face. "That bad, huh?"

"Worse." He confirmed.

They stepped out of the alley and approached Valhalla. Wendy led the way, trying to look as casual as possible as she moved off to one side of the main entrance. When they had walked just a few yards down along the wall, she checked if anyone was looking. With no one watching, she confidently pressed her hand on the wall once, then looked confused. And a second time.

Her brow furrowed. "Well, that's new."

"What?" Randy whispered.

"There's a magical barrier up that is preventing us from just walking through it. They're serious about security these days! Hang tight, I think I know a spell that can bypass it." She chanted the words of the spell and waved her arms and wiggled her finger in a way that would have seemed rather foolish to the uninitiated. The bizarre display ended in a glowing white oval of energy appearing on the wall beside her.

"Quickly! This hole won't last long!" she said as she darted through. Randy made to follow but was distracted by the sound of approaching feet. He turned to see a Valkyrie running toward them.

"Halt! What goes on here?" the Valkyrie cried.

"We've been spotted!" Randy declared, rooted to the spot until Wendy's muscular-appearing arm reached through the hole in the wall and pulled him through it. "Hey!" he protested and landed atop her on the other side.

They looked on in unison as the Valkyrie stopped on the other side of the hole, her eyes tracing its edges before she saw them. She was about to step into it when it disappeared.

Randy looked down into Wendy's eyes, their magical beards practically touching. "What's the chance she'll forget about us?" he asked miserably.

Before she could answer, the Valkyrie's voice boomed from the other side of the wall. "Valhalla has been breached! Intruders are inside!"

Randy disentangled himself from his teacher, and offered his hand to pull her up. "They're onto us! Maybe we should leave now?"

"We'll be fine!" she demurred, and sauntered off down the corridor after brushing herself off. "If they come for us, we can always just wake up, remember?"

Randy followed, mulling over what she said. Technically he wasn't here, and his body was back in his bedroom in North Brunswick, NJ. All he had to do was will himself into waking up and his spirit would snap itself back into his body. However, it was an inelegant way of coming out of the trance, and the few times he'd done it had left him feeling hung over for days afterwards.

No sooner had Wendy turned the corner when she came face to face with a particularly fierce looking Valkyrie, who brandished a spear pointed directly at Wendy's midsection. Wendy sighed, defeated. *I really was looking forward to showing him around this place.* She turned to Randy. "Randy, get ready to wake–"

A wide glowing net shot out of the tip of the spear and entangled them both, Wendy flinching against the magical webbing. "Awww shit!"

Randy's eyes closed, then opened again, this time in panic. "I can't wake up! Why isn't it working?"

"They must be using weapons they bought from Paradise," Wendy said through clenched teeth. She hadn't anticipated this, and kicked herself for failing to do so, even as a fog settled over her mind.

Paradise was another Afterlife realm where the people had developed a more scientific understanding of the Aether. Their scientists used this knowledge to create powerful weapons that could ensnare or even destroy a spirit. They then sold these weapons to their neighbors in exchange for Ambrosia, which were concentrated packets of psychic energy generated by prayer. They served as a kind of universal currency in the Aether.

The Valkyrie was joined by another who appeared from the opposite direction in the hallway. She carried a pair of glowing shackles in her hands and shoved them toward Randy and Wendy through the gaps in the net. "Put these on," she commanded.

Randy and Wendy numbly obeyed, snapping them shut over their wrists. Through her mind-fog, she hoped once the net was removed, she could figure a way out of this. The net dulled their perceptions and made them susceptible to suggestion.

The first Valkyrie twisted the shaft of the spear and the net retracted into the spearhead. The effect did not dull, to Wendy's distant-feeling disappointment. *The shackles must work the same way.*

The Valkyrie then removed the weapons that had appeared on them as part of the glamour spell, but as she continued to search them, she found the Wayfinder Stone as well, giving it a quizzical look.

"Walk forwards!" The second Valkyrie commanded forcefully, and poked Randy in the small of his back with the tip of her spear to punctuate the point.

"Owww! Geez! Okay, okay, I'm going, I'm going!"

"Where are you taking us?" Wendy inquired.

"To see the Allfather. He shall decide your fate, trespasser!"

"The Allfather? We're gonna see Odin?" Randy asked with an excitement not usually found in people pointed at by spears

Wendy winked at him. "Relax. I know Odin, we go way back. Everything's going to be fine."

That "reassuring" remark made him nervous again. He'd noticed that when she got too cocky, she tended to make bad decisions, and the last few hadn't exactly been winners.

Wendy and Randy were ushered into the main part of the building where Odin held court in a vast high ceilinged hall. A number of long wooden tables ran parallel to the walls with several fireplaces roaring away beside them, and on the tables were arrayed an amazing variety of foods and drinks.

Burly warriors crowded each other at each of the tables, rowdily arguing. A few groups belted out bawdy songs. There were even some Gods seated at the tables, who were easy to spot as they were about three times larger than the typical human. Hung from the walls were torn and bloodied banners commemorating long ago battles. Flickering torches provided what light the roaring fireplaces did not.

They crossed the room to the throne of Odin, which was covered in runes that glowed in a faint amber color. His throne appeared to have been carved from the base of a massive tree, whose roots still dug into the floor. Two humongous wolves flanked the throne and slept peacefully at Odin's feet.

The Allfather himself also looked as if he was carved from wood, his face deeply lined and his skin the quality of old tree bark. His gray beard, stained red in places by drops of wine, curled to his waist. He had a missing eye, but the other twinkled with equal portions of malevolence and grace. A somewhat ridiculously oversized helmet crowned his head, antlers curling up out of it like tree branches reaching for the sky. Engaged in some great debate with his son, the God Balder, he seemed to take a good swallow of wine from his drinking horn whenever he took a breath. It was said he subsisted entirely on wine and had no need to eat meat.

Balder, for his part, was an impressive sight. A tall, fair-haired and handsome God who radiated a soft yet intense light from every portion of his body.

Wendy relaxed in his presence. She'd met him before and had done some dealings which had gone amiably. He was a kind and considerate God, as Gods went, with a generally sweet disposition that endeared him to everyone he met. Most importantly of all, he could be a moderating influence on his more impulsive and unstable father.

That said, she observed that the pair of ravens who usually sat perched on Odin's shoulders were missing, and that was a very bad omen indeed. They were Hugginn (thought), and Munnin (mind), and those weren't just names. Without them, Odin was, to some extent, literally out of his mind.

She steeled herself as Odin's eye finally turned to them, looking mildly irritated as the Valkyrie bowed before him.

"Great Allfather, pardon my intrusion. These two were found trespassing here. They used magic to penetrate the east wall."

Odin motioned for the Valkyrie to rise. She obeyed wordlessly and stepped to one side, revealing her captives fully to him.

He squinted critically at them, giving Wendy the distinct impression, he was looking *through* them, which wasn't far off. "As I suspected! A pair of sorcerers! You can't fool me with that cheap glamour spell!" He waved his hand, and they were revealed in their true forms.

They shifted nervously on their feet. Randy grumbled that he didn't get to use the cool Viking aliases they'd created for each other.

"How dare you invade my great hall like this!" Odin bellowed, his face red in anger. "This is a sacred place, reserved only for those who have fallen bravely in battle and who have pledged to stand with me at Ragnarok! If you wanted to exchange some Ambrosia for my assistance in working some kind of magic, this is not the way to do it. There are protocols which must be observed! You don't come barging in here like a pair of amateurs!"

Wendy bowed her head. "Great Allfather, we beg your forgiveness. My name is Wendy Sommardahl. I am Pontifex Maximus of the Temple of the Old Gods. I am accompanied by my apprentice, Randy, to whom I wanted to show the wonders of your great hall, so he may know your glory and always show the proper respect to the Gods of Asgard."

As she spoke, she made tribute of a tiny golden sphere of Ambrosia, the stuff the Gods were made of and which sustained them. It emanated from her chest and flew into Odin.

He smiled in appreciation as he absorbed it, which left him feeling a little high, but even so Odin remained determined to maintain an air of authoritative displeasure. "So just because you're the Pontifex Maximus, you think you can go anywhere you want to without getting permission first? Arrogant mortal!"

Wendy bowed deeply and sent him another shot of Ambrosia. "Again, my Lord, I beg your forgiveness for this intrusion. I admit it was foolish of me to come here in this manner."

His manner softened – a little. "Wendy Sommardahl, eh? I know that name!" He scrunched up his face in concentration, as without the raven that held part of his memory nearby, it could be difficult for him to remember anything. "You're Clark Kismet's apprentice! How is the old fool? He barely ever bothers to stop by anymore!"

"He's enjoying his retirement," Wendy reported. She hoped it was true, though the deeper truth was she hardly ever saw her old mentor anymore. She really needed to rectify that one day.

"Why, you were barely more than a girl the last time you were here! I see you've grown into *quite* the woman! Care for a roll in the hay? You know what they say, don't you? Once you go God, you never go back!"

Wendy struggled not to roll her eyes but managed a curt smile instead. "Would that it could be, my grace, but the Allfather knows I am only interested in women." What was it about so many of the Gods that headed up these Pantheons that made them into such horn dogs? Zeus, Yahweh, they were all the same! It was one of the reasons she tried to avoid them. She supposed it must be an alpha male thing.

"Do I?" he asked doubtfully.

"You tease me, sire, feigning ignorance! Of course you do. Your knowledge *is* legendary." She wasn't sure if he was still trying to flirt, or truly didn't know given the missing ravens. Best to split the difference with flattery, she thought, which seemed to work well with these guys. Especially the drunk ones.

"Well, no matter! I can be anything you like me to be. Why, Loki here once took the form of a mare, seduced a horse and gave birth to my favorite steed!" Odin chuckled at the memory, pointing at Loki, who sat at a nearby table gnawing on a turkey leg. The God of Mischief paused long enough to give Odin the finger, then returned to his meal.

With a blinding flash of light Odin transformed into a beautiful, statuesque woman dressed in his clothes. Long, white tresses of hair hung from her head in elaborate braids. Disturbingly, one eye socket still yawned emptily out from her otherwise comely face.

"Well? What do you think? Not bad, huh?" Odin thundered proudly, in his original – male – voice.

She hadn't seen this coming but had an answer. "Err . . . most tempting, Allfather! But regrettably, I must still decline. You see, I'm a married woman now!"

"Eh? Marriage? I never let that stand between myself and a good time!"

"I'm afraid that I do," Wendy said firmly, tiring of this game. "I'm a woman of my word." Too, oaths were a gravely serious matter in this culture, and she used that to her advantage.

"I admire your integration . . . irritation . . . no, that's not right . . . irrigation?" He (she?) scratched his chin then took another swig of wine. "Integrity! Yes! That's what I'm trying to say!" With another flash of light he returned to his male form.

Balder leaned forward, speaking gently. "You must excuse my father, Wendy. His ravens aren't around right now, and he's been drinking rather a lot these days."

"You'd be drinking more than usual too," Odin said boisterously, "if your religion started attracting lots of Nazis and skinheads! I hate those guys! Always trying to get in here!" Indeed, while it was hardly true all of Odin's modern-day worshippers were white supremacists, it was also unfortunately true many of these racists found themselves drawn to his religion.

"I may be many things, but racist isn't one of them. I love black folks, they're so much fun!" he went on. "I really need to talk to my High Priests on Midgard, maybe start an outreach program? Heaven gets all the best entertainers. It isn't fair! We need that kind of quality talent here!"

Wendy had to suppress a laugh at how the supposedly all-knowing Allfather was ignorant of how incredibly racist what he had just said was. It wasn't as if an entire group of people existed solely for his entertainment, as if that was their only value in the world. Unfortunately, he wasn't done either.

"Mr.T is awesome. Such spirit! *'I pity the fool!'*" Odin pantomimed badly and laughed. Perhaps he was laughing at the poor quality of his own attempt at an impression? One never knew with Odin.

"Yes, we could certainly use more warriors like that around here!" Balder agreed.

"I especially love Whitney Houston! Why, I was just telling my favorite son here the other day how much I enjoy that woman's voice, isn't that right?"

Balder nodded obediently. "She's very talented."

"Magnificent set of pipes on that young woman!" Odin enthused.

"Most remarkable indeed," Balder echoed.

"Honestly, I kind of like Mariah Carey better," Randy interjected.

Wendy flinched and buried her face in her hands. Of all the things he could have opened his mouth about . . .

Odin's good mood vanished. He leaned forward to address them both. "Hmmm, if you're not here to ask me to do some kind of a magical favor for you, and you're not here for a bit of fun, then what are you here for?"

Wendy took a deep breath. "We're on a mission to map the various Afterlife realms here in the Aether."

Odin leaned back, his back thumping into his throne. "Mapping the Aether? Why bother?"

"Because it's there. Because nobody's ever done it before," she intoned, as if imparting the wisdom of the ages.

"It's not like climbing a mountain, woman!" Odin scoffed.

She felt her face grow hot, and her teeth ground so hard they squeaked. "Also because such knowledge will be invaluable to future generations of magic users," she added after several seconds.

He scratched his wine-stained beard, his intense gaze seeming to burn into her soul. "Hmm. You can't kid a kidder. You've got some other motivation for doing so, which you hide even from yourself. You will never find that which you truly seek until you can be honest with yourself about what you're really after."

His musings were interrupted by the Valkyrie who captured the pair. "She speaks truthfully, Allfather. I found this on the boy." She held up the Wayfinder Stone

"Perhaps she speaks a truth, but not the truth." Odin took the stone from her hand and examined it. "I haven't seen one of these in ages!" He smiled broadly and looked at Wendy. "Did you know it was I who first taught one of your ancestors how to make these things? Only back then, I don't think that I was called Odin yet. It must have been one of my previous selves. It was all so very long ago."

An odd thing about the Gods was they were constantly changed by the whims of how mankind perceived them. Some were combinations of multiple earlier Gods that humanity's collective imagination had merged together.

Odin wasn't wrong, and the names and natures of the Gods he had evolved from were lost to history.

His mood changes like a weathervane, and it's blowing in my direction, Wendy thought. Better use that before it changes again. "If you would be so kind as to let us have that stone back, we won't trouble you any further, mighty Allfather."

"No," he said, his eyes narrowing. "No. I don't think so.

"But what possible reason could you have for keeping us here?" Wendy nearly shouted, all patience and pretense gone. Even though the real Wayfinder Stone was with her physical body back on Earth, she needed to bring the astral copy back with her to sync them up. Otherwise, the mapping information they had gathered today would be lost forever.

"The magic is strong in you, woman. I can see it! You have grown in power as surely as you have grown in beauty. I have need of a sorceress of your ability. Yes, you might just be the one! Truly, the Norns have sent you to me this day!"

"What service could I possibly provide which the mighty Allfather cannot accomplish on his own?"

"I have a great quest for you! You must return to Midgard and use your magic to find . . . my backscratcher."

"A backscratcher? You've got to be kidding!" Randy said, as Wendy gaped

"I *never* kid around!" Odin replied.

Randy stepped forward. "That's not true! You literally just said Wendy couldn't kid a kidder like two minutes ago, ergo you must be a kidder!"

Wendy recovered enough to place a hand on his arm in warning. Now wasn't the best time for him to indulge in his habit of showing off how clever and right he often was.

"Silence!" Odin said. "I will not be contradicted in my own hall. By a mere stripling of a lad, and a *Mariah Carey fan* at that!"

"I never said I was a *fan*," Randy said as he took a step back and crossed his arms. "Just that she has a few good jams, is all."

Wendy broke in to try to salvage the situation. "We will be happy to help in any way, great Odin. Tell me more about this, err, backscratcher. What's so special about it? Is it enchanted?"

"No, it's not enchanted! It's just a regular old backscratcher," Odin replied irritably.

"It's not magic at all?" Wendy inquired.

"Not even a little bit?" Randy wondered.

"Does it have to be? It's a very nice backscratcher! Regin made it for me. It was my favorite one. It has great sentimental value to me."

So Regin, the Norse God of metal workers, made Odin one fine backscratcher, Wendy thought to herself. God-forged or not, she couldn't quite understand how a mere backscratcher could hold such sentimental value, but on the other hand, people could form emotional attachments to all kinds of odd things, and apparently Gods were no different.

"Perhaps if you told me something about how and where you lost it, it would help me to find it for you, great Allfather?"

"That's the trouble! I can't remember *how* I lost it! I still go down to Midgard occasionally, to have a bit of fun. I lost it recently. I can't recall exactly how, or where. I was quite drunk at the time. All I know is when I returned, it was gone. My ravens are out now, searching the nine worlds for any word of it, but so far, they have heard nothing. They've been gone for quite some time now. I want it back! That's why I need you! Perhaps the apprentice of Kismet, and the Pontifex Maximus, can succeed where my ravens have failed?"

"And in exchange we will get our freedom and the Wayfinder Stone back?"

"Yes, you have my word on it."

"Well, that's good enough for me, Sire." She smiled brightly. "Can I see a picture of this backscratcher?"

Odin waved his hand. A giant glowing image of the backscratcher appeared in front of Wendy and Randy. Its "business" end appeared to be made of a bright silver, with three claws shaped like those of a dragon, the dark wooden handle covered in runes.

Odin flicked his finger and the image buried itself inside Wendy's head. "There. Now you can refer to it whenever you need to."

"Mighty Allfather, may I also take a sample of your aura, so that I may use it to backtrack your movements on Midgard?" Honestly, she had no idea how else she'd be able to fulfill this quest if he didn't grant this request.

"Oh! Good idea! Why didn't I think of that? I *knew* you were the right one for this job! Please proceed."

Wendy withdrew a golden dagger from her purse and pointed it at Odin and chanted out the words to a spell. An emerald glow briefly surrounded him before condensing and returning to the tip of her dagger, where it embedded itself within.

Wendy placed the dagger back into her purse. "Thank you. Well, I think that's all we'll need to begin our quest. If someone will remove our shackles, Randy and I will get going now!"

"No! The boy stays!" Odin declared.

"What? Why?" Randy demanded.

"Father, this hardly seems necessary–" Balder interjected.

"Stay out of this!" Odin hissed. He turned his terrible gaze upon Wendy. "The boy is collateral. How else can I guarantee you will return?"

"Don't be absurd! The Wayfinder Stone is collateral enough!"

"You're in no position to bargain with me, witch! If I say the boy stays, he stays!" he bellowed. Then in a softer tone, he said, "Don't fear, I will see to it that he's treated well."

"Very well," Wendy agreed, as though she had a choice. She turned to Randy and placed her hands on his shoulders. "I'm sorry. I'll be back for you as soon as I can. I swear!"

"I know you will," he said with a reassuring smile. "But don't worry about me, I'll be fine. I always *did* want to learn more about Norse mythology, and what better opportunity than this?"

She had thought he was just trying to make her feel better, but she realized maybe he was being sincere. "Always looking on the bright side of things, huh?"

"You know it! Run along, and find the totally uninteresting, completely non-magical backscratcher. I'll be fine."

"Really?"

"Yes, seriously."

"Okay then. Sit tight and try to enjoy yourself. I'll be back in two shakes of a lamb's tail!"

Odin snapped his fingers and the shackles fell from her wrists, landing on the ground with a thud. "May the Norns watch over your quest and favor you, Daughter of Sommardahl."

"I will not fail you, Allfather. Or my apprentice!" she replied.

Then she recited the incantation that would open another portal like the one that had taken them to the Aether. She manically waved goodbye to Randy with a cheerfulness and confidence she didn't truly feel as her form was distorted and sucked through the portal.

As soon as she was gone, Odin pointed at one of the Valkyries.

"Take him to the dungeon!" he commanded.

"*What?*" Randy protested. "I thought you said I'd be treated well!"

"It's a very nice dungeon!" Odin replied with a toothy smile which reminded Randy of how a shark looks at his dinner. "And there will be *entertainment.*"

Entertainment for who, was all Randy thought as he was led away.

The Valkyrie took hold of a short chain that dangled from Randy's shackles and pulled him roughly away from the throne. She dragged him down countless dark corridors deeper and deeper into the fortress, which became increasingly dank and musty. He tried to engage her in conversation once or twice, but utterly failed.

Finally, they reached a level of the fortress that was filled with jail cells. They all seemed to be empty, except for the odd skeleton or two that was chained to a wall. This was particularly confusing to Randy considering that they were already in the Afterlife. He decided it must just be an affectation to make the place look suitably spooky. There was one cell that they passed which held a rather forlorn looking dwarf. Eventually they came to a cell that was completely empty. The Valkyrie removed a set of keys from her belt, unlocking it. The door creaked loudly as she opened it and shoved him inside.

He looked about and turned, rubbing his arms despite that his astral form could feel no cold. "Cozy," he said drily to her.

"It gets better," she replied, and produced from behind her an enormous boombox. Randy blinked, wondering where she'd gotten it from, as there was no such thing sitting outside of the cell a moment ago. In her other hand she produced a CD jewel case with *Whitney Houston's Greatest Hits* on the cover. She set the boombox down on the floor in front of the bars and placed the CD inside. There was nowhere to plug it in but he was sure it wouldn't matter.

"The entertainment, as the Allfather promised. He wants to make sure you get a proper appreciation for the musical stylings of Whitney. You are to listen to this CD on repeat the entire time you are our guest."

Randy wondered how Odin had communicated this plan to her. He imagined it must be through some kind of telepathy. She pressed a button on the boombox, and *I Wanna Dance With Somebody* started playing.

Loudly.

Very loudly.

From elsewhere in the dungeon, Randy heard the dwarf groan loudly enough to be heard over the din.

The Valkyrie walked off. Randy ran to the bars and shouted at her retreating form. "I never said I didn't appreciate her! I just said I liked Mariah Carey a little better! I'm a musician too, ya know? Believe me, I know how hard it is to hit those notes, I sure as hell can't do it! There's no need for this!"

The Valkyrie laughed and disappeared into the shadows.

Randy turned and sighed, pressing his back to the bars and sinking to the floor. He really didn't mind the music – yet – but over time it would drive him insane.

Then he remembered he had more control over his etheric body than he did his physical one. Could he simply turn off his sense of hearing like he had turned off his sense of smell earlier?

He concentrated, and all the sounds around him ceased . . . *except* for the sounds of Whitney.

"Damn!" Randy cursed. Even drunk and half out of his mind, Odin had managed to think of everything! The music played within his mind, despite his hearing being turned off. Odin had enchanted the boombox in a way Randy couldn't counter.

How many times could he listen to the same CD before he lost his mind? Even something you love can become maddening with too much repetition, and he didn't *love* this music. At best, he only sort of liked it. He was really more of a punk and alternative rock kind of guy.

"C'mon Wendy, find that backscratcher and get back here pronto!" he whispered as if in prayer. He believed in his mentor. She was the world's most powerful witch, after all. He was confident she'd find the lost backscratcher . . . eventually. Whether she'd do so while he still had all his marbles . . . not so much.

It's not that *much of an impossible task is it?* he thought to himself sarcastically. She only had to search the entire Earth, and she didn't even know where to begin. Simple, right?

Randy sighed and placed his head in his hands.

Yup, I'm fucking doomed, aren't I? He realized with forlorn certainty as Whitney continued to hit those seemingly impossible to reach notes.

Part Two: Doggie Demigods

Wendy emerged from the other end of the portal, her astral body floating high above Earth. She picked this spot to get a better idea of where Odin had been lately. The ultimate bird's eye view on the problem before her, so to speak. A satellite passed right through her, and she didn't even blink, her mind focused on how to accomplish her quest.

Time passed differently for the souls that inhabited the Aether, and a few hours' time in "the real world" translated into days for them. Our days were their weeks, our weeks their months and so on. She had gotten the impression that Odin had lost his favorite backscratcher fairly recently from his point of view. This meant she probably didn't have to backtrack his movements *too* far back in time . . . maybe only a week or so, at most?

She sighed. At times like this she wished she was a detective, like her friend Matt. She could ask him for advice on how to handle an investigation like this.

But he'd no doubt flip out on her when she told him she'd gotten Randy into this kind of trouble. She didn't want to hear it, not needing that kind of stress in her life right now. She already felt bad enough about the situation without other people heaping additional layers of guilt upon her. Guilt would just distract her. There would be plenty of time for self-recrimination later, once she'd completed her task.

So how best to proceed?

She could return home, to the headquarters of the Temple of the Old Gods on the hidden island of Elysium. Her physical body was there, and she could put the full resources of the Temple behind the search.

But she didn't think she would, at least not right away. For one thing, she felt too embarrassed by the entire episode. She didn't even feel like telling her wife April about this incident. They'd already had enough arguments about the dangers Wendy had exposed Randy to during the course of her efforts to map the Aether. This latest turn of events only seemed to prove that April had been right all along about the recklessness of this whole enterprise, and Wendy wasn't quite sure she wanted to give her that satisfaction quite yet.

More importantly, if word got out that the Pontifex Maximus had let her apprentice be taken prisoner, her political enemies would have a field day with the information and use it to undermine her efforts to reform the organization.

No, it was better to see if she could handle this on her own first. She would only seek help if the task seemed too enormous for her to handle on her own or if it was taking her too long to complete. The time differential between the physical universe and the Aether meant Randy's spirit would spend several days as a prisoner in Asgard, even if she wrapped this all up in one Earth day. Therefore, it was imperative she find the missing back scratcher as soon as possible.

She retrieved the dagger from her purse and pointed it at the planet spinning below her. Gathering the imprint of Odin's aura in her mind, she recited the words of an enchantment that would make anything it had come into contact with for the past week glow a bright green that only she could see.

She almost cried when she saw how many brilliant green dots appeared on the globe below her.

Great Goddess! He sure does get around, doesn't he? The dots did not just concentrate mostly in Europe and Scandinavia as one might expect. She had to admit she was surprised. Not because of how far he'd traveled – Odin was known as a God who liked to wander – no, what astounded her was this only represented how often he'd visited the planet in *the past week*. It took a great deal of Ambrosia for a God to manifest bodily on the physical plane. Many of the Gods whose religions were in decline hoarded their Ambrosia zealously, but Odin was obviously comfortable burning through it like this, and that amazed her.

She felt overwhelmed by the enormity of her task and reconsidered whether she would have to swallow her pride and get some help after all.

Why was all of this happening to her? Was the universe trying to tell her something? Is that why this was happening? She knew that even though Odin seemed to be something of an uncouth and boorish God, many of her fellow magic users also believed he had a special connection to what they called the Divine Consciousness of the Universe.

Supposedly, he acquired this connection when he sacrificed his eye to drink from a special well at the base of the World Tree which granted him great wisdom. Ever since then, he became an agent through which the Divine Consciousness of the Universe sometimes acted and spoke. Whether or not Odin was even conscious of this, and to what degree, was debatable among the magic users who believed it in the first place. Her own mentor, Clark Kismet, believed it, which was why he visited Asgard so often to seek Odin's wisdom.

As for herself, Wendy believed more in a core teaching of the Temple of the Old Gods, which went, "everything is a coincidence, and yet there are no coincidences."

Contradictory on the surface, what it meant basically was that it was all a matter of willful perception. If you decide to interpret a series of seemingly coincidental events as being an intentional message to you from the Divine Consciousness of the Universe, then it will take on a more significant meaning for you, and you will alter your behavior accordingly. It becomes a self-fulfilling prophecy because you are the self who actualized it into reality based upon how you decided to interpret it. And because you assigned it more importance, it *became* important.

Otherwise, it just remains a random set of coincidences. Whether or not it could ever empirically be shown to really be some sort of divine message or not is irrelevant because how *you* decide to react to it personally, and let it shape your destiny, is all that truly matters.

So how was she inclined to interpret this latest set of circumstances? What was the universe trying to tell her by allowing this to happen?

She was in this predicament because of her decision to map the Aether, and the real reason why she was mapping the Aether was because she still hadn't come to grips with Autumn's death. That was the unavoidable truth of it. She needed closure, and she was looking for the ultimate kind of closure by trying to find a way into the Summerlands so she could speak with Autumn again, despite the impossibility of it all.

Why did she need this closure so badly? It had to be because she blamed herself for Autumn's death. Wendy had spotted her potential early on, singled her out and taken her under her wing. She promoted her to work as one of her aides. In no time, Autumn proved to be her most reliable and trustworthy assistant. It wasn't until she was gone that Wendy fully appreciated precisely how much she'd allowed herself to become dependent upon the younger woman's counsel to keep her more flighty and unfocused nature in check. Losing her had been like losing a vital part of herself. Autumn had trusted Wendy too, looking up to her like an older sister, constantly seeking her approval.

It had ultimately cost Autumn her life.

She'd been shot in the head while trying to capture one of the ringleaders of a misguided scheme to take over the world hatched by the previous Pontifex Maximus. The bright flame of her life snuffed out by a madman with a gun.

What if I hadn't taken such an interest in Autumn? Hadn't facilitated her career? Would she still be alive today? The question tortured Wendy on the few occasions when she allowed herself to ask it.

And now here Wendy was, doing the same thing all over again, putting another talented young person who looked to her for leadership in danger!

No! I'm not to blame for what happened to Autumn! She thought hotly. *She knew the risks and she volunteered. If I'd ordered her not to go, she still would've done it. She did it because she knew it was the right thing to do. The people running the Temple of the Old Gods back then had to be stopped! They perverted everything we believed in, plotting to abuse magic to dominate the world. Autumn was as dedicated as I was to making sure that would never happen. She died fighting for what she believed in. If I don't respect her choices, her sacrifice, isn't it the same thing as disrespecting her?*

Wendy knew it was foolish to go on blaming herself for Autumn's death. She knew this logically, but she could never convince her heart. She tried to counter it with more logic, hoping an avalanche of reason could bury her emotions.

She focused on the idea that Autumn herself probably wouldn't blame her. Nobody blamed anyone for anything where Autumn was now. They were all in the most perfect state of peace of mind. Forever beyond such petty concerns.

Ah, that's it, isn't it? That's what you're really after! It's not guilt that's motivating you, it's greed. You want another taste of that perfect bliss. A cruel voice inside her head told her. Cruel, but brutally honest as cruelty often is.

So that was it then. She knew better too. She knew that kind of unending bliss could not be found on Earth, except in small doses here and there. What an idiot she'd been! She needed to give up on this idea of finding a secret way into the Summerlands. It had almost cost her her apprentice. And if she did somehow find a way back there, what would she do?

If she could stay there, would she be strong enough to ever willingly give up such bliss and return to Earth? Would she abandon her duties as Pontifex Maximus? How about to her family, and her apprentice? How could she respect herself if she did that? If she got to experience it again for even longer than she had before, and was kicked out of the Summerlands, then everything on Earth would pale in comparison. She'd never be able to properly experience joy again. Even if she got what she wanted, even if she won, she would lose. There was no winning in this situation. The Summerlands belonged to the dead, not the living, and for good reason.

No, she had to abandon this idea before it completely destroyed her and the people closest to her. She had to learn to recognize that the bliss she really wanted already existed in the world around her, in her daily interactions with her friends and family, not in some inaccessible other world. It was just so hard nowadays to find that joy and still to hang onto being the happy go lucky person she'd always been, she had so many different responsibilities weighing on her lately. She felt some of that bliss when she was in the arms of April, or when she held her daughter Celine and heard her laughter. Or when she shared with Randy some new wonder of the universe. She had to make herself more aware of when those moments presented themselves and hold onto them as tightly as she could.

She resolved then and there this would be her last Aether-mapping mission with Randy.

They'd already hit most of the important Afterlife realms anyway. Perhaps she would open up the project to volunteers and let anyone who was interested continue it, just to see it through to the end? But for her, the project was over. Whether or not coming to this realization was Odin or the universe's real purpose in sending her on this quest was irrelevant. She was making it *her* purpose.

Randy was already paying the price for her hubris. She prayed that Odin really was treating him well. Loki might be the trickster God, but Odin could be crafty and unpredictable too.

She turned away from her troubled thoughts, and back to the planet rotating silently below her. It was time to get started. Where to begin? The greed dots where he'd been most recently burned brightest. Was it better to start with the most recent place where Odin had been, or the least? She didn't know. It was exactly the sort of thing she would have loved to ask Matt's advice on, but she'd already resolved to keep him out of this.

She decided to start with the oldest place on the list and directed her flight to the faintest spot on the globe. If she knew her geography, it was somewhere in China.

Randy sat cross legged on the floor of his cell. He had discovered a way around the madness that was sure to come from listening to *Whitney Houston's Greatest Hits* on replay for the foreseeable future. He realized that if he put himself into a meditative state, where he felt like he was one with each note, each beat, he didn't mind it at all. As he *was* the music, how could he mind it? He was both the experience and the experiencer now, and he wanted to experience it all.

None of it could hurt him anymore, not in his present state of transcendent consciousness. The answer as to how to deal with all of this had been obvious. This was how he typically dealt with the pain in his life, the trauma of his past. Why not also use it to overcome the obstacles of the present?

He was in that groove when the music unceremoniously ended, bringing him crashing down to his normal perception of reality. As his eyes popped open, he found a Valkyrie looking at him intently from the other side of the bars with an odd expression on her face.

An expression of deep longing.

She was quite possibly the most beautiful woman he'd ever seen in his life. And something about her seemed oddly familiar too. He couldn't quite put his finger on where he might have seen her before, and she wasn't one of the Valkyries who had captured him earlier.

She looked about the same age as himself, with bright green eyes and a small, slightly upturned, impish nose. Her hair, capped with a helmet sporting horns, swept in a long wave of red that pushed its way down to the back of her knees. No, not red. More of a strawberry blonde than the deep red of Wendy's hair, or the rusty auburn of Penny's when she neglected to dye it some unnatural color. Her scale mail shirt's neckline plunged invitingly in front and was much shorter than the ones worn by the other Valkyries, being cut more like a mini skirt. On her feet she wore sandals laced to just below her knees. All in all, her outfit was far more sexy and far less practical looking than those of her sister warriors.

She carried a silver platter with a small portion of meat in one hand, and a drinking horn slung over her shoulder by a leather strap.

He looked at the boom box. "Won't you get in trouble for turning that off?"

"Probably. It is of little concern to me," she said, sparing it a scarce glance before drilling her gaze back into his." The Allfather might be my master, but my true loyalty lies with my creator."

He swallowed. "Your, err . . . creator?"

She moved forwards to unlock the cell with a large key and enter it. "I've brought you some food and wine." She unslung the drinking horn and sat down beside him on the floor, placing the platter between them.

He took the horn from her and gratefully drank from it, the alcohol already warming his insides. "Thanks. You know, where I'm from, I'm still considered too young to drink this stuff?"

"There is no legal drinking age here in Asgard," she said noncommittally.

Randy thought he knew why. He and Penny lived with his friends Matt and Naomi. Naomi was a history major, and he'd learned a lot from her over the years just through casual conversation. He recalled a talk they'd once had about why in ages past people consumed so much alcohol, and thought he'd try to dazzle this amazing looking young lady with his knowledge.

"It's because the water is too contaminated, isn't it? That's why even little kids used to drink beer back in the day. The water wasn't safe." He figured the same thing must be true around here, since this place was the product of the imaginations of people from such times.

"No," she said with a tinkling laugh. "It's because legal drinking ages are *no fun*. We like to have fun around here!

Randy had to laugh, too – hers was infectious – but with nothing more to say, he sampled the meat she'd brought him. While he didn't need to eat or drink anything because this wasn't his real body, he could still taste, and this tasted amazing.

Speaking of hunger, she wasn't eating – she hadn't touched the food, not even glanced at it. But there was hunger in her eyes, just not for the food.

She placed her hand on his knee. "We could have some fun together, you know. Like we did before?"

"Um, before?" It came out high-pitched.

"Yes, before. Don't you remember?" she asked and leaned toward him in a way that all he could focus on was her moist, parted lips.

All in a rush, he *did* remember.

Yes, he'd seen her before, imagined every inch of her body in excruciating detail. It had been a few years earlier, after he'd been up all night reading a book on Norse mythology, and he nodded off while reading a passage on Valkyries. In that bizarre state of mind halfway between wakefulness and dreaming, he had a rather lurid fantasy about making love to a Valkyrie, and he'd given her a ridiculous name because doing so had amused him at the time.

"My God, you're Gertrude!"

She threw her arms around his neck and hugged him. The smell of her being so close to him was intoxicating. Her hair smelled like strawberries. Her skin, like peaches. Just like he'd imagined it.

"I knew you'd remember! I came as quickly as I could once I heard they were keeping you here, my love," she whispered in his ear, the heat of her breath arousing him.

"But how can this be?" he stammered. "You were just a fantasy!"

"And you are in a place where fantasies become reality. Especially for someone with an imagination as powerful as yours. The same imagination which makes you such a great wizard."

Randy blushed, not so much because she thought he was a great wizard when he was only an apprentice, but because he was hardly accustomed to discussing the contents of his masturbatory fantasies with anyone, let alone attractive women he'd only just met! Even if said attractive women were both the subject and the product of such fantasies . . .

"The same imagination that gave me life! I'm very grateful to you for that. I'd like to show you *how* grateful I am, if you'll let me?"

How desperately she longed to be with her creator! She believed it was the only thing which could remedy the deep well of emptiness that dogged her, the nagging feeling of purposelessness she often struggled to evade. She tried to distract herself from this ennui with training and battle, but it was never enough. No, *this* was what she needed to feel complete, she was sure of it! What was she, other than an extension of her creator? She *had* to be near him, to reestablish that connection with her source, her lost half. She leaned in toward him, softly kissing his neck. Yes, he *would* be hers!

He flinched away. "Wait! If I created you, doesn't that kind of make me your father?"

Gertrude screwed up her face. "No. Ewww! You dreamed me up, it's not the same thing. It's completely different!"

"It is? Really? Because I don't see quite how–"

She placed a slender finger against his lips. "Shhh! Stop overthinking everything. It *is* different. *Very* different!" she said firmly. "Don't you *want* it to be different?" She leaned in and kissed him again, this time fully on the lips. He couldn't help himself and drew her in closer. He did indeed want it to be different, but–

He pushed her back again suddenly.

"What now?" Gertrude asked in irritation. She couldn't believe he was rejecting her advances! Hadn't he created her with this very purpose in mind? As a creature born from his desires, she knew exactly what he wanted most. *She* was what he wanted most! All this resistance made no sense!

"I have a girlfriend back on Earth! I can't do this. It's cheating!"

She let out a breath. So that was it! Since she'd been born from his psyche, she knew him better than he knew himself, despite just having met him. She understood his deep sense of honor, his need to feel that he was doing right by the people he cared for. It was a code of conduct he strove to live by. Much of his feelings of self-worth revolved around being true to it. As a warrior, she also had a highly developed sense of honor, albeit one that was centered around displaying her skill and valor on the battlefield.

Hmm, how to get over these objections? Words had never been her weapon of choice, but she knew that a good warrior must be adaptable if they expect to snatch victory from the jaws of defeat. She thought a moment, concentrating on sharpening her message into something able to slice through all his protests. She smiled to herself, as she realized what the perfect tactic was to shatter his shield of self-control with her spear of seduction.

"I don't think it's cheating at all! Isn't this all just a kind of dream to you? Why should you torture yourself with guilt over something you did in a dream? You see, this is your whole problem. You take everything too seriously, and it prevents you from really enjoying yourself or living life to the fullest."

Her fingers got to work unbuttoning his shirt. "Besides, she's not here and what she doesn't know won't hurt her."

Yes, but I'll know. And I won't like knowing, thought Randy. Worse, he'd end up telling her. *And then she'll probably rip my head off, and I'l help her do it because I will have deserved it.*

Penny was more than just his girlfriend, she was his partner, his best friend. He always told her everything sooner or later. Yet despite all of these misgivings, he felt powerless before the onslaught of kisses Gertrude peppered his shirtless torso with. How could he resist her? He couldn't. Maybe it was the effects of the shackles he still wore? Maybe it was the wine? More than likely though, it had more to do with the fact that she quite literally was his dream girl!

And he was obviously her dream man.

Wendy floated towards a ramshackle barn on a small farm in the Chinese countryside. Inside, she found the object (objects?) of her attention which had drawn her there.

Inside was a mother dog suckling a litter of puppies. The mother had Odin's aura all over her, and the puppies had part of the aura *inside* of them. The puppies looked fit and strong, *all* of them, not one runt.

Almost unnaturally fit and strong, Wendy thought, and realized what she was looking at. And laughed. These dogs were demigods. Doggy demigods! Every one of them!

Countless stories had been told of the Gods descending to Earth and taking on the form of an animal, and in some of the stories, these Gods even had sex with animals. She didn't really understand why, except certain Gods seemed to be unusually horny in general.

Some magic users theorized this had something to do with their origins, with them springing forth from the creative energy of the human race's collective dreams. Since sex was the literal act of creation here on Earth, and they were intrinsically linked to creative energy, it made them basically want to fuck just about everything they encountered. However, not all Gods behaved in this way, which seemed like a major hole in the theory, in Wendy's opinion. It was a mystery, and Gods were inherently mysterious, and she was content to just leave it at that.

What a weird and wonderful world it was, where the random dog from down the lane that knocked up your dog might turn out to be a God in disguise! Did most people have any idea how bizarre and miraculous this world truly was? She doubted it. Perhaps people in ancient times had some inkling, but this awareness was something that had been lost by most people living in these modern times.

Hell, even she forgot it sometimes! Yet it was exactly the sort of thing she needed to keep in mind so she could properly appreciate the real world, instead of endless pining over the siren song of the Summerlands.

So Odin sometimes enjoyed running around the Chinese countryside as a dog, and even had himself a little doggy girlfriend. He'd obviously been there in the past week to check in on his canine family, which she found to be rather sweet of him.

Well, she wouldn't find the backscratcher here. He would have had to have been in human form when he lost it, and it was time to move on to the next place. She said goodbye to the female dog, who could see her in her astral form, but had decided that she was no threat to her pups. Wendy guessed this was probably because the mother dog could sense some of Odin's aura on her.

As Wendy went on, she would find that Odin's title of "Allfather" was far more literal than she had ever dared to suspect. Scenes like the one she had found in China were repeated around the planet, with various kinds of animals and a healthy number of humans of all races too. His lust seemed to know no bounds.

And that could be useful. Wendy took special note of where the human offspring lived. They'd make good candidates for the Temple of the Old Gods someday. She'd have to assign some of her people to watch over them until they became of age to begin their training. She was certain a demigod would test quite highly on the Potts/Rudolph Test, the test of psychic potential her organization had been using for centuries.

In fact, she wondered if this was the origin of all the people on Earth who had higher than normal psychic sensitivity? Were they all demigods, or descendants of a demigod?

Seeing how far and wide Odin appeared to have spread his seed, it seemed possible. And he was only one of the Gods that was known to sometimes indulge in such activities! Perhaps in this way, the Gods were unwittingly raising the consciousness of the entire human race? She hoped so. Humanity could use a little evolution of consciousness, in her opinion. Humans who were able to perceive more of the hidden layers of the universe also tended to be more aware of the interconnectedness of life, which sometimes made them nicer, better people in general. The world needed a few billion more of those sorts of folks.

This was an interesting discovery, but so far it had brought her no closer to finding the object of her quest. There had been no sign of the missing backscratcher in any of the homes of Odin's various human conquests. Although she could move around the planet at a blinding speed in her astral body, she was still mindful of how much time must be passing in the Aether for poor Randy. If she didn't get results soon, she'd have to ask for help, no matter how much doing so might gall her.

Not all of Odin's wanderings involved copious copulation, and he had visited his share of bars, wineries, pool halls and bowling alleys all over the world. And, to her astonishment, a few libraries and research facilities. She couldn't imagine what he'd been up to in these places, but it was nice to see that he sometimes thought with something other than his dick or his insatiable appetite for alcohol.

At long last, in a sauna in Iceland, she found the object of her quest: the backscratcher itself. It sat next to a wooden bucket of water beside a brazier of hot coals. Evidently it had been used to stir the coals. Her jubilation at finding the backscratcher was tempered by the realization it was at nearly the last place Odin had visited that week, so if she had started her search at the most recent place he'd been, she would have come across it far sooner.

Since the backscratcher was an object from the Aether in material form, it could be broken back down into a purely ethereal object by sucking out the Ambrosia that had allowed it to manifest physically. Easier said than done, though. Wendy had only read about doing something like this in an old book, and if she screwed this up, she could destroy it. Then what?

Of course, she could just make an astral copy of it, but so could Odin. It was very clear that he wanted the original back, not a replica. Making an astral copy would also leave the physical version still on Earth. No, she was certain Odin would see through such a deception and punish her for it.

She could always wake herself up out of her trance, go find the book that held the spell she needed and study it. She cursed. That would mean more delays, but she couldn't risk screwing this spell up. She'd already taken enough unnecessary risks today.

Hang in there, Randy. I'll get you back home soon enough!

A half an hour later, after consulting her spell books back at home, Wendy was once more in that Icelandic sauna. But this time she was not alone. Sweaty old men dressed only in towels lounged all around her, and they were engaged in an animated conversation which made it difficult to concentrate on the spell. She was forced to temporarily turn off her sense of hearing, and with a rush of satisfaction, the backscratcher disappeared from its spot beside the pail of water and reappeared in her hand.

One of the old men saw it fade out of existence before his astonished eyes and shouted, pointing to where it had been. Wendy didn't speak Icelandic and wasn't curious enough to do a translation spell so she could understand what they were saying, but she didn't have to because it was clear from their tone and body language that they thought their companion was either out of his mind, or trying to play some kind of a silly prank on them.

Why is it that the people who are a bit more tuned into the weirdness of the world are often branded as lunatics? She wondered. Ah well, she had successfully completed her quest and that was the important thing to focus on.

She smiled to herself as she opened a portal in the ceiling and allowed herself to get sucked up into it. This time, when she arrived in Asgard, Wendy arranged for the portal to deposit her right outside of the front doors of Valhalla.

She boldly marched right up to the pair of Valkyries that guarded the entrance. "I am Wendy Sommardahl, Pontifex Maximus of the Temple of the Old Gods, and I demand entrance. The Allfather is expecting me."

Somewhat to her surprise and without a word, the guards pushed open the massive wooden doors for her and stepped aside.

As she entered, there was a bounce to her step that had not been there before. A natural, unconscious swagger, as opposed to the false, self-conscious one she normally projected. It was the walk of a woman with a newfound sense of purpose.

The Valkyries escorted her to Odin's throne. The scene looked much as it had the last time she'd been there, except Odin's ravens were back now, one each sitting on either shoulder. And Odin looked even more drunk than he had before, if that could be believed. He regarded her with one heavy lidded, bloodshot eye as she approached.

She marched right up to him and stopped. "You've got quite a lovely collection of families back on Midgard. I suppose congratulations are in order. I especially liked the puppies, although the llamas were adorable too."

If he realized he'd been insulted, he didn't show it. "Well? Did you find what you were after?" he asked testily.

"You could say that," she replied with a cheerful tone, and pulled the long back scratcher from her magically short purse and playfully tossed it to him.

He greedily snatched it from the air. "No, I meant did you find what you were really after with all this Aetheric mapping nonsense?" He eyed her again as he impatiently tapped the backscratcher on an arm of the throne.

Wendy's mouth gaped for a moment as understanding dawned. "Yes. Yes, I believe I have," she replied with a newfound confidence. "Thank you."

"Good!" Odin thundered as he flipped the Wayfinder Stone back at her. She nearly fumbled it before catching it, and with a sigh of relief she stuffed it back into her purse. Sports had never been her forte.

He shoved the backscratcher down the back of his shirt and worked it up and down his back vigorously. "Ah! Yes! That really hits the spot! I knew you wouldn't let me down!

You Sommerdahls always were such a clever lot. A bit reckless, but clever."

The raven on his right shoulder spoke, firelight glinting off its tiny, night black eyes. "I'm glad she's finally come to her senses. There's no way for the living to get into the Summerlands."

"Oh yes. Quite a foolish exercise," the one on the right shoulder agreed. "Life is for the living. With plenty of wonders abounding for those with the eyes to see them. It's not healthy to focus so much on what comes next." It spread its wings and flapped lazily before folding them back against its body.

Talking ravens? She cleared her throat. "Yes, I understand that now, but how did you–"

"Let's go fetch that apprentice of yours from the dungeons!" Odin interrupted. He dropped the backscratcher into its custom leather sheath hanging from his belt.

She did a double take. "The *dungeons*? You said he'd be treated well!" An entire week, perhaps more, had passed here while she was gone, and the thought of Randy languishing in a dungeon for that entire time made her blood boil.

"I suspect he's had an unusually pleasant time down there. Come along, you'll see what I mean soon enough." Odin winked at her with his one remaining eye as he rose from the throne.

As they made their way down, Odin and Wendy were met by the raucous sound of Ska music floating towards them from somewhere down the corridor. Soaring electric guitar riffs and trumpet blasts assailed their ears.

"By the head of Mimir!" Odin shouted, holding his ears. "What is that horrible sound? That's not Whitney! It's even worse than Mariah!"

"I know that music," Wendy said half to herself.

"It's Lung Collapse," One of the two ravens put in.

"Eh?" Odin remarked. "Isn't that a medical condition? Talk sense you accursed corvid!"

"That's my apprentice's band," Wendy explained, wondering what they'd find.

As they turned the corner, their eyes were greeted by the sight of a mostly naked Randy and Gertrude lying on the pillow covered floor of the jail cell, their heads bobbing in time to the music. Their bodies were intertwined beneath an animal skin blanket with empty bottles of wine scattered around them. The boombox played an astral copy of Lung Collapse's recently recorded demo disc that Randy had recreated (with some effort because of his chains) from his own memories. Apparently, Gertrude had smuggled not a few items of contraband into his cell over the course of the past week.

"Apprentice!" Wendy cried.

"Gertrude!" Odin bellowed as he sent a bolt of lightning into the boombox, silencing the rocksteady sounds of Lung Collapse.

"Mistress!" Randy shouted in surprise.

"Allfather!" Gertrude gushed.

Wendy scowled. "Here I was, worried sick about you, and all this time you've been living it up and partying!" Despite her words and facade of outrage, though, she was relieved to see that her apprentice was not only safe, but evidently having a wonderful time.

"It's not his fault! This was all my idea, and I will happily accept the full punishment for it!" Gertrude pleaded.

"Please, don't punish her. Punish me instead!"

"Oh please, calm yourselves!" Odin directed. "You two are so sweet it's making me sick! 'Punish me!' 'No, punish me instead!' Bah! Nobody is going to be punished here today! I expected something like this might happen, once you heard your creator was here, Gertrude."

"You did?" Randy and Gertrude said together.

"Aye, didn't I say there'd be entertainment, boy?" Odin laughed.

"Wait a minute. Her 'creator'?" Wendy asked.

"Yes, your apprentice here dreamed her into existence quite a while ago. She just appeared here one day since this is where Valkyries belong, and we took her in. She's been pining after him ever since. It's quite pathetic, actually."

"Oh Randy, what about poor Penny?" Wendy wondered.

"This doesn't count! It's like having a dream," he said, rationalizing. Beside him, Gertrude nodded her agreement.

Wendy raised her eyebrows. "I doubt she'd see it that way. Anyhow, get dressed, we're going home."

"So, you were successful?" Randy asked her, although he already knew the answer. People have an annoying habit of doing that sometimes, don't they?

"In more ways than one," Wendy replied enigmatically.

"What about these?" Randy asked and held up his still-shackled wrists. Gertrude had been unable to remove them. Only Odin could, and with a snap of his fingers the shackles clattered to the ground.

Randy then simply willed himself back into his clothes and stood up. Now that he was free of the willpower sapping effect of the chains, such a thing was child's play for him. Gertrude stood up too, carefully covering up her nakedness by wrapping the blanket tightly around herself.

"Promise me you'll come back to see me again, my love!" Gertrude cried out. The idea she may never see Randy again was an unbearable thought to her.

Randy looked to Odin questioningly.

"Oh, I don't really care what you two decide to get up to, just so long as you keep it outside of the halls of Valhalla."

"I will!" Randy said and turned to Gertrude. "I'll always be grateful to you for making my stay so . . . pleasant." He sealed it with a long, lingering kiss.

Dream or not, it made Wendy uncomfortable, and she interrupted it by tapping him on the shoulder. "Okay, enough of that, you smoothie! Time to get back to reality. We can't live in our dreams forever. There are people who still need us back home."

Randy pulled himself from Gertrude's embrace. He wouldn't mind living in this particular dream forever if he could, and resolved that he'd be back again, and soon.

He looked over at his Mistress, who seemed different in the way she carried herself. More focused, more at ease. He hadn't seen her look so carefree since he'd first met her, back when Autumn was still alive. "You seem . . . better."

"I am," she agreed, and smiled as she weaved the spell for the portal which would take them home. It was true, she was better. She had a renewed sense of purpose. For too long, she'd been focusing on all the wrong things, and overlooking the deepest and oldest kind of magic. The magic of love, which had been right in front of her all along.

She couldn't wait to get back home to hug April and Celine again.

As it turned out, there was no place like home.

GRATITUDE FOR GERTRUDE

At the rainbow's end

That is where

All my love I send

She awaits me there

Unto Valhalla's great hall

On winged mare she doth bear

Those whom in battle so valiantly did fall

How fortunate am I

To have captured her affections

Even tho I have yet to die?

Always still she heeds my call

She comes to me without pretension

Sweet Valkyrie! How blessed I be

'Twas I who caught your eye

And to whom you bestow all your love

OTHER BOOKS IN THE DEAD END WORLD SAGA:

The Shadow of Death

Tales from a Dead End World

Beyond the Veil of Death

And coming in 2023:

Tales from a Dead End World Volume 2

Matt Spike and the Vampire's Curse

and also *Jersey Devils*

9 781959 860020